ELLE HARTFORD

Cry Big Bad Wolf

The Alchemical Tales #4

*This one is dedicated to everyone out there
who's facing down their shadow.*

You aren't alone.

Contents

Welcome

Long, long ago, a coven of witches created a world just
beyond ours—a realm of fairy tales.

In Beyond, humans rub shoulders with mythical creatures,
and magic mixes with science.

There are only three rules:

Happily
accept that we share the same home

Ever
remember that what you take, you must also give

After
struggle will always lead to new beginnings

So, if you are ready . . . you are welcome here.

* * *

Belville & nearby forest
abandoned castle grounds
police station
Curiosities & Museum
Ginger's Bakery
Antiques by Cairn
Red's Alchemy & Potions
Market Square
Hair & Beauty by Gloria
A Petal in Time
Lavender's Tavern
Luca's bookstore
Witch's hut
local beach
N
W
E
S

Cast of Characters

Top twelve, in alphabetical order

Dusty: handy-gnome and jack of all trades, best friend to William

Gavin Goodwin, Doctor: new arrival in town and neighbor to Red

Gloria: phoenixkin, owner of Hair & Beauty by Gloria; recently friendly

Luca: bookseller and scholar, complicated past; friendly to a fault

Marguerite: mayor of Belville, a glassblower by day

Red: alchemist and child of Seers, full name Cinnabar Sunset

Rowan, Sir: old-fashioned knight; works at Red's Alchemy & Potions

Ryuko: snakekin, local ne'er-do-well; generally keeps to himself

Sakura: nickname Saki; shadow witch, adopted sister of Ryuko; new in town

Thorn, Officer: half-orc policewoman in charge of keeping law in Belville

Trent: young Witch, lives in a Hut outside of town; eager to help

William: canine familiar, capable of protection magic and plenty of sass

1

All Hallow's Eve

As I made my way across Market Square from the bakery back to my potions shop, I dodged a ghost, sidestepped a zombie, and nearly put my boot right through a carved pumpkin.

Fall in the tiny alpine town of Belville was a dangerous time. The grassy Square, always the center of the town celebrations, was littered with decorations for All Hallow's Eve. I'd traveled all across Beyond, a world of vibrant cultures and locales all tied together by magic and fairy tales, and yet nowhere—not even in the gleaming magitech cities or the spookiest of swamps—had I seen a place that took Halloween, or more properly, All Hallow's Eve, so seriously. My somewhat bull-headed friend Officer Thorn had volunteered to oversee the decorating, perhaps because Belville's one-person police station didn't give her much opportunity for bossing people around. I could hear her voice booming from the other corner of the park and instinctively put a tree (decorated with monstrous wolf-like masks) between myself and her, thinking as I nursed my chai latte, *William probably asked me to go out and get cinnamon rolls this morning because he was hoping I'd get roped into decorating and he wouldn't have to get up and help me run the shop.*

"Hiya, Red!"

The thing about trees is they only keep you hidden from people in one direction. Caught unaware, I gave an un-stealthy jerk as I wheeled to face Luca, town scholar and book seller. To be a "scholar" was a lifelong profession, which came with its own rules and protocol—and was invaluable to any town. Like all scholars, Luca wore a simple black robe and hood no matter if it was rain, sun, snow, or perfectly crisp autumn weather like today. And as usual for him, his green eyes twinkled against his dark skin as he grinned at me from under his hood.

But his smile faded much more quickly than usual, and behind his eyes there was worry as he added, "Why isn't William with you? You weren't going out alone, were you?'

"Only to the bakery and back," I said, showing him my basket of rolls—and a bonus quiche for myself—with a reassuring smile. "No one's going to abduct me in the town square. Besides, aren't you out alone?"

"Of course not. I have Frank," Luca informed me. Sure enough, a wizened white mink doing a very good impersonation of a woolly scarf lifted its head and nodded at me from Luca's shoulder.

I pursed my lips. Luca's mink had made a sudden appearance over the summer and ever since had been his inseparable companion. And while I thought it was nice for Luca to have a companion—"pet" wouldn't be the right word for an ancient, sentient mink, just as it would offend William, my dog-shaped magical familiar—I really wasn't sure how much protection it provided.

But then, appearances can be deceptive, and I had realized recently that maybe some of my preconceived notions were holding me back. Case in point: Frank had come in very handy during a fight with some bad guys at a wedding.

I shrugged away the argument, and the reminiscing. It was too early in the morning for both; I needed more chai. Or more accurately, I needed more of the caffeine my chai included.

"In any case," I said, sipping my drink, "I still think we're perfectly safe in the town square. Maybe not from all the paper ghosts and jack-o-lanterns, but definitely from roadside bandits. I'm not even *on* a road right now, for goodness' sake."

Luca fell into step beside me as I made my way toward the northeast corner of the square, where Red's Alchemy and Potions sat. "Red, you may be right—I mean, of course you're right—but it's that kind of thinking that could get you in trouble. Remember, that's exactly what got you into trouble last year at the castle, and then again last winter with the miners, too! I'm not saying you did anything wrong, exactly, and I know everything's fine now, but still—people worry about you, you know? And they aren't wrong to worry. You've been here more than a year now, Red. You know how weird and scary these attacks are for everyone here. It isn't something to take lightly. I know Officer Thorn can be—bossy, but her idea about sticking together is right. I think it's right, anyway. Just in case."

Luca's gaze on me was earnest—so earnest I had to turn away, staring instead at the crinkly red and yellow leaves under my feet. I got the feeling at that moment that perhaps what Luca was really worried about wasn't miners or robbers or even Officer Thorn, but *me*. I got the feeling—as I often had, especially since our attendance at my friend Taiwo's wedding over the summer—that perhaps what Luca was trying to say was something more like *I wish I could look out for you*, or even *I need you to stay safe because you are important to me.*

A fallen twig snapped beneath my boot. I dismissed my feelings. The cold, hard facts of the matter were that Luca had never said any such things aloud, and furthermore that he was a kind, caring, somewhat-over-enthusiastic soul to *everyone*. Not to mention he was one of my oldest friends in Belville, and had never indicated he wanted to be more.

Alchemists look for facts. That's what Paracelsus, my old teacher, would have said to me.

"Listen," I said as we approached my shop's front stoop, "I'm usually very safe, I promise. It's not like I go looking for mysteries. I've hardly even had time to leave my lab lately, what with all of Thorn's requests for ever-sticking glue and glow powder for her decorations. Today was just a blip. William woke up grumpy, and he wanted baked goods to cheer him up."

Luca stopped on the sidewalk and looked up at me innocently as I unlocked my door. "Why go buy them?"

The pure force of his faith in my baking—which is one of my favorite hobbies, but nowhere near good enough to consider actually opening a storefront—made me chuckle. "I would've made some, but like I said, I've been busy."

"I get that. I have been too. I'm putting together a display on ghost stories," Luca said absently as he glanced out at the Square.

This got my attention. The scholar before Luca, in addition to being a terribly cruel person, had always insisted that seasonal displays were "frivolous." When Luca had worked as his assistant, there had never been any such fun or levity. It made my heart swell to see how much better Luca was making his life now that he was free of Owl.

I paused before I went inside, following Luca's gaze out into the Square. Thorn and her ragtag group of volunteers marched from tree to tree, looking more like a class of trainees from the police guild than a bunch of holiday decorators. I could hear the officer yelling something that sounded suspiciously like *"Hut! Hut! Hut!"*

"Luca," I asked, my good feelings faltering again, "do you think we really will have the All Hallows celebration? What with everything that's been going on."

"I wondered that too," he admitted. "I actually looked back through the town records, because I was curious. Turns out the town council has *never* canceled a holiday celebration, not even for blizzards or droughts or one wild purple-sprite infestation. So I don't think they'll cancel one now—especially All Hallows. After all, the whole point of the party is to scare away evil spirits, right?"

* * *

William, who had specifically demanded *three* cinnamon rolls still warm from the oven, ate two at the register during the first hour the shop was open. I'd arranged my shop to have an open floor plan: upon coming in through the front door, a customer was greeted with rows of waist-high shelves and displays, mostly potions arranged by specialty or raw ingredients for various kinds of alchemy. The walls were lined with more potions and books. In the back right corner, tucked under a spiral staircase that led to my apartment, was a snug nook with two plush armchairs and a pot of free tea for customers waiting for special orders—or friends who wanted to visit, more often. To the left was the sales counter, which was usually William's domain; he used curls of blue magic to operate the cash register and keep up his protective wards on the shop. Behind the register was an internal wall that separated my lab from the public space. I'd knocked out a large window so that I could see William and anyone else in the store, but I often kept the door to the lab locked. The last thing I needed was for someone to barge straight into a chemical reaction or, even worse, the ceramic kiln I kept in one corner. From my lab, I had access to a patio full of potted plants and a teeny backyard.

Punctually at nine o'clock, a rap sounded at that back door. I left my vials of specialty glue on the workbench and pushed my alchemists' goggles up over my forehead as I went to answer it.

"Hey, Sir Rowan. You know, you could come in the front. As I've told you every morning since you started work here last spring," I added with a weary chuckle, standing back to wave my part-time employee in.

"Good morning, Miss Red," he said cordially. "And as I have answered you every morning since you were kind enough to employ me, I am quite comfortable with things the way they are."

Quite comfortable, indeed, I thought to myself as I let Sir Rowan into the shop and closed my lab door behind him. I had to smile. Sir Rowan had arrived in town last winter, hard on the heels of a string of murders and all kinds of trouble at the mine. Throughout the investigation he had clung fast to his *miss* thises and his *my lord* thats and his stuffy, yet rather charming ways. Most likely a human with water-fairy blood, he still wore the armor and the habits of an actual knight, despite having settled very happily into Belville (and into a relationship with Daisy, a dragon-in-human-form who lived nearby . . . but far be it from me to gossip). I had to admit, Sir Rowan had a calming, steadfast presence that came in handy around the shop, and he knew his flowers like no one else outside of the proprietors of Belville's floral shop, A Petal in Time. Plus, William adored him.

"This cinnamon roll is extra," I heard my grumpy companion saying through the open lab window. "You could have it. If you want."

"Why, thank you, William. 'Tis convenient indeed, for I came down early this morning, and it has been a long time since my breakfast."

'Extra!' I'm so sure, I thought, shaking my head. But Sir Rowan's answer was more interesting than William's deceit. 'Came down early,' I'd learned, was Sir Rowan's discreet way of saying that he'd come to work straight from Daisy's home high on the mountain, rather than his own magical campsite outside of town. The commute was long and, of late, dangerous. Since I knew we had no customers in the shop, and Luca's worried eyes were still haunting me, I decided to ask about it.

"Hey, Sir Rowan," I called through the window without looking up from my glue. "What does Daisy think of you traveling on the roads nowadays?"

"You refer to the reports of highway robbery, I presume," said Sir Rowan, his tone measured despite the fact that he was eating a sticky cinnamon roll.

William whined. "More than just reports. You should have seen the torn up tarp Officer Thorn brought in last week while you were out. It'd been clawed to pieces."

"Indeed?" Sir Rowan sounded interested. "And what did the officer wish Miss Red to do with it?"

"She wanted me to run a few preliminary tests on some liquid found on it. I *can* hear you," I reminded them both. "Apparently she was doing it at the behest of the person who was robbed, some former mayor or something. And yes, before you ask, some of the traces were definitely blood."

"Magical blood?" Sir Rowan asked.

"I think so. Or mythical creature, maybe. Which begs my question again—aren't you and Daisy worried at all, living out in the woods?"

Sir Rowan's tone was delicate. "One would have to be a fool indeed to attempt to rob or kidnap Miss Daisy."

"More like *dead*," William agreed with a snort. "They'd be dead."

I rolled my eyes, but I smiled too. Daisy was something of a recluse, but I'd met her a few times—enough to know that a) she was terribly shy, but almost as sweet as Luca and b) William was right. Anyone who messed with her or Sir Rowan would have one extremely angry and terrifyingly huge dragon to deal with.

"That makes sense," I said. "I just wondered if you were uneasy, that's all. We can figure out a way for you to stay in town if you ever need to."

"It strikes me that most of the targets so far have been wagons and travelers with expensive luggage—a far cry from myself and my horse," Sir Rowan said serenely. "However, I appreciate the sentiment, Miss Red."

Well, that answers that, I thought to myself as I stoppered up my last vials. *And he does have a point. The attacks of the past two weeks would just seem like normal highway robbery, if it weren't for . . .*

"Are you and Daisy coming to All Hallow's Eve next week?" William was asking Sir Rowan.

"I am not certain. While it is our wish to be friendly with our neighbors, neither of us is particularly fond of made-up spooks."

. . . if it weren't for all the ghoulish tales.

2

Knights and Masks

Before William and Sir Rowan could continue talking about the party—before I could decide whether to voice more of my misgivings—the bell above the shop's front door tinkled.

"Good morning," Sir Rowan called cordially to the new-comer. "If there is anything we can assist you to find, please do—"

"No need for that, lad, no need for that." The voice, and the step, that interrupted Sir Rowan were unfamiliar. I popped my head up from washing my tools in time to see the stranger, a man with graying hair and a heavy limp, glance dismissively over William. "Where is the 'Red' advertised as owning this shop? Finder of lost objects?"

"Back here," I called, before William could say something rude. He hated being overlooked almost as much as he hated people calling him a "dog." "I'll come out in just a minute."

Hastily I dried my hands on my rough apron and blew strands of my long black hair out of my face, thinking. Clearly, the man was new to Belville. In thirty seconds, he'd already created a rather condescending impression—in my experience, the only people who looked at William dismissively were snobs, self-important sorcerers (so, pretty much snobs), or criminals who were about to learn the error of their ways. I wasn't especially interested in helping *any* of those three groups find missing objects, but my shop's sign did advertise "object finding services," and I figured it would be better if I dealt with the newcomer myself.

I hung up the apron and squared my shoulders before emerging into the shop. I suppose I was bracing myself for a confrontation—but the stranger caught me by surprise.

"Ah, here's the alchemist," he said, stepping toward me at once and holding out his hand. "Of course you are Red. It's a pleasure to meet you. I'm Doctor Goodberry. You can call me Gavin. I just moved into the shop next door."

My head spun a bit as I processed all this. Dr Goodberry—or rather, Gavin—seemed to be human, or perhaps half elf, well into his middle age. For elves, that would mean perhaps a hundred years old. Gavin's stoop as he leaned upon a time-worn cane made it difficult to judge his height. His handshake was warm and firm, his fingers pale compared to my tan skin, and his blue eyes lit up as he introduced himself. Salt and pepper hair, a mustache and trim beard, and a thin silk scarf and fine coat over knee-high boots all combined to give him a very self-contained, respectable air.

A self-containment that I did not possess. "Not Gloria's?" I blurted. Hair and Beauty by Gloria, the salon next door to my shop, was a fixture in Belville. Furthermore, Gloria was my friend—despite a rather rocky start to our relationship.

"Of course not," William snorted from off to the side, behind the counter. "He must mean Cairn's old place. I heard it was rented, finally."

"Your assistant is correct," Gavin agreed, with a curt little nod to William that made me think maybe he hadn't been dismissive before, just determined.

"That's William," I said automatically, and continued by introducing Sir Rowan, too. In the meantime, I thought, *Ah—that makes sense. I was wondering what would ever be done with the old antiques shop.* My shop sat on the corner, and the antiques store sat catty-corner to it, across the road leading out of the Square. I'd been in the store often before it closed a year ago. "That space should make a very nice doctor's office," I continued. "That's assuming you're in Belville to practice medicine?"

"A prudent question. There are many branches of science, as you know yourself," Gavin answered with a twinkle in his eye as he squared off with me after nodding to the others. "But yes, Red, that's what I'm here to do. It seems there's a lack in Belville. I've been on the road some years now, and needed a place to settle down. Fortune brought us together, then."

"Uh huh." I could tell that Gavin wasn't planning on a quick stop-by-then-leave sort of introduction, so I decided to make us comfortable. "Would you like to sit for a while in our tea corner, there? William, Sir Rowan—"

"We'll watch the shop," William said hastily. I raised an eyebrow at him. It wasn't often William passed up a chance for new gossip.

But before I could comment, Gavin took me up on the offer. "Very kind of you, Red. The old bones aren't what they used to be. Ah, to be young again, eh? Though I've actually had this injury a very long time," he said, indicating his leg. Of course, I couldn't see anything wrong with it past his boot and trousers, but his use of the cane certainly indicated some fragility. As we took our seats in the plush armchairs, he added, "Makes me a better doctor. Gives me some idea of what my patients are going through."

"Empathy," I supplied, nodding. "Would you like some tea? I'm trying out a new blend of maple-flavored green today. Of course, I could go get a different one if you prefer."

"Caffeine," said the doctor, with a momentary severe glance at my floral teapot on its miniature burner. "Never touch it, myself."

I hesitated. I'd already started pouring myself a cup. "I could get an herbal blend—"

"Don't trouble yourself," Gavin interrupted, smiling again. "I won't be holding you up long. I'm sure you must be very busy. I see you do all kinds of potions and trinkets," he said, looking around the shop. "Do you do any tinkering? Magitech, automation, that sort of thing?"

Momentarily, I made a face. I couldn't help myself. In my opinion the only thing most magitech could do really well was break. Magitech puppets, or automatons—complex machines of gears, levers, and pulleys designed to mimic living beings—took that to its extreme. Besides, automatons and their magical counterparts, animated objects, raised all kinds of havoc and moral issues, in my experience. I avoided them like the plague.

But as customers came in and began to browse, and Gavin turned back to me, I rearranged my frown. "I, um, I don't, as a rule. I prefer botany and geology, myself. I know the town Witch, Trent, loves to animate objects, though, if you're looking for that kind of thing."

"No, no, I prefer to rely on science. Much more precise than magic," the doctor replied, glancing away. When he glanced back, though, his gaze was kindly. "It was only an idle question. I really don't know much about the topic. More importantly, I may need to pick your brain about running a business in Belville. Not now, of course, but outside of work hours sometime. If you're amenable?"

"Um," I said again, struck a little strangely by the way he said 'outside of work hours.' *He may not drink caffeine, but I think I still need more of it,* I thought wryly to myself.

"Purely as one neighbor to another," Gavin assured me, smiling now. "I happened to see you earlier this morning with your young man. The town scholar, I take it?"

"Uh—Luca," I corrected, feeling my cheeks fire up with a blush. "We aren't dating, but he is a very good friend. And yes, he's the town scholar. In fact, he would know even more than me about town customs and so on."

"I'll bear that in mind," Gavin said, with a look in his eye that seemed very much like a grandfatherly *you aren't dating yet, you say.* "Actually, I was curious because I believe I've found some things of his in my new office. Just scrolls and the like—elven history, if I had to guess. They were piled in the back corner of a closet."

"Probably an oversight of the previous owner's," I said, not sure how much to divulge. "You don't have to rush, but I'm sure Luca would love to have them back. If you find you're too busy unpacking and settling in, I'd be glad to take them over."

"I appreciate it, Red, but I think it will be good for me to get out and meet more of the town. After all, they may end up in my office sooner or later." Gavin said this with the briskness of a seasoned medical practitioner, someone who had seen many injuries, deaths, and sicknesses come and go.

"They might," I agreed, glancing out at my customers. Everyone was perfectly fine; Sir Rowan was helping a family with neon green glow powder for holiday decorations, and William was ringing up a new soap order for Johann, Gloria's assistant from next door. "We've done okay so far between my own salves and Trent's charms, but I'm sure most people will be very glad to have a proper doctor around."

"Especially with this business of the roadside attacks," said Gavin, with a serious air that made me think we'd reached another subject he'd wanted to talk about.

I surveyed him carefully. "Were you attacked too? Did you lose anything?"

"I was, and I did," the doctor said, chagrined. "It happened in the very early hours of the morning. I'd left while it was still dark, hoping to get to town early. Little did I know! It was over so fast, I never even got a glimpse of the perpetrator. Whoever it was, they got away with a crate of my best tools and a spool of copper wire."

"Oh, no," I said, with true emotion in my voice. All of my tools were very dear to me—I couldn't imagine any of them being stolen. "I'm so sorry. But if you were hoping we'd help you find them, I'm afraid we don't deal with stolen objects—more objects lost to time, and that sort of thing."

"Naturally, naturally," agreed the doctor. "No, I did not come to engage your services, Red. In fact I think it best if you and all of Belville's citizens stay out of the forest. Whatever attacked me was too fast—it swooped out of the trees, right into my cart and back up again. No, I would not ask anyone to face it. I was merely intrigued by your many talents."

"Ah, okay." I smiled at Gavin. It was a relief not to have let him down, but it was also nice to have someone *not* tell me to help them with something dangerous, for once.

"I've already ordered replacements," he continued. "There's no need to dwell on unpleasantness. I'd rather think of the upcoming celebrations. Samhain is important to the town, I take it?"

"It is indeed," I answered, my smile growing. That the doctor used *Samhain,* an archaic name for All Hallow's Eve, did not surprise me. Many traditional folks still did call it Samhain, and took it seriously as a time when the barrier between our world and the world of the dead grew thin. "You probably saw Officer Thorn out there setting up the last of the decorations. If last year was anything to go by, I think it'll be quite the event. They set up a bonfire in the Square, and have trick-or-treating and pumpkin carving and games for the young at heart. There's plenty of spooky stories and good food shared, too."

"And costumes?" the doctor asked, curious.

"Absolutely. Do you have one? I didn't have one last year, personally, and I was the odd person out. Nearly everyone will have at least a mask on," I explained, laughing.

Gavin smiled. "Thank you for the warning. I think I can rustle something up. Are there any guidelines you would suggest? What will you go as?"

And William says I'm *methodical,* I thought, grinning over someone asking for costume guidelines. "Most people dress as something traditionally considered 'spooky,' like ghosts, demons, or zombies. This year William wanted us to be undead, so I suppose that's what I'm going with."

"Friends can be so insistent, can't they," Gavin mused

indulgently. "Excellent. That gives me some good ideas to start with. Thank you, Red. I'll let you get back to work."

"No problem," I said as we both rose. "And if you do end up wanting to talk about business in Belville, just let me know."

Gavin acknowledged this with a firm nod, and made his way out the door. I took a moment next to the counter to get a feel for how things were going in the shop. Sir Rowan was still helping the same family, his hands now full of a veritable rainbow of glow powder. They were clustered in the far corner, examining jars of a fun, viscous potion I'd created just for decorative purposes, because it looked a little like fake blood. A few other lone customers browsed quietly.

"Bit full of himself, wasn't he?" William murmured so that only I could hear.

I understood that he meant the doctor. "Is that why you didn't want to talk to him?" I teased, glancing down at my companion.

"He wasn't all that nice to Sir Rowan, either," William replied with a sniff. "Besides, I knew whatever he told you, you would tell me. Eventually."

"Yeah, I get the impression he's used to being on his own," I said thoughtfully. I ignored William's comment, because to be honest, it was true. "But he seemed nice overall. He's going to return some old things of Cairn's to Luca, and he didn't end up asking me to go out into the forest to get lost stuff for him."

"Good," said William. "Because if he had, and you had said yes, I'd have had to have Thorn lock you up. We're *not* getting involved in theft."

"I know, that's what I told him," I said, chuckling. "You don't have to worry. I think it'll be nice to have a doctor as a neighbor," I added, still thinking. "I know he didn't make a *great* first impression, but I'm trying to work on getting better about making assumptions. Maybe it's the leaves changing colors or something that makes me feel like it's time for a change in myself, too."

"Or maybe it's *love*," said William.

"What?"

"Nothing," William rumbled. "You know, some people think of Samhain as the start of the new year."

"Oh?" I grinned as I took his meaning. "Well, perfect, then. That'll be my early resolution: no more letting myself get hemmed in by preconceptions."

3

Spooks and Ghouls

Later that afternoon, I'd just finished setting up a batch of lightstick liquid—my home-made lightsticks were selling faster than I could put them out on the shelves—and Sir Rowan was putting together our monthly order from the glassblower's shop down the mountain when the decorating party in the Square broke up. I knew this not because I could see them (I'd covered the shop's two picture windows with black silk, cobwebs, and other fun reminders of the season) but because of the sound.

Officer Thorn marched herself up the shop steps with purpose, and when she opened the door, the shop bells jangled like a brass band in a hurricane. Strangely, though, she didn't announce herself—and I didn't hear her voice at first. Instead, a dozen other voices flooded in: the volunteer decorators, making use of my free tea.

They swarmed around the waiting nook and the sales counter, and it seemed every single one of them was talking.

"Did you hear? Another cart was attacked, just two nights ago. The night was so cloudy no one saw anything—no one even knew what had happened until the next morning, so there never was any chance to help," said a werewolf named Sarya, who ran the bakery along with her husband.

"I don't see why *she* should be so worried about it. It's clear that *some people* are in more danger than others," hissed a voice in the corner, one I recognized vaguely as belonging to one of the servers at Lavender's Tavern.

"Nothing like a Samhain with a real criminal about, eh?" the local handy-gnome, gossip, and (apparently) seasonal volunteer, Dusty, was saying loudly to William. "Rangers still haven't found a trace of anything that's been taken. And if you ask me, they're never gonna."

I was about to pop my head out the lab window and ask Dusty to keep his voice down—and maybe ask for some details, too, because no one was ever as well-informed as Dusty—when the door to the lab rattled. I turned down the heat on the magical burner under the pot of lightstick fuel and went to join the fray, pressing a hidden button on my gloves as I went. Like my goggles, my gloves are almost *always* on my person. Alchemy isn't a profession, it's a way of life, as my old teacher would say. At least with my goggles on my forehead and my gloves converted to fingerless accessories, I looked a tiny bit normal.

But I shouldn't have worried about my looks. On the other side of the door was Officer Thorn, crowding so close that she was practically one with the wall.

"Red," she said, in perhaps the quietest tone I'd ever heard her use, "we have to talk. Upstairs."

"Lead on," I replied, waving her up the spiral staircase to my apartment. On a normal day I might have teased her for simply assuming my living quarters were open to her, but something about her struck me as too serious to be questioned.

***

My apartment sits directly over the shop, with a landing at the back that the stairs open on to. Technically I have two staircases: the spiral one that leads into the shop, and a more conventional one leading to an exterior door. Both share the landing. Even inside my kitchen with the door to the landing closed, we could still hear the murmur of voices below.

Officer Thorn paced, which in my little studio meant that she walked back and forth from the fireplace in one corner to the dining table in another, passing by the front windows and messing with my light. Fortunately, over the winter, a songbird-sized pixie called Sugar had taken up residence in my kitchen. I *could* have used a spell or magical traps to kick her out—pixies are like teeny tiny fairies, and since they usually prefer not to talk, a lot of people see them as pests— but like Luca's mink, she'd been very helpful in the past. As far as I was concerned, she had a home for life. We'd settled into a routine: I cooked, and she watched. With Sugar hovering over my shoulder, I could use her faint pink glow to pour water and start the tea kettle boiling.

And *still*, Officer Thorn had said nothing. I glanced surreptitiously at my friend. This had to be a record. Unfortunately, it was one that made my stomach clench.

"How was the decorating?" I ventured as I pulled mugs from the cupboard. Sturdy, elven-made ceramic for Thorn, and for me, my personal favorite, a shell-inspired mug with a rainbow sheen on it from my merfolk friends.

Officer Thorn stopped pacing and pivoted so she could

look out over the Square, as though considering my question. Instead, she just said, "I saw you this morning with Luca."

You and everyone else, apparently. "Oh. Well, we weren't trying to hide."

"Hmph."

"I had to get William some pastries this morning. Have you had anything to eat?" I kept talking partly out of embarrassment and partly to fill the unusual silence. Officer Thorn shook her head and kept pacing.

"Ooookayy," I said quietly to Sugar. The pixie shimmered at me, which at least was more of a response than I was getting from Thorn.

Since I hadn't had lunch yet, I pulled some leftover cheese out of the icebox and set it on a plate with some apples and a jar of peanut butter. Taking the platter in one hand and my tea tray with a steaming pot and our mugs in the other, I crossed the kitchen to set everything down on the table in the corner.

"Sit," I told Thorn, pointing to the nearest chair. "And drink your tea. And eat something. And then for goodness' sake, tell me what's going on before all this tension makes me implode."

For once in her life, Officer Thorn did as she was told.

I sat next to her and waited. Though I usually thought of her as bold and brash, truthfully, Thorn was beautiful too, and extremely orderly. I had never *once* seen her out of her police guild uniform with its shiny buttons and high collar. Her hair was long and black, like mine, but instead of shoving hers ruthlessly in a ponytail every day, she wore it loose and shiny and perfectly cut. To me, that made no sense; but I suppose when you're half-orc, little things like getting your hair in your face might not matter so much. Officer Thorn's heritage made her broader, taller, and much stronger than me, and in fact many people in Belville. I have to admit though that I privately thought the coolest part of Thorn being half-orc was her mossy green skin. It seemed to underscore her status as a force of nature.

She nibbled at an apple, made a face, then ate half of it in one go. "Tell Luca not to wander around alone," she said as she swallowed.

I chuckled. "That's what *he* was telling *me*. And he says he's not alone, he's got Frank the three-legged mink."

"Not enough." Officer Thorn shook her head and then drained her tea. "I don't want any of you involved in this business with the roadside attacks, Red."

"Why? What happened?"

Officer Thorn paused in the middle of pouring herself a new cup, and sighed. "It isn't just thievery, Red, it's something worse. I *know* it is."

I frowned. Technically, since the attacks had all occurred in the forest rather than in town, a special unit of the police guild called the "Rangers" were supposed to be investigating them. And they weren't telling anyone in Belville very much. So anything Officer Thorn "knew" was likely based on a hunch, not on evidence.

"They're bringing in a witch hunter," Thorn admitted abruptly.

"Yikes, that sounds intense." I had heard of witch hunters only vaguely—to the rest of us layfolk, witchy affairs are very mysterious. Of course, everyone in Beyond has heard scary stories about witches who went "rogue" or "bad" and started wreaking havoc. Those tales are especially popular at this time of year. But even in all my travels, I'd never *met* such a witch. And I'd also never met a witch hunter—a mercenary-like person tasked with tracking down witchy rule-breakers.

A witch hunter on the outskirts of Belville? Seems extreme. Since Officer Thorn wasn't volunteering any details, I asked, "Do they really think the attacks have something to do with rogue magic?"

Thorn glowered, and her answer wasn't an answer. "The town council's official policy is to let the Rangers handle it, so I haven't been involved." But she rapped her fingertips on the table and added finally, "I don't like it, and I don't want you or Trent involved. Or William."

Ah. Things were starting to make sense. I could see how Officer Thorn might feel protective of her primary magical helpers—Trent and William, and by proxy, me—in the face of accusations of nefarious magic.

"It's probably all show," Thorn continued at a growl. "If they were spending as much time investigating the attacks as they are talking about how dangerous they are, they'd have caught the culprit already. Or at least have a profile. Instead they just have a mess of contradictory clues, from the sound of it. They're probably sitting on it just to get back at me."

"To get back at you?" I echoed, confused.

"When Officer Ebb called me in to help with that business in Seaside, some of the other officers got jealous," she explained. With a loud *bang* as her fist came down on the table, she finally broke. "Why don't they see this is more important than professional squabbles?"

Though I could understand why Officer Thorn's growing reputation as a crime-solver—aided by myself and William, of course—might cause jealousy, I was still in the dark. "More important how? You mean because people's things are being taken?"

"My uncle called earlier today," she replied, in a somewhat startling non sequitur. But her voice was as intense as ever, so I let her run with it. "He called to check in on our plans. I had to tell him to stay home. Because mark my words, Red, when highway robbery is let to go on like this, sooner or later it ends in murder, and I can't take that chance!"

"You don't want him to be in danger," I theorized, trying to fit the narrative together.

"He was coming to see me," Officer Thorn continued, her voice thick with emotion. "My—my whole family was going to come. They wanted to see Samhain in Belville. It's a big time for us, you know, we—it's considered the end of the year. Most orc families think of it like that. The end of the harvest season. Gods, now I'm babbling," she said, abruptly turning to hide her face in a handkerchief fished out of a pocket. "I—I told them not to come. This morning. Because those blasted Rangers haven't solved a thing. I had to tell them to stay home."

While I had known about Samhain being a big deal in orcish culture, I hadn't known about this family visit. Thorn rarely discussed her family at all, aside from humorous tales about her brothers. I'd always thought that this wasn't because she didn't love them, but because she loved her found family in Belville with equal ferocity. I could readily understand that for Thorn to tell someone she loved *not* to come see her had been a very difficult task indeed.

"I'm so sorry," I said, and I meant it. "I can see how it must be really frustrating."

"And they continue to *not* share a single thing that's going on if they can help it," Thorn said, grinding out the last few words as though determined to carry on without stopping. "The Rangers have been *useless* if you ask me. *You* are more helpful than those pigs."

"Gee, thanks," I said. "But really. You know I'll have your back on this one."

Officer Thorn brought her cup down on the table, hard. "No."

"But think about it, Thorn, if we look into things from our end—"

"No one but me is getting themselves hurt on the Rangers' watch, and that's final!"

We paused, staring at each other, each having spoken over the other. Usually, I made it a point not to fight with Officer Thorn. But every once in a while, she crossed the line.

"You're wrong," I told her, crossing my arms. "Did you hear what you just said? You're clearly already investigating this case, even though you keep saying you know nothing. You aren't thinking straight. If you're investigating, then you're probably in danger, and you need back up. And you need to tell the council what you're thinking, too. In fact the only thing you *don't* need to do is go rushing straight into a violent problem without thinking everything through!"

"I can't just sit by," Officer Thorn replied, leaping to her feet, upsetting her chair. "I'm not losing anyone because of this bureaucracy, Red. *None* of you, do you hear? Of course I'll tell the council, I'm not stupid. I already called a town meeting for tonight. But I'm telling you right now, if you start poking into this case I'll—"

"You'll *what?*" I challenged, standing too. "You'll do what, exactly? When *you* shouldn't be investigating either, and technically you came to *me* in the beginning to take a look at that tarp?"

"The tarp was a one-time thing," Thorn yelled. Her reticence had clearly dissolved into frustration. "I just needed enough evidence to take up my case with the council!"

"If you can admit you need evidence, why can't you admit that you need *me*?" I shot back.

Officer Thorn steamed. "If I get the all-clear to investigate tonight and I take anyone with me, it'll be that blasted dog. *You* stay right here and look after your shop, like you're supposed to do."

I'll admit, the barbs about my shop and about William being a simple "dog" hurt. That's the problem with fighting with friends—and why I often did my best to avoid it. But I let Officer Thorn stomp down the back stairs without complaint. A concession made with poor grace is still a concession, after all. She'd gone from being determined to go it alone to declaring that she'd drag William out with her.

Whether she knew it yet or not, *I* knew that I'd just won the argument.

4

Snake in the Grass

I may have won an argument, but I'd also committed myself to investigating robberies—something William had *just* told me not to do. *That'll be a conversation to be approached carefully,* I decided, sighing.

After Officer Thorn stomped down the staircase leading straight outside, there was silence. Worried that I hadn't heard her slam the back door, I decided to go after her and check. And maybe sit on the back patio for a moment to calm down. William and Sir Rowan were no doubt fine in the shop, and we still had a precious hour or two before we needed to close up for the day.

I went down the back stairs, bypassing the shop altogether. Officer Thorn *had* closed the door, it turned out—mostly; it hadn't actually latched, and hung open just by an inch or so. I made a mental note to get William or, even better, Trent to make a spell that ensured the door closed every time. And, having reached the maximum level of how responsible I felt like being in that moment, I shut the door behind me and took a seat on the rim of an ancient pot holding a miniature orange

28

tree.

I'd better move or cover the fair-weather plants soon, I thought, distracting myself from my worries as I glanced around the crowded patio. Even as a traveling alchemist, I'd kept potted plants. Impractical as it was to travel with living plants, I just couldn't force myself to rely on dried herbs alone. Plus, I liked them. Plants, in general, smell good, look nice, and above all, they don't cause trouble.

And since I'd settled in Belville, my plant collection had easily tripled in size. Many of them were ones I used often in potions and experiments, though some—like a wizened old dragon's blood tree—were simply botanical friends. I cast a glance over to the taller trees and bushes in the corner, still thinking about how to prepare for the winter weather.

I abruptly stopped planning, though, when I noticed an unfamiliar shadow.

My heart caught in my throat. *Jade?*

But I shook the thought away. *Jade* had been the name I'd given to a ghostly presence which had turned out to be an alter ego of Luca's—an effect of a curse. Before we'd realized what was going on, I must admit I'd almost fallen for Jade. Now that Jade was actually Luca, well, things were . . . different.

No; the shadow was an intruder, and while it might have been hidden so well that Thorn hadn't noticed it, I certainly wasn't going to give it the same grace.

"In exactly two seconds, I'm going to call my familiar out here," I told the shadow.

The briar's woody stems shimmered and rustled, and from between them, a tall man in dark clothing stepped forward. His spine stooped in habitual bad posture, and his mouth was set in one long line. Dark green eyes and a once-broken nose didn't distract from the reptilian scales that covered his gray head, neck, and arms in crisscrossing patterns.

"Ryuko," I said, recognizing the assistant at Belville's Curiosities Shop and Museum. "Why were you hiding behind that bush?"

Ryuko shrugged. "Didn't want to talk to *Thorn.*"

He said her name the way some people say *white and black hairy mold on bread.* I had no idea what Ryuko's life had been like before he came to Belville—he'd settled shortly before I had. But it was pretty clear that in his past life, he and the police had not been friends. And Officer Thorn suffered for that.

Not that she would care, I reminded myself, letting his tone slide. "So that means you were sitting on the patio until she came out? Why?"

Ryuko glanced around my backyard once more, as though searching the bare dirt and ancient fence for someone else. "I have to talk to you, Red. But not because you're an alchemist."

I waved him over to sit next to me and kept my mouth shut. Truthfully, my heart was racing. *The only reason Ryuko could have to talk to me aside from alchemy is my family in the desert, but I thought our friend Clare promised not to tell him I'm technically a Seer! I don't do that any more. Do I really need to have that conversation again? William bothers me about it enough!*

I drew breath, readying myself to say, *Sorry, Ryuko, I don't do the Seer "thing," go somewhere else if you want someone to intuit your fortune or read your palm.* But before I could get the first syllable out, he said,

"You, uh, you traveled a lot before you got here, right? You and William?"

Is that *what this is about?* I breathed a sigh of relief. "Oh. I mean, yes, we did. Why?"

Ryuko glanced over his shoulders. I half expected him to stick out his tongue and taste the air—but that was unfair of me. Though Ryuko *was* snakekin, meaning that for some magical reason—be that a curse or a blessing or the gift of a god—he and, presumably, his family had snake-like attributes, there's always a fuzzy line when it comes to -kin. It varies from person to person how much like their animal they might be.

"Did you ever run into . . . summoning?" he asked at last.

Summoning? I'm not an expert in magical matters but I did know about summoning, or to put it simply, conjuring up creatures using magic. Technically William, as a familiar, was a summoned creature. But much more nefarious beings could be summoned, too. From Ryuko's manner, I had a feeling that was the kind of summoning he was talking about.

"I'm not the magical expert. That's William's realm," I said.

"Obviously." Ryuko rolled his eyes at me, like we were twelve years old. "So do either of you know anything about it?"

"What are you hoping we'll know?" I asked suspiciously. "Neither of us have been involved with anything like that, if that's what you're asking."

"No, it's not. I know that." Ryuko shook his head, looked down at the stone patio beneath his feet, and seemed to come to a decision. "Look. I know what's going on in the woods. It's going to be a summoning."

I blanched, thinking of Thorn's determination to solve the case. "I thought it was just theft so far."

Ryuko shook his head again, this time vehemently. "That's just it. It's *what* they're stealing. Stones, herbs. Everyone at the shop was saying how the old mayor's luggage was ransacked and he lost a set of obsidian crystals and all the wine he'd packed, but not his fancy jeweled shaving kit. It's a pattern. I—I've seen a gang do something like this before. I don't think it's the same people, but it's the same thing. I *know* it is."

I paused, weighing this. Despite their differences, Ryuko sounded a lot like Officer Thorn. And I couldn't help but respect his conviction. Even if he wasn't quite making sense yet. "Okay, so how do you know?"

"I just *know*." *Hmm,* I thought, *maybe he's a little too much like Officer Thorn on this case. There seem to be a lot of hunches going around.* Ryuko continued, "That's why I came to you. I was hoping you could help me prove it. We *have* to prove it, Red. I'm going to tell everyone at the meeting tonight."

"Tonight?" I echoed, wondering how that would play into Officer Thorn's plans.

"I have to. Everyone here is in danger."

Again I paused, looking Ryuko over carefully. As a rule, he and I didn't spend much time together, and I didn't know him well. I didn't think anyone in town did, honestly. As delicately as I could, I said, "Are you *positive* some kind of summoning gang is involved, Ryuko? Because after the thing with the carousel horses. . ."

"So I was wrong about the shadow organization and the worldwide ring of thieves," Ryuko said, batting the memory of the last time we'd worked together on a mystery aside. "In that case. That doesn't mean things like that don't happen. I've seen it before."

"Sure. But after the way you got everyone riled up last time . . ."

"I *know*," Ryuko said impatiently. "Even without that, no one ever wanted to trust me. Even *you* just think I'm some good-for-nothing shop assistant who'll steal anything not nailed down. I know what you all think of me. But it isn't true. Like I told you, Red, I came here to make a better life."

"One without magical gangs, presumably," I mused, watching him. "I'm not saying I don't believe you now, Ryuko. I'm just saying you're going to have to make a good case to the council, especially if you want them to believe something so . . . dramatic."

"Again, that's why I came to *you*," Ryuko said. He shifted on the planter of rosemary he'd perched on, rubbing the leaves and releasing their spicy scent.

Rosemary, for memory. What a coincidence. I sighed. "I get it. And I would help if I could," I told him. "But you have to help me here, too. Tell me everything that makes you think 'summoning' about these attacks, and we can go from there."

Ryuko nodded, leaning forward over spindly knees in black trousers. "It's like this. I—well, to start off, did you ever hear of the Big Bad Wolf Gang?"

The "Big Bad Wolf Gang?" I raised my eyebrow at him. "I'm familiar with the fairy tale character, if that helps." After all, Beyond *is* a fairy tale world—all kinds of tales are familiar here, and we often see new versions of old stories playing out with little twists. Or spooky twists, in this case.

Ryuko shook his head. "Look, I know it sounds silly. That's just what the newspapers started calling them. They called themselves the Dogs of the Moon. They wanted to summon the actual Moon Dogs, who some people think guard the gates of the afterlife. The gang leader wanted to distract the Moon Dogs so that he could bring someone back."

"Wait—are we talking about necromancy?" I asked, startled.

Again, Ryuko shook his head. "That's just the one example I know of. That gang was caught because they stole this massive cache of obsidian from a jeweler and then a ton of wolfsbane in one night. They used weapons like claws and daggers made of fangs. *Really* obvious. I'm not saying that whoever's doing the thefts now wants to summon the Moon Dogs. They could want to summon an actual wolf, for all I know. But all the stuff they're taking is similar, and their weapons are, too."

"You mentioned the obsidian from the mayor," I agreed slowly. "And, what, you're thinking the wine is meant to be a magical offering of some kind?"

"Maybe," said Ryuko, maddeningly. "It's more the other stuff. The old mayor was the first one attacked, but did you know right after that—the very next morning—a shipment for A Petal in Time was raided? They stole club moss and wolfsbane that was supposed to be for the town's Samhain celebration. And a cart going *out* of town, from the mine, was attacked and the robber ran off with just a bunch of bloodstone, even though there were gold nuggets in the cargo, too. Plus one of Priya's shipments got attacked and she lost a ton of special black candles. And everything was slashed up, like with claws."

Priya, Ryuko's boss, ran the curiosities store along the northern end of the Square. It made sense that Ryuko would know about that firsthand, but the depth of the rest of his knowledge of the robbers' movements left my head spinning. *He may have moved on with his life, but he certainly keeps tabs on his old world.* Aloud, I said, "So, obsidian, club moss, wolfsbane, black candles, and bloodstone—that's all stuff that would be used in a summoning?"

"The wolfsbane was what really tipped me off," said Ryuko, nodding. "But that's not all. Think about it. It's almost

Samhain. That's the perfect time to summon something like the graveyard Black Dog or even Cerberus or the Hounds of the Wild Hunt—"

"Whoa." I held up a hand to interrupt him. If he was going to sit there and list mythical wolves or big dogs, we'd be stuck until well after sunset. "I get how wolfsbane makes you think there's some kind of wolf or doglike creature involved, but seriously, why would someone go to the trouble?"

"Why does anyone go into crime?" Ryuko shot back impatiently. "Maybe they want to get ransom money from the town. Maybe they want power or revenge on someone here. It could be anything. The main thing is we can't let them do it. Once you start messing around with this kind of stuff, there's no going back."

I gazed at Ryuko speculatively. I wondered if by 'this kind of stuff' he meant summoning wolf creatures, or criminal gangs, or both.

"Do you believe me?" Ryuko pressed.

"I . . . I might," I told him, and when his face fell, I said, "Don't take it personally, Ryuko—it's just my nature. A good scientist doesn't come to premature conclusions. Let's just say I agree with you that there's something here we need to look into. And you're right. Someone *does* need to tell the council."

"I will," Ryuko said, stubbornly. "I don't care what they say. I just have to do this."

I nodded and, for the first time that day, I smiled at him. "Alright. I'll do some of my own research, too, and maybe check with William and Trent. I may not be done by tonight, but I'll be at the council meeting, and we'll back you up."

And just like that, I'd made the last in a string of decisions that would upend the safe appearances of my little world.

5

Full House

Of course, at first, the rest of the afternoon seemed completely normal. The shop was busier than ever, and I didn't have a spare moment to talk with William or track down Trent. Forced to bide my time, I decided to fill in my companion on our way to the town meeting that evening.

William and I made it into the town hall, just a few blocks north of the shop, an hour after closing. We'd been held up by some intensive cleanup and not a little dithering on Sir Rowan's part (the knight had finally decided that it was more important to go spend time with his "lady" than to hear the complaints of Belville, but it took him easily half an hour to get to that point).

"Should've got here earlier. 'Specially if there's going to be talk about summoning cursed wolves or the like," William grumbled as we squeezed our way into the back of the huge—and hugely crowded—hall. Belville's town hall was actually the blacksmith's guild with all the metal-working equipment magically shoved to one side. It underscored the town's

37

origins as a mining town. And, when arguments got heated, all the weapons lining one wall really added an element of excitement.

"Exciting" was usually the last word I'd use to describe town politics, though. I rarely came to meetings, although William never missed a one. And despite my promises to Ryuko and Thorn—or perhaps *because* of them—I had my misgivings about being there that night.

"Blame your idol the knight," I mumbled back, doing my best to smile and nod politely at a family of dwarves as we shuffled by them looking for breathing room. The eldest of the family coughed on me. "So do you think there's truth to what Ryuko was saying?"

"Actually, there might be." William carved out a space for us in the very middle of the back wall, using his fluffy tail almost like a broom to sweep away other onlookers. Someone else in the crowd to the right coughed, too, and William added in a whisper, "Hope you took your vitamins."

I made a face, thinking of the orange tree on my patio. Some vitamin C certainly wouldn't go amiss if a cold was sweeping the town; it *was* the season for such things, after all. And thinking about colds was suddenly much more palatable than thinking of fairy tale demons. "If there's something going round the town, then it's probably good we have a new doctor after all."

"Didn't you hear?" William asked, his gruff voice undercutting the constant murmur of the crowd around us. "There's a sign in his window saying he has to postpone opening until he has his replacement tools."

This announcement distracted me from looking around wondering why the meeting hadn't started. "Really? That's got to be pretty hard on him, losing days where he could be making sales and helping people."

"Yes really," William said, in the tones of a teenager dealing with a basically fossilized ancestor. "Dusty was telling me all about it while you and Thorn were yelling earlier."

"Are you talking about the new doctor? He's really nice!" A sunny new voice added.

"Luca," I said, turning to find the ubiquitous scholar behind me. "I guess he found you and gave you the stuff Cairn left behind, then?"

My reference to Cairn, whose history with Luca was beyond complicated, showed how distracted my mind still was. I cringed as Luca's excitement at finding us faltered. *I really seem to be stepping in it with everyone today.*

Of course, Luca saw my reaction. Despite constantly wearing a hood that *had* to have narrowed his field of vision, he seemed to see everything. "It's okay, Red," he said, divining my regrets with ease that would have put my mothers to shame. "And you're right, he did. It's just elven records— nothing—well, nothing about curses, or anything. Just generic stuff. Shows you how worried she and Owl were, at the time, that they found even that to be worrisome enough to hide!"

"I'm glad it was nothing too bad, and that you got it back. But I didn't mean to bring up bad feelings," I said awkwardly.

"Don't worry about it. It was a good excuse to meet Doctor Gavin," said Luca, smiling. After a moment's hesitation, he reached out and put a hand on my shoulder. "That's all in the past—thanks to you."

"Thorn and William helped," I mumbled, growing suddenly way too hot in the unheated hall.

"*Shhh,*" said William, very loudly. "Stop flirting, you two.

The mayor's starting the meeting now."

The sound of a gavel against an anvil rang through the hall, interrupting my mortified glare at William. The mayor, a no-nonsense glassblower by day, cleared her throat and quelled the unruly audience with one sweeping look.

As she began her preliminary remarks, I have to admit my attention wandered. I was looking for Officer Thorn—or Ryuko.

And I didn't have to wait long. Almost before Mayor Marguerite was done explaining why we were all present, Officer Thorn strode out of the shadows, magic twinkling around her throat indicating an (unnecessary) amplification spell.

"Most of you know the facts of the recent attacks. But for those who don't, listen up," she said, immediately taking over the makeshift stage. "First known attack was two weeks ago, on the former mayor's caravan. Three more attacks following that, all at night, all on the eastern road out of town. One more attack as recent as this morning, on our new doctor's wagon. Wire, tools, and other valuables missing. So far, no one injured.

"Now," continued Thorn, pacing with a vengeance, "because these attacks took place outside of town, the council ruled to let the Rangers sort it out. I understand that this is the policy. But I ask you: have any of you, councilpersons or otherwise, heard any kind of report from the Rangers since they took over two weeks ago? Have you even *seen* them?

"Add to that the fact that apparently the case is serious enough that they're making a move to bring in a witch hunter, and you can see that this is getting too big for them. We're the ones who know these woods—I say it's time we get involved.

"Ms Mayor, Council, I want to *officially* suggest that the Rangers are out of their depth on this one. They don't know the woods like we do, and they don't know the victims like we do, either. We don't have to kick them out. But we have to give them help. *We need to be involved in this case.* More people—relatives—will be coming to town for the holiday next week. We *must* solve this case and catch the criminal by then."

I had to admire Officer Thorn's matured sense of subtlety. Though it was pretty clear that when she said "we" she meant "I", at least she hadn't started yelling.

Marguerite, the mayor, came up to stand beside Thorn on the stage. Behind her, lined up along the wall like a row of suspects, stood the town council—the true power in Belville. I didn't know any of the six members very well, except Lavender, who ran the local tavern. No doubt William could have rattled off biographies of all of them.

"We hear you, Officer Thorn," Marguerite was saying, "and the Council will carefully consider your request, I'm sure. There are still six days before Samhain. It is my belief that—"

"We don't *have* days," someone called from the front row. "Not unless you want a hellhound loose in Belville!"

Ryuko.

***

Officer Thorn looked like she might burst—whether at the interruption or at the idea that Belville might fall prey to a spectral wolf, I couldn't tell. Even the mayor, usually unshakable, was taken aback.

And clearly, Ryuko wasn't one to wait for permission. In

their silence, he leapt up onto the stage. Without the benefit of a spell, he began to shout, alternating between facing the crowd and the Council.

"That's what this is. How can you not see it? This is bigger than any of us and bigger than the Rangers. They *have* to be stopped! I've seen all of this before. If no one does anything, then whoever's behind this will summon something demonic and take over the town and there won't *be* any holiday to worry about!"

"Something demonic like what?" asked the mayor warily.

"How do you know any of this?" Officer Thorn growled.

"It's *obvious*," said Ryuko. "Obsidian? Wolfsbane? Ritual wine and candles? That's exactly what a summoner would need. If they were honest and this wasn't something to worry about, they'd just buy the materials themselves. Instead, they're stealing it, to try to keep attention off of themselves. And they're using weapons based around what they want to summon. It's like an obsession. It all fits together. And they're getting away with it, because no one will admit the pattern!"

"Trust Ryuko to insult the people he's trying to help," William muttered. In fact, the entire crowd around us was muttering, most of them very uncomfortably. "If he wants people to listen to him, he's not going about it very well."

"He came to me earlier and said this stuff too," I told Luca, since William had already heard the story. "I'm sure he believes it. He was pretty worked up. I told him we'd help look into it, at least."

"I wish I'd known about this before," Luca agreed. "I'd have looked it up before I came. I don't think there's anything specifically in Belville's history about summonings, but I *did* come across some stories about a ghostly wolf in the woods when I was putting together the All Hallow's display. And there were stories about night attacks on the roads, too, but I think the two were always separate. How awful, to think of the two together!"

Luca glanced at me earnestly, and I realized that—inappropriate as it was—I was smiling at him. I had never imagined that when I settled down in a little rural town I'd find friends so erudite and kind at the same time.

Though he couldn't possibly know my thoughts this time—*could he?*—Luca smiled back. "What do you think, Red? How will you help?"

My response was cut off as Officer Thorn, still at the front of the room, found her voice. "If all this is true, then what do you propose we do about it?"

"Find the summoner. It could be anyone. Make a test," Ryuko said at once. "Test everyone. Anyone with ties to dark magic or the occult has to be kept inside and under watch at night. It's the only way!"

6

The Drop of a Hat

I watched in shock as the town Council, supported vociferously by the people around us, not only agreed with Ryuko—but began to plan how the tests would be done *right that moment.*

"Hey. Hey. Ground to Red," William said, nudging at my leg. "Focus. There's nothing we can do about it."

I shivered.

"What's wrong? Are you okay?" Luca asked beside me.

I tried to turn to him and laugh it all off, but my mouth wouldn't work.

"We don't do checkpoints," William told Luca, his voice low. "Why do you think we've never stayed very long in a place until now?"

I can't imagine that explanation made any sense to Luca. The truth is, even though alchemy is useful, it's also weird. It's science without being magitech and miracles without being magic. A lot of people don't understand it—after all, I've studied it for years and barely understand it myself. And things that people don't understand are usually the first to fall when towns start instituting "tests." William and I had left more than one place in the middle of the night when things got dicey. One of my old friends, a girl who'd been an apprentice with me in another corner of Beyond, had actually been imprisoned for three years—a truly unheard-of amount of time in most civilized places—because a local tinkerer's experiments had created tiny monsters and she'd taken the fall for it.

And now, not only was I an alchemist, but William was, well, *William*—a giant, fluffy, wolflike creature in a town about to be overcome with a fear of magic wolves.

My feet itched and my thoughts roared. Just the very *idea* of imprisonment makes me want to run. I turned, a half-formed plan in my head, some vague thoughts about jumping past everyone and heading for the door.

But then my heart rate slowed, and I was rooted to the spot. My side was reassuringly warm. Luca had put his arm around my waist.

"Nothing's going to happen, Red," he was saying in my ear. "No one's going to do anything to you. It's just a few questions, and then we'll leave. Remember how you stuck up for me, when Officer Thorn thought I killed Owl? I'll stick up for you. That's something you have now that maybe you didn't have before. I'll stick up for you. Everyone knows you have nothing to do with dark magic summonings; that'd be absurd."

I turned infinitesimally so I could see Luca's face. "I didn't realize *this* was Ryuko's plan," I whispered, licking my dry lips. "Sorry."

Whether I was apologizing for my reaction or for the inconvenience of a "test," I couldn't say. Luca was supremely unbothered, though. "You don't have anything to be sorry for," he assured me. "Come on, everyone's making a line to the right of the stage. Let's join in, and then we can get it over with and go home. I'll make you some of my famous hot chocolate."

As we walked, William on one side and Luca on the other, I chuckled. I had to—the other option was crying, which was a highly irrational reaction. "Luca, I don't think I've heard of any of your cooking being described as 'famous.'"

"Infamous, maybe," supplied William, who seemed very unbothered for someone who fit Ryuko's description of a nefarious summoned creature.

Luca beamed at us both. "Making hot chocolate isn't cooking. It's stirring. And boiling milk, I guess. You don't mind if I make it with milk, do you? I tried it once with almond milk and it was just as good. One old recipe I found in the storeroom suggested using water, but—"

"Luca," I interrupted, "if you're talking about recipes and stirring, that's cooking."

"Well either way, it's very good," he promised. "Just you wait. We'll be making some in no time."

William rumbled as he looked up the line to the stage ahead of us, not quite growling, but not agreeing either. "What do these tests entail? Red distracted me and I didn't hear what the mayor said."

"I think they called Trent up to see if people have magic," Luca said. "That's easy peasy, right, Red? You and I don't have any magic at all."

It *was* reassuring, though I felt bad for Trent, getting sucked into all this. He was probably used to it, though—in spite of, or perhaps because of, his easy-going nature, Trent got dragged into lots of hijinks. He was Officer Thorn's other favorite "unofficial assistant." And from what I understood, it was fairly simple for a Witch to discern if someone else had magic or not—the same way I could test for magic in blood.

Easy peasy, I thought, trying to hold on to Luca's optimism. But I wasn't so sure that Luca *didn't* have magic. Though an off-the-shelf glamour spell on his robe made him appear like a dark-skinned human, he was actually descended from a race of tree elves, and the curse on him left him with a twisted, dark unicorn-like horn and the ability to fade into shadows. *How detailed is Trent's spell going to be?* Technically, even my Seer heritage could count as magical blood. It certainly was *mystical.* And William was straight-up a magical creature, so there was no way he was getting out of here easily.

"Miss Krinkle's also going to ask people some questions, since she's neutral and respected," said a newcomer. "It's a two-part test. You have to pass both parts. What's wrong with Red? Panic attack?"

As one, Luca, William, and I whipped around to see my neighbor Gloria behind us. Her laser-like gaze narrowed on me, and she gave a thin-lipped smile.

"I'm not panicking," I said, immediately embarrassed. *To think, I chose Belville to settle down in because I thought things like this didn't happen there,* I added silently. *And I thought I'd finally grown enough so that I could face these fears . . .*

"When did you get here?" William asked Gloria.

She shrugged. "A little later than you. I saw you guys going in ahead of me."

But she didn't say anything or try to stand with us. For Gloria, this was not surprising. Phoenixkin, tall and voluptuous, with burnt orange skin and deep red plumage instead of hair, she could be as standoffish as she was beautiful. It was actually kind of flattering that she'd noticed me having trouble.

That is, it *would* have been flattering, if I wasn't so embarrassed.

"So you heard everything they said?" Luca was doing his best to be friendly. "What do you think of it all?"

Gloria glanced from Luca to me, then tilted her head as though thinking. Through lips painted a striking maroon, she blew perfect smoke rings. She wasn't actually smoking—this was just an ability she had, because of the phoenix blood in her veins. I privately thought she did it to show off. "Don't care," she said coolly. "As long as I don't get accused of anything again."

William snorted. "Easiest way to make sure *that's* the case is to not break the law in the first place."

"And did I ever?" Gloria challenged, glaring down at him.

"Did you?" William shot back, uncowed.

"The line is moving pretty fast," Luca observed. His arm wasn't around me any more, but he was still standing very close.

"Yeah. Not like they're going to catch anyone tonight," Gloria said through more smoke.

"Why do you say that?" I asked, trying not to think about how cold my body felt all of a sudden.

"Because. What dark mage or whatever comes to town hall meetings? Anyway, they probably have some kind of hideout out in the forest. Not *here*."

She has a point there, I thought. Taking a look around, I noticed that we were near the back of the line—not too surprising, since I'd delayed us with my anxieties. The line, which had wrapped around the hall at first, now had shortened to just one side wall. Above everyone's heads, I could just see the faint glow of Trent's purple magic on the stage ahead. Behind him, off to one side, stood a tall lady I took to be Miss Krinkle. A portion of the crowd trailed away from her, out the side doors; but several people sat along the back wall with Officer Thorn.

There's nothing to it, I assured myself, channeling my inner Luca. *All we have to do is tell the truth.*

* * *

"Hey, Red." Trent smiled at me as I took my place on the stage with him. "Woulda figured you'd be first up here."

I could feel Luca's encouraging gaze from the wings behind me, and Gloria's less kindly eyes as well. William sat off to one side, already pronounced "obviously magical." Despite the gravity of the situation, he was wagging his tail.

A stool had been placed in front of Trent, so I sat. I tugged at my tunic and wiped my palms on my tights. My palms were sweaty. "Well, we were late getting to the meeting. We were standing at the back."

"Yeah. I'm starting to wish I hadn't shown up, myself."

I glanced up and, just for a moment, smiled at Trent. He was a young Witch, barely out of school, which Witches graduated at twenty-one. His shoulder-length black hair with purple streaks and habitual t-shirts with goofy slogans spoke to how he felt about things like conforming and town meetings and using up lots of magical energy to appease a council. But I knew for a fact that Trent really wanted to fit in amongst the folks in Belville, and probably was glad to be of use—even if the bags under his eyes showed how tired the tests had made him.

49

"Anyway, this'll only take a sec," Trent said. As he spoke his eyes glowed purple and his hair lifted from his shoulders, and I could feel the warmth of magic washing over me like a scan. When he was done, his shoulders dropped. "Man, I'm going to sleep for days after this. I already spent a lot of energy doing Hut repairs this morning. If I'd've known they were going to ask for a million personal scans tonight, I would've stayed in bed."

Despite my nerves, I laughed at his exaggerations. "I wouldn't count on getting too much rest, given the way things are going. I'd have warned you if I could have—Ryuko came over this afternoon and was talking about this then, too. But we were slammed at the shop after that."

"Well, after this, it's *your* turn to be assistant tomorrow," Trent informed me with a grin. "You're clear, by the way. You can go follow William."

Was it my imagination, or did his eyes change when he said I'm "clear"? I wondered as I stood to walk away. Automatically, my hand went to the end of my ponytail, tugging at the strands. Though my hair is black, in the right light it has sparkly strands that give away my heritage—the same way Trent's purple highlights underscored his.

He's a lot more proud of his, though, I thought, brushing back my hair and making sure my goggles were in place over my head. My feet faltered as I crossed over to Miss Krinkle. *Not that I'm not proud of my family . . .*

"You're Red, the alchemist, aren't you?" Up close, Miss Krinkle was tall indeed—a forest elf, a common sight in alpine Belville. Her skin had a birchlike paleness to it and her brown eyes were friendly as she smiled at me. "I have wanted to visit your shop for too long now. Perhaps you know this already—

your familiar certainly did—but I'm one of the teachers at the childrens' school across town. I feel certain you must have all sorts of things in your shop which would enhance our science experiments."

"Experiments?" I swallowed and willed myself not to sound so guilty. "Of course. I'd love to help you, and the students, some time. I mean, some time when we're not all—ah—worried."

I failed my hands about, gesturing to the hastily-made system of lines and stations on the stage. Miss Krinkle inclined her head benevolently before gesturing for me to sit down.

As I did, I couldn't help but feel like one of her kindergartners.

"Officer Thorn asked me to survey everyone as a matter of routine," Miss Krinkle began. After dozens upon dozens of townspeople, she clearly had her talking points down pat. "I am, as you may know, considered something of an expert in finding untruths. Please don't bother to lie to me."

"L-lie?" My eyes widened. *So much for not sounding guilty.*

"Just a routine caution," Miss Krinkle assured me. "Nothing more. Now, Red, tell me: have you ever dabbled in magical arts?"

"Um—no, I—I thought Trent said I was clear?"

"Of course. But sometimes those of us without magic still seek it, isn't that so? We find other ways to get what we want, like divination or ritual worship. Have you ever considered anything like that, Red?"

"Uh—no. Not exactly. No."

"Not exactly?"

"Well—no. Just no." *Better not to get into the family thing . . .*

"Very well. And have you ever had any interest in summoning?"

"No, definitely not. Of course not." *Aside from the fact that my best friend in the whole world is a familiar, of course . . .*

"Do you know how those things might be done?"

"Me? Why? Because I'm an alchemist? I never—I mean, magic isn't really my thing. I certainly don't, you know, know any spells or anything. I just never really got it. I'm an experimental alchemist, like tinkering and—well, not tinkering, exactly, but making conveniences and doing research, that kind of thing. I like plants and minerals." *Great, Red, way to sound like a guilty scientist . . .*

"Mmhm. And do you know anything you'd like to share about the attacks recently?"

"Um . . . not anything that anyone else wouldn't know. I mean, I know my friends are worried about them. But everyone just heard all that, you know, from Officer Thorn. And Ryuko." *Who I am going to ban from the shop and the back patio after this!*

"Hmmm. Thank you, Red. Go and have a seat with Officer Thorn, please."

What?

I stood, dazed. *It's over? Why didn't she say I could leave?* I glanced at William, who was sitting by the side door, waiting for me. But Miss Krinkle's words could not be denied. I turned, and walked on autopilot to the back of the stage.

Officer Thorn stood hovering over two seated people and someone I vaguely recognized as a councilperson. She turned and cocked her head as I approached. "What is it? Did Trent have a message for me?"

"Um . . . no," I said, still feeling unsteady on my feet. "Miss

Krinkle sent me."

"Why? Does she need something?"

"Uh . . ." I glanced over my shoulder, then at Thorn. "I think
. . . I think she thinks I'm responsible somehow."

7

Fire Burn

"But you aren't magic," Officer Thorn kept saying.

"Gee, thanks," I said, still pacing along the back of the stage. My pacing put Thorn's to shame. I think the two seated miscreants were getting dizzy watching me go back and forth. "How about, 'you would never summon an evil wolf creature'?"

"Don't be silly. Of course you wouldn't," Thorn said, sounding very much like Luca—Luca, who, like William, had passed his test and now was waiting by the side door with wide eyes. "But I wouldn't want to jump to conclusions."

Reasonable, said a part of me, rising above the confusion, *because after all, if anything happened to William and he had to be re-summoned, I would absolutely do my best to make it happen. Not that he's evil . . .*

I stopped. "What?"

"It's in the guild handbook," said Officer Thorn complacently. "Never jump to assumptions. *You* never do. That's why you're such a good assistant."

"Not on *this* case, apparently!" I hissed, resuming my frantic walk.

"I still don't see how you could pass Trent's and fail Miss Krinkle's," Thorn called behind me.

I bit my tongue before explaining Miss Krinkle's thoughts about ritual worship and the like. The fact of the matter was, she was right. There was a small but real chance that the summoner—if in fact there *was* a summoner, *thanks very much, Ryuko*—wasn't "magical" at all, but was relying on the power of magical offerings (wine or candles) and inherent magical properties in herbs and crystals to carry out the deed.

Luca and William had already tried making a scene to get me out, to no avail. Gloria had already yawned and went home. It was late—past midnight. The last few townspeople were sitting for Trent, and in the corner I could just barely hear the mayor talking with the council about what to do next.

By the time they finally decided to take down our names and information and let us be on our way home, it was two thirty in the morning.

I nearly ran right through William and Luca, who were still standing by the door. Luca caught me—which must have taken a lot of effort on his part—and marched me outside, while William lingered behind to glare for good measure.

"I just can't believe it. I knew it," I was saying on a loop. Actually, I was so tired and wrung out that I thought I was just *thinking* those two sentences until Luca finally stopped us on the street corner and said,

"Red, we can't believe it either. And no one else will. This was just a fluke. They were just doing these tests to make people feel better."

"Political theater," William agreed, catching up to us. "It

doesn't mean anything."

"It means something to Officer Thorn!" I protested.

William shook out his fur, sparkling in the cloudy night. Unlike the rest of us, he actually got his energy from being out under the night sky. "I doubt it. But I'm going to go follow her, just in case. You two can get back alright, yes?"

"Of course," Luca said, and William galloped back toward town hall.

"You see," Luca continued, turning to me. "If William was *really* worried, it'd be you he was following."

Luca's insight caught me off-guard. "What, to make sure I didn't attack anyone?"

"I meant more to keep you safe, but either way, you know he wouldn't leave your side," Luca said with a smile.

I chuckled half-heartedly. "You know, I actually think you're right."

"Of course I am. I'm right all the time, and no one notices," Luca said cheerfully, taking my arm and beginning to walk toward the Square. "But that's alright. I don't mind. I just want everyone to be happy," he added, stealing a glance at me.

I was preoccupied—not with thoughts about summoning wolves and tests, finally, but with memories of moonlight walks with another old friend, Jade. When I met Luca's gaze, I blushed. "I really am sorry about all this, Luca. I didn't mean to cause so much trouble. You really didn't have to stay."

"Of course I had to," he insisted. "I promised you, didn't I?"

"Yes, well—I'm sure you didn't actually think your promise would keep you up half the night like this," I protested.

"I don't mind," he repeated, looking at the quiet steeped roofs and rustling trees around us. "I like the night time."

Of course. I'd forgotten, once again, about his heritage. The

Drus were a people who worshiped the moon.

"That said, it *is* a little spooky now with everyone's All Hallows decorations up," Luca added, smiling again. His hand on my arm tightened. "Maybe with the town council watching everyone so closely, whoever is doing the attacks will stop."

"If they were even there. Gloria may have been right," I couldn't help but say.

"Well, you'll be safe, at least."

In the shadow, Luca's green eyes were so deep that I had to look away. My shop loomed up on the corner, a familiar beacon. It helped me refocus. "Thank you for staying. You didn't have to."

"Red." Luca stopped and took my shoulders, turning so we faced each other. "Yes, I did."

We were almost nose to nose. Something in my chest went liquid, like molten gold. It was too much. After the stress of the evening, I buckled like a tin can.

"I—I should go in. I should eat something," I mumbled. "We missed dinner. Did you get anything to eat? Should I send something home with you?"

"No, Red, I'm fine," said Luca. "Are you going to be okay?"

"Of course," I said, willing it to be so. "Of course I am."

* * *

I was not.

More accurately, I was moderately okay for the rest of the night—even without William at home, I had Sugar buzzing about my head until I finally fell asleep. I never remember my dreams usually, but they must have been restless that night, because I woke up to blankets hanging off the bed. William snored in the window seat, like always. The thought of warm black tea with coconut cream and crystallized sugar got me up and into the kitchen.

But even as the scent of caramelly tropical goodness hit my nose, there was a knock at the back door.

I pulled my plush bathrobe—a shockingly neon pink—tighter around me and trudged down the stairs, mug in hand. When I opened the door, the heavy gray sky overhead reminded me that I'd overslept and would have to open the store soon.

And the sight of Officer Thorn reminded me of everything I'd been trying *not* to remember.

"Got a minute?" Thorn asked, eyeing my attire as if to add, *you obviously busy and important merchant, you.*

"Sure," I sighed, reminding myself that Officer Thorn was not the enemy here. *No one is the enemy,* I continued. *Except the summoner, of course. If there is one.*

Before the door had even closed behind her, Officer Thorn blurted out, "Last night Miss Krinkle was attacked. By something magical."

8

Cauldron Bubble

"Excuse me?" It took all my concentration not to spill my tea on Officer Thorn's navy blue uniform. "How? Where? Is she—"

"She's fine," the officer assured me. "Are we going to talk in your hallway, then?"

"You're the one who broke the news before you were in the door," I reminded her. "Let's go into my lab, actually. I can make you some tea there if you like, and I have to be getting ready for the day anyway. But seriously—what *happened?*"

"You're going to work in your pajamas?" Thorn asked, trailing behind as I led us back out to the patio and through the lab door.

"I'm going to set everything up and then make William cover for me while I run up and change, *mother,*" I said, giving her a pointed—if teasing—look. "Now are you going to talk or not?"

"Since you're so anxious." Thorn settled into pacing along the back wall of my lab while I set the kettle over my burner and began checking my overnight experiments. "She just came to me at the station and reported it. Said it happened last night on the way home from the meeting, but she didn't see any point in 'keeping me up,' since she knows I don't have any trainees or other help at the moment."

"So it can't have been too bad," I prompted.

"No. Couple of bruises, a banged-up knee. Said she was cutting through the alley behind Lavender's when she heard a noise behind her. When she turned, she caught a glimpse of a large, ungainly assailant, and possibly a second, slimmer one behind the first one. Could have been a shadow, she said. Anyway, the first one brings down a club or some other weapon—she was unclear—on her, she dodges, trips, and manages to get away."

"Yikes. Good for her. But how did she know they were magical?" I asked, shuffling through my cabinets for the stash of tea I keep for the store—and for Thorn.

"I asked that too. There's the ungainliness, of course. Something that awkward should have been noticed around town, but it wasn't. And then it disappeared. Plus, she said they *smelled*."

I turned to look at Officer Thorn, shuddering. "Well, I guess that makes sense about the disappearing. I hate to ask, but did she say *what* they smelled like?"

Officer Thorn pointed at me, as if to say, *good question*. "She said it was like decay, mixed with another odor. Evil magic, maybe?"

"I don't think magic of any kind has a smell," I said, wrinkling my nose.

Just then a new odor filled the room—not an evil one, fortunately, but a cheesy, eggy, basily one. A rap sounded against the wall, followed by, "Red? The back door was open."

"Ah, the meddling bookseller," Officer Thorn said jovially as Luca walked in with a paper bag in his hands.

Just the sight of him made me blush—probably because it reminded me of my behavior the night before. I turned to Thorn. "Some police officer you are, leaving people's doors open."

"I have a lot on my mind," she protested.

"Did something happen?" Luca asked, setting the aromatic bag on my workbench.

"Yes," Thorn answered, "but right now I'm more curious about what you've got in that bag."

"Oh," said Luca. "Well, I figured Red probably didn't have time to make breakfast again, and so I thought—I thought you might like a quiche," he said, turning to me. "I got some croissants and things too—you could have one of those, Officer Thorn, if you haven't eaten."

"I haven't and I will," she said, taking a seat.

I bit my lip. Normally I have a strict rule against eating in my lab. (Tea doesn't count, naturally.) However, since this had been a strange day already and was likely to continue that way, I decided to let the rule slide. I grabbed my quiche from the bag before Thorn could steal it, and gestured for Luca to sit with us.

"There was an attack last night," I told him, because I wanted to say *thank you* but the words wouldn't come.

"Oh no," he replied, eyes wide. "Is everyone okay?"

"She's fine," Thorn said through a mouthful of pastry. She caught Luca up to speed, and then turned to me as if we'd never been interrupted. "Ask that dog of yours if magic smells. Especially evil magic."

"Yeugh." Luca set down his muffin—which, I noticed, was

toffee and white chocolate chip. Muffins at the bakery sold out fast, especially the sweet ones, and yet somehow whenever I saw Luca eating one, it was exactly that kind. "What if it was just a person who smelled bad, though? Not a spell?"

I nodded. "That was going to be my next question."

"Miss Krinkle also said she never heard them breathe," Thorn informed us.

I raised an eyebrow. "She must have very good hearing."

"Oh, she's famous for it actually. She always tells everyone it's because of being a teacher," Luca offered, nodding emphatically.

For some reason, I felt a little annoyed Luca knew more about this than me. *But of course a teacher would often deal with a bookseller,* I reminded myself.

"That," said Officer Thorn, agreeing with Luca, "and keep in mind their situation. Anyone'd be breathing heavily while trying to attack with a heavy weapon."

"But she never got a good look at them?" Luca asked.

I frowned again. *There he goes, stealing all my questions!*

The officer shook her head and poured herself some tea, which I had completely forgotten to do. "Said it was too dark, and it happened too fast. She just wanted to get out of there."

"And they didn't say anything?" I hastened to ask.

"Not a word," Thorn affirmed. "Any more croissants in that bag?"

"So," Luca thought aloud as Thorn fished for more breakfast. "Whoever set up the attack probably knew about the town hall meeting, and when it ended."

"Which no one could have predicted, unless they were there," I said.

"Right, and how else would they have known what route

she would take, unless they followed her or happened to see her out?" Luca added.

"Especially since this was the first attack in town," I said.

For a moment, the three of us were quiet as the weight of this settled in.

Officer Thorn drained her tea. "More reason than ever to solve this as fast as possible. There's no *way* the council can insist on leaving it to the Rangers now. Guild politics be damned. Say, you two make a pretty good team. Maybe I could use another assistant," she said, looking over at Luca.

"Oh, no," I cut in. "Weren't you just telling me yesterday that this is too dangerous?"

"But if the roadside attacker is coming into town now, then everyone should be on deck," Luca said, looking over Thorn at me.

"My thoughts exactly," said the officer. "This is my turf now."

I shook my head, refusing to budge. "No. Everyone should be *careful*, not 'on deck.' That's the rational response here."

"Well, I can tell you who I'm *not* asking for help," said Thorn, standing. "That Ryuko. It was his plan that made us stay so late last night. He has a lot to answer for."

Luca yelped and leapt to his feet. "Sorry," he said as we looked at him in surprise, "it's Frank. He just bit me a little bit, is all. He's helping me keep time because otherwise I'm always late opening the shop. I should—I should go."

He looked past Thorn at me, curiously, as though he wanted to say more—or *hear* more. I felt my cheeks growing hot again, and I resented that feeling. *First he has to witness everything last night, and then show up here this morning all perfect with breakfast, then get himself thrown into this investigation on top of everything else?* I wasn't having any of it.

"That means I need to get ready, too," I said, standing and shooing them both out the back door. "Officer Thorn, thanks for stopping by. Luca, thanks for breakfast. But I don't think either of us should do anything more until we have a better idea of what's going on!"

* * *

As it turned out, neither Luca nor I ought to have hurried to open our shops. Word about the late night attack on Miss Krinkle spread like wildfire through the town. By lunchtime, I was peering out my front windows at a Market Square populated only by jack-o-lanterns and fake ghosts.

"Good time to go to Lavender's," William suggested from the back of the shop. "There won't be a line."

"I'd be happy to procure the necessary food order," Sir Rowan offered. I had him inventorying all the potions along the northern wall, poor man. He was probably itching for a chance to get out.

But so was I. "Actually, I have something else on my mind. I want to go check on Ryuko."

William growled. "The snake whose fault it is that you stayed up half the night and had a panic attack, and that Miss Krinkle got attacked?"

"Don't call him 'snake,' that's rude," I replied automatically. "And I did *not* panic. That was just . . . me trying to adjust some of my preconceived notions. Like I said I would yesterday. See?"

"I am not sure whether to regret or be glad that my lady and I missed the event," said Sir Rowan ruefully.

The comment sparked a little light in my otherwise drab mood. *"My lady," huh? Things must be going well with Daisy.* It was fun to see Sir Rowan, so reserved and downright severe at times, in love.

"Be glad," I assured him with a brief smile. "Anyway, yes, William, I'm worried about Ryuko. I think his actions last night were innocent—if unfortunate. How about this: I'm just going to go out for a walk and take a glance at his place to make sure nothing bad has happened, okay?"

William grumbled. "Walk fast. Actually, scratch that. I'm coming with you."

"But—"

"Rest assured I will be quite content," Sir Rowan said, interrupting my protest. I sighed. He *had* watched the store by himself on several occasions, so I had no grounds on which to argue. *Looks like I've got company whether I want it or not.*

William stretched as we hit the cobblestone street outside the shop. I was worried at first that he'd berate me for something—as I saw it, there was a laundry list of possibilities: my anxiety the night before, my foolish answers to Miss Krinkle getting me marked as a suspect, my being worried about Ryuko or planning to go out alone. Instead, we walked along in companionable silence.

I grew up in a desert climate with two seasons only, but in my year at Belville, I'd come to realize how marvelous a quiet walk in autumn could be. Though the sky was still gray, the clouds felt like a thick cozy blanket, and the riot of color from the trees' leaves and the towns' All Hallows decorations was endlessly fascinating. The usual noise of feet and carts and sales was missing, of course, but the bird calls from the forest around us were comforting. And, my favorite part, the air was laced with wood smoke and a faint but undeniable trace of pumpkin spice.

Too bad Ryuko doesn't live near the bakery, I thought, my stomach rumbling. Despite that one defect, though, my mood had definitely lifted by the time we made it to the outskirts of town where Ryuko lived.

"We're just walking by, remember," William said as I craned my neck at the two-story wooden row house. Since it was squished in among many others, all with identical little yards and peaked roofs, I wasn't sure at first which one was his.

"I know I said that," I admitted, "but I think I see a light on. Shouldn't he be at work, though? Let's go and check. We'll be quick."

William's huff said quite articulately that he didn't believe me for a moment. But I was already charging past the front gate.

Ryuko rented rooms on the second floor of a multi-family home, and it took me a moment to recall exactly how to get to his staircase. But as soon as I arrived at his door, it opened.

"Saw you coming. Might 's well come in," Ryuko mumbled. The scales covering his head looked dull and tarnished, and there were huge bags under his eyes. *If he's slept even a wink since last night, I'll eat William,* I thought.

I followed Ryuko into his living room, William hard on my heels. Ryuko's apartment spanned one half of the second floor, as it turned out, and was incredibly simple: kitchen and bathroom in the back, living room in the middle, and a bedroom behind a closed door in front. I had no idea what the other rooms looked like, but judging by the dingy, monochromatic, barren living room, there wasn't much to see.

"Well," said William, plopping himself down on a ratty sofa—the only furniture in the room aside from a wooden chair, a trunk, and an old empty crate that served as a coffee table. "If you *are* performing dark magic, I think it's safe to say you aren't doing it here."

"William!" I reprimanded.

"Don't bother," Ryuko told me as he sank onto the chair. "Everyone's saying it. Customers at the shop this morning were saying how I'm probably the one behind the attacks and wanted to set up Miss Krinkle and that's why I made the meeting go on so long last night. Priya put me on leave."

"She sent you home?" I clarified, surprised. I didn't know Priya well, but she seemed like a no-nonsense sort of person. As far as I knew she'd always been less judgmental about Ryuko than anyone else in town.

"Had no choice." Ryuko ran a hand down over the scales covering his neck. "I don't blame her."

"Still, that's rough," I said sympathetically. "Um—we just wanted to come see how you were, after last night."

"Yeah. Sorry about that, I guess. I just wanted to help," Ryuko told the dusty wood floor. And then as if the whole situation had hit him all over again, he said, "Gods. I just wanted to help, and look what happened. I never should have said anything in the first place. I thought I was doing the right thing. I really thought it . . ."

"Oookay," I mused, as his voice trailed off. "You clearly need lunch. And a change of scene. Why don't you come to Lavender's with us?"

William startled, most likely unhappy with the idea, but I ignored him.

"I don't think so, thanks though," Ryuko said. "Anyway, I

can't leave."

"What do you mean, you can't leave?" asked William, a canine whine in his voice.

Ryuko opened his mouth to answer, but at that moment, a scream floated up the stairs.

"What in Beyond was that?" I jumped, turning toward the door.

Another scream came, a ghostly sound. They seemed to be coming from outside the house. *But it's broad daylight! No one's been attacked—*

The light coming through the windows, faint already, dimmed. The temperature in the apartment plummeted. I shivered. A third scream split the air, this one much closer. Next to me, William was glowing. Ryuko had leapt up and was trying to tell me something, but I couldn't focus on his words. I ran to the front door and threw it open.

9

Shadows and Bones

"Hello!" A short person dressed almost entirely in pink bounced in the hallway, grinning like there was no tomorrow. But then she blinked at me. "Wait—*you*'re not Ryuko."

"No, I'm not," I agreed, leaning out of the door to peer around her. "Did you hear those screams?"

"Yep! It's how I say hello to Ryu. Is he there?"

Just as I was peering out, she began peering in, bending to look under my arms and around my waist. I sputtered.

"Hey, Saki," Ryuko called faintly from behind me.

His visitor brightened at once. "Oh good, he is. Can you let me in? Nice to meet you, by the way. Your name is—?"

"Red," I managed finally, turning to let her in and shut the door behind us. "I'm sorry—the lights, the cold, the screams. That was all *you*? That's how you say *hello*?"

"Only to Ryu," the newcomer assured me. She went straight to Ryuko's chair and gave him a side hug, since he'd sat back down. "Seeing as we're related and all."

I sat hard on the arm of the sofa next to William, and stared at her. She was five foot tall at most, her arm slung over the sitting Ryuko, who could've easily topped six feet if he stood up straight. What I'd taken for an all-pink haze at first was in fact a striped knee-length sundress, matched with thick tights, a fuzzy white cardigan, and an absolutely adorable pair of pumps. The only accessory she wore was a long necklace with a pendant in white and blue. Her bobbed white hair was tucked under a pink bucket hat adorned with live flowers. The smoothness of her fair skin seemed to give her away as young, as did the energy in her shockingly blue eyes.

"I wouldn't have done it if I'd known you were here," she continued. "Usually Ryu doesn't have visitors. This is good! You're making progress!" she added, turning to him.

Ryuko pulled a face. "Sakura's my sister. We adopted her ages ago."

"Twenty-two years," she corrected him. "Almost two dozen!"

"You were a lot quieter back then," he muttered in reply.

"Are you here for All Hallow's Eve?" I guessed, trying to get a word in edgewise.

"Not exactly," she said, "although it *is* my favorite time of year, and I'm glad to spend it with my big brother! But no, Ryu sent me a note yesterday about all the attacks, so I came as soon as I could."

William sneezed. "Are you his protection?"

"I will be if I need to," said Sakura easily. "You see, I'm a shadow witch."

* * *

I've said it before and I'll say it again: magic is William's responsibility. I could never understand it before he came along, and even after he did, he pretty quickly gave up trying to teach me. It goes in one ear and out the other for me. I couldn't even recall ever being told that there were different kinds of witches, aside from official town Witches and the rogue kind that drew attention from witch hunters.

As I processed Sakura's simple statement, trying to gather up all my questions, William snorted beside me. "If that's what you are, why do you smell like fairy dust?"

"You must be magic too, to notice that," Sakura observed. She smiled as she stuck out one leg. "It's because of these. See? I lost my original legs, so the fairies made new ones for me. Fairy dust keeps them working properly." Noticing my frank admiration, she added, "I get the shoes specially made. Cool, right?"

"Very," I agreed, deciding not to wonder about how she could so easily say she'd "lost" her legs, as though they were a pair of keys. "Oh, and this is William, and he gets kind of rude with new people—sorry about that. But can we back up a minute? I'm not a magic person. What's a shadow witch? I thought pretty much all witches had to go to magic school and then get assigned to villages and such."

"That's Witches," Sakura said, giggling. "That's if you want to be official. But there's lots of other ways to be a witch. We're just not as common. Shadow witches are probably the least common of all, so don't feel bad. It just means that my magic comes from things that some people see as dark or scary. Like the fake haunting I made for Ryu just now. See?"

"Huh." I didn't quite see, but since this was supposed to be a quick visit, I figured an in-depth exploration of how "shadow witch magic" worked could wait.

"Everyone's surprised at first," Ryuko told me quietly. "You get used to it. Saki, look, I know I asked you to come, but things got worse last night. You should probably—"

"I figured," she interrupted. "Why else would your friends be visiting you at home if things weren't bad? You *are* here about the robberies, aren't you?" she asked William and me.

Despite the situation, I smiled back. Puzzling as she might be, it was clear that Sakura was sharp. "We are. There was a full-on attack last night, this one right in town."

"And people think I did it," Ryuko added glumly.

"But that's not based on any hard evidence," I added quickly. "In fact, what happened last night was really different from the other attacks, when you think about it."

"It was? I have a lot of catching up to do," said Sakura, swaying as she thought.

"And *we* have a shop to get back to," William reminded me with a growl.

But Sakura was still thinking aloud, and I wanted to listen in. "Ryu, I wanted to make sure I told you, about wolfsbane," she was saying. "It *could* be used to summon and control a spectral wolf of some kind, but I think it might also be used for protection. Some shadow witches I know use it, especially when dealing with Hecate."

"Who's Hecate?" I couldn't help but ask, even though I knew I might regret it.

"One of the ancient patron deities of shadow magic. A lot of people really fear her," Sakura told me brightly. "And she's often associated with hounds or dogs, so that's probably the reason for the wolfsbane. It might be nothing, really, but I wanted to make sure I said it. You never know what people's reasons might be."

William huffed, and I knew exactly what he meant: *wanting to make sure you bring up a shadow magic deity in conversation sounds like asking for trouble.* Also, if Sakura was coming up with reasons for someone else to use wolfsbane, why did they sound so much like reasons *she* might use it?

From the way Ryuko's eyebrows bunched together, I had a feeling he could tell what William might be thinking, too. He said, "Did you say you have to get back to your store?"

"True. We should go," I admitted. "But I do want to help—"

"Don't worry," Sakura assured me. "Ryu will tell me all the other details, and we'll come find you this evening. Together, we'll get to the bottom of this!"

10

Trick or Treat

William waited precisely until the moment we were on the road in front of Ryuko's house—and not a second longer—to voice his opinion.

"Shadow witchery? Seriously, Red? This is what you're getting yourself mixed up in now?"

"Better to be able to watch her than to be surprised," I returned, reasonably. "Besides, it seems like we have the same goal: help Ryuko, and clear up this mess in town."

"Never mind the fact that she's exactly the type of person the Rangers' witch hunter will be looking for," William growled. "*She* could do summonings."

I tucked the ends of my knitted scarf around my neck, shivering as the wind swept up the road we walked. "Aside from the fake haunting thing, she seemed pretty harmless to me."

"And did it occur to you that she seems 'pretty harmless' on *purpose?*"

Clearly, William didn't buy into my new "question preconceived notions" campaign. I sighed and let the matter drop, knowing that we wouldn't get anywhere discussing it further. *Maybe after lunch, we'll both feel a little more gracious about everything,* I hoped.

In silence, we paced back toward the Square. We didn't quite make it to the shop, though—nor to Lavender's. Instead, as we emerged from a side street onto the tree- and decoration-filled park, I got the shock of my life.

I'd just been walking quietly along, pondering Ryuko and Sakura and why anyone would be interested in summoning demonic dogs in the first place, when a monster stepped out in front of me and tripped me up.

"Ack!" I yelled, very bravely and gracefully tumbling to the ground.

"Hi Red!" said the monster.

The familiar voice sliced straight through my panic, and I paused. "Luca?" I asked, suspiciously.

"Of course," the monster returned. Then, hastily, Luca removed the enormous green mask from his face and emerged grinning bashfully. "Oh, sorry, I forgot how it might look. I was just stopping by the new doctor's office on my lunch break and I wanted to show him my costume so that he had an idea what people might be wearing next week, and then I thought on my way back I ought to test it out to see how well I could see out of the eye holes, and then—well, and then I ran into you."

Oh, Luca. For a moment, all I could do was shake my head and smile at him as he helped me up. My boots slipped on the wet leaves, and Luca dropped his mask to steady me with his free hand.

William plopped himself down on the cobblestones and cleared his throat. "I think it's pretty clear that you *can't* see," he observed sourly.

"Hm?" Luca had been looking at me. When he turned to answer William I realized I was blushing. Again. "Oh, through my mask, you mean. Yeah, I guess you're right. It's a good thing I tried it out before the actual night, huh? Now I know what to fix."

"True," I agreed, brushing myself off belatedly and a bit self-consciously. "We'd hate for you to run over anyone else."

William cocked his head to one side. "Although, it does seem like there's a lot of spare children running around these days . . ."

"*William*," I reprimanded. "They're excited about All Hallows—that's the point. There will be no squishing of children."

"I'm still hoping the party will be safe in the first place," Luca added, the more serious look on his face indicating that he meant the roadside attacks and threats of dark magic. "You two haven't seen anything more, have you?"

"We haven't," I said hastily. Suddenly, my annoyance from the morning returned, and I wanted Luca as far from the case as possible.

Luca gave me another curious glance, as if he knew what I was thinking. I tugged at my ponytail and did my best to keep a straight face. While it was true that Luca had been a big help over the summer, and in fact in every mystery I'd happened upon in Belville, it was also true that . . . Well, this felt different, even if I wasn't exactly sure how. Relying on friends was one thing; getting them involved in some big bad wolf scheme was quite another.

I knew I was acting oddly like Thorn. And I knew I was being irrational. And I knew it wasn't fair that I was particularly scared about involving *Luca,* of all people. But I wasn't about to admit any of that aloud.

As Luca continued staring at me, and I continued struggling to come up with *anything* else to say, William spilled the beans. "Red's making friends with shadow witches now," he announced.

"What?" Luca asked, distracted.

"I am not!" I protested, with all the desperation of a teased younger sibling. Recollecting myself and bringing my voice down a notch, I explained, "We've just been to check on Ryuko. His sister's in town. She seems nice, but as William has pointed out, we don't know much about her."

"Well, I guess it is worth bearing in mind that we don't know if the criminals are camping outside town, or have lived here all along, or recently showed up—or were camping out and *then* showed up," Luca mused, seemingly in danger of getting lost in his own thoughts. "I have to admit I haven't really talked to Ryuko since the carousel business. We just never cross paths. He kind of keeps to himself most of the time, doesn't he? I don't think I'd ever seen him at a town meeting until last night."

"No, but that doesn't stop everyone in town from knowing about him," William observed.

"Ryuko's reputation aside, I don't see how he *or* his sister would benefit from this whole summoning thing," I said, hands on my hips.

"Anyone can benefit from theft," William sniped back.

"Well, any *thief* could benefit because of their stolen goods, but that would probably only be temporary—eventually they'd be found out," Luca chimed in, continuing his musing.

"Maybe the snake never changed its scales," William said,

the tip of his tail wagging.

"I've already told you not to be so rude," I returned with a grimace. "And besides, if they were stealing stuff, why would they sound the alarm about summoning?"

"To sow division in town," William said promptly. "Or cast suspicion somewhere else. Like on magic users. Don't look at me like that, Red—I'm only saying what I bet everyone else is saying from the safety of their own homes right now!"

"I don't believe you," I murmured, shaking my head again.

"He isn't wrong, but he may not be right either," Luca said. As William huffed at us and trotted ahead to the shop, Luca laid his hand on my arm, almost hesitantly. "It's just too early to tell. Are you alright, Red?"

"I don't like it," I blurted, to my own surprise. But Luca's green eyes on mine were patient and understanding, and I found myself adding, "This whole business of suspecting whoever is new in town, or whoever seems strangest. I—I hate it. It makes me think of all those years when William and I were always the strangers in town. Why doesn't he remember what it's like?"

"Maybe because he didn't ever feel like he was a stranger," Luca said gently. "Because he had you."

I stared at Luca, startled. It felt like an eon passed before I finally blinked. "I—I mean, I didn't mean to say it was all bad, traveling. I loved it. And I loved—I still do love—having him with me," I ended in a whisper.

"I know." Gone was the distracted musing and the bubbly enthusiasm; Luca's voice was level and warm and kind. "And I think he knows it too, Red. He's just trying to protect you. We—your friends—we know that this is hard for you. We're just trying to help."

"Trying to help get to the bottom of the mystery," I assumed, confused.

"No." Luca's hand on my arm tightened, and in a quick but careful movement, he hugged me before stepping back. "Trying to help you feel at home."

I could all but hear the sentence end with *my friend,* the way Jade would have said it, in his archaic tones. The memory rooted me to the spot. I'm not sure if I said anything to Luca at all—I thought vaguely he might have said something; he was probably itching to get back to his shop, and Frank—but then someone else was calling my name.

Luca faded away, continuing down the street with a smile. I turned to see Doctor Goodberry hailing me from the front stoop of his office.

Shaking my head, trying to clear it, I made my way over to the doctor. The quick walk through wet grass and vibrant leaves helped me regain some control over my racing heart.

"Red, I apologize if I interrupted something," said Gavin as I approached. "I was just setting up my front parlor and saw you there. Isn't Luca something? A very fine scholar," he declared, waving me into the office. "Come in, come in. Might as well be warm. I just have a quick question for you."

I stepped into the new office and pivoted, taking a look around. Gavin had turned the front room into a combination waiting room and small store, with glass cabinets along the back wall behind a fine counter. Boxes on the counter contained all manner of vials and powders which would no doubt line the cabinet shelves. Some chairs and a small table, more fine wood furniture, took up the rest of the space. A fire crackled at one end of the room. *I hadn't realized Cairn had a fireplace in here,* I thought, a little surprised, but also charmed by the overall effect.

"Coming together," Gavin commented, seeing my glance around the room. "I've worked in larger offices, of course, but none that could beat the location of this place. I hope to open tomorrow. I still don't have my replacement tools, but with the cough and hints of hysteria making their way around town, I didn't want to delay any longer."

"Hysteria?" I asked, following the doctor toward a pair of chairs.

"Mild so far," he returned briskly. "Surely you noticed it at the meeting last night?"

I flushed, wondering if he was referring politely to my own fears. "Tensions certainly are running high, I'll give you that."

"So I gathered," he said dryly. "I myself had to escort the baker—Ginger, I believe—home. His wife, Sarya, said he's taken it very hard."

"Oh, poor Ginger," I said, though secretly I was a little relieved that Gavin hadn't been around to witness my pacing. And I could completely understand why Ginger, a werewolf, might have been upset by Ryuko's thoughts about Big Bad Wolf-type gangs in Belville. "I hope he's okay now?"

"Perfectly well," came the reply. "Now, Red, I was wondering if you would take a look at this for me."

From the side table he brought forth a small box with a little mechanical device in it. As I obligingly pulled my goggles over my eyes and began examining the thing, Gavin explained, "Of course, I recall that you don't consider yourself a tinker of any kind. But I've found that it is useful to have some conveniences on hand. This one was damaged during the attack. I'm afraid I don't have the proper knowledge myself to fix it. Any suggestions you have would be welcome."

At a nod from him, I lifted the device out of the box. It was a little automated desk clock—nothing I'd ever owned or made myself, but a familiar enough design. I turned it this way and that, but could see nothing wrong. Then, struck by an idea, I lifted it to my ear and listened to it as I tilted it from side to side.

"Oil," I declared, and at the word, Gavin's eyes lit up. I went on, "I think it probably got knocked over and lost all its lubrication—you might not have noticed, if everything else was wet and in disarray. If you need some replacement oil, I do have some on hand for the local farmers and smiths. We have a couple different kinds, in fact."

"Perfect," said Gavin. "How much would it be for me to buy some from you?"

"I have an even better idea," I replied, thinking of Sakura's plans to investigate. A doctor's perspective on hysteria and attacks could be useful. "Call it a favor. There's a chance I'll be calling on you for your expertise pretty soon."

"How mysterious," said the doctor with a smile. "Very well. I'll be over this afternoon to pick it up."

"Don't worry about that—I'll send it over with William," I said, standing. "Couldn't be easier."

"How fortunate," Gavin said as he rose too. He smiled. "I can see now how useful it will be to have an alchemist as a neighbor!"

"I keep trying to tell Gloria that." I grinned. "When you meet her, be sure to point that out for me, will you?"

11

House of Straw

It turned out that "this evening" in Sakura-speak meant about four o' clock in the afternoon, which was actually a good thing, considering that the sun set earlier each day. When she and Ryuko came into the shop, raring to go investigate a lead, I left William and Sir Rowan to close up on their own.

"So explain to me again," I said, steering Sakura out the door before she made William antsy with unspoken arguments, "where are we going, and why?"

"Ryu told me that there were three people detained last night for questioning about the potential necromancy," Sakura said.

"Plus you," Ryuko said to me. He managed to make waiting on the sidewalk for exactly two seconds look like what Officer Thorn would call "loitering."

"Plus me? Wait, how many people are we going to see?"

"Just the one for now," said Sakura, tugging her hat over her ears with a cheery beam. "He's at the graveyard!"

Ryuko's number of suspects still puzzled me, but I reminded myself that the answer was simple: I could just ask Thorn when I saw her next for the names of everyone there. My own memory of the night was not entirely to be trusted. *Wait,* I realized belatedly. *Did Sakura just say we're going to the graveyard?*

As I jogged across Market Square to catch up with Sakura and Ryuko, I noticed Luca going the opposite direction. His eyes were fixed on Sakura at first, and without thinking about it, I frowned. Then he saw me frowning, and his eyes widened. Then he frowned back.

"I thought we weren't supposed to be doing anything!" he called to me.

I waved him off and caught up with Sakura and Ryuko.

"What was that about?" she asked innocently.

"Honestly? I have no idea," I said.

* * *

Rumor had it that the town of Belville had actually had several different graveyards over the years—a lost fisherman's graveyard somewhere near the lake, a cemetery specially for a local sect of druids, even an elusive (and highly unlikely) pixie graveyard. The stories were quite popular around All Hallow's Eve. Rumor had it that this year—if everything went to plan—the celebration might even include a cemetery scavenger hunt. I almost felt a pang that we *hadn't* brought Luca along to talk about the history and lore of Belville's one working graveyard, but I quickly brushed the feeling straway.

The current graveyard lay in a hollow on the northern edge of town, a place sure to get dark and creepy before anywhere else nearby. The mountains behind it rose up jagged and rocky. We were within spitting distance of the mine. I wasn't sure what bothered me more—the thought of getting caught out there in the dark, or the proximity to the mine's formidable owner, Lark.

Sakura, however, was not bothered at all. She clasped her hands like a girl at a fancy ball as she turned to Ryuko. "Where did you say they live?"

"Far side," he answered. As she led the way through the scattered headstones, he turned to me and explained, "Orby's family. Dark elves. Think they prefer the forest to the town. His dad's pretty proud actually, I guess the graveyard's kind of a family business."

"I'm sorry," I said, "his name is 'Orby'?"

Ryuko nodded without looking up. "That's what everyone calls him. Think it's 'cause he sees ghosts and spectral orbs all the time. Comes into Priya's a lot. I don't think he's, you know, as reliable as his dad wishes he was."

I let this insight go without comment, as we'd arrived at the gravekeepers' home. It was squat but respectable, with a thatch roof and massive trees rising from its backyard. From the front door an older elf with shadow blue skin peered out, and waved us along when Sakura asked for Orby.

We found the son in question sitting by himself beside a small pond at the edge of the cemetery. He, too, had dusky blue skin and the high cheekbones and pointy ears of elf heritage. Though he was reasonably well-dressed, the rumpled state of his jacket and the mud on his shoes testified to Ryuko's estimation of his reliability.

He leapt to his feet as we came up. "You," he said, looking immediately at me. "You're the pacer."

"I'm an alchemist," I said dryly. "Hi, my name's Red."

"I saw you last night," he added unnecessarily. His gaze

drifted down to Sakura, and he smiled. "You're cute."

I caught Ryuko's eye—his grimace matched mine. But Sakura, apparently, knew exactly how to handle the situation.

"Thanks! You're nice," she replied, smiling widely. "We came out here to meet you. Say, could you tell me something?"

"Anything you want to know." Orby returned her smile with a leer that made my stomach turn.

Sakura tilted her head to one side. "Did you and your friends attack Miss Krinkle last night?"

Orby stepped back, stunned, and in the silence I had to swallow my chortle. Ryuko patted my back reluctantly as I pretended to cough.

"My friends attacked Miss Krinkle?" Orby asked finally. In the afternoon light, his surprise was written clearly across his thin face.

"They said *you* were the one in charge," Ryuko put in.

I eyed both Ryuko and Sakura in turn. I doubted very much that Ryuko had ever been told any such thing. Sakura seemed entirely unfazed by the lie, but I wasn't. My mothers had always been disapproving of brazen dishonesty.

However, it seemed Orby didn't share my skepticism. He puffed up his chest. "Of course I am. It's *my* club, after all. I'm the one who started it."

"The club for summoning, you mean?" Sakura asked sweetly.

"What—the—" Orby slipped on the muddy shore of the pond. "No, it isn't for *summoning*. Who told you that? That's a lie. It's for reincarnation and occult magics, that's all."

I pursed my lips. "Those things all sound pretty similar to me."

"Well, they *would*, to someone like you, wouldn't they?"

Orby gave me a pretty scornful look for someone who was doing such a good job of incriminating themselves. "It's for *past* lives, not *ending* lives. Or—or summoning lives. Otto and Sloane should know that better than anyone. Why would they go off and attack someone?"

He sounded genuinely perplexed to me, but Sakura pushed him harder. "They'd do it if you told them to, wouldn't they?"

"But I wouldn't," sputtered Orby. "I didn't."

"Are you sure? I hear it was a pretty busy night," said Sakura.

"We were just *sitting* there. It was *boring*. But I wasn't mad. I actually thought you had a pretty good idea," he said, shaking a finger at Ryuko. "Too bad it didn't turn up anything."

"Actually, it did," said Ryuko.

Orby's face creased. "What?"

"You," Ryuko answered, stuffing his hands in his pockets casually.

Orby's arms pinwheeled. "But I didn't, I tell you. It wasn't me. Why would I do it? Miss Krinkle is terrifying. She used to make me sit in the corner when I was a kid. I wouldn't go within ten feet of her. No one could attack her and live!"

"If you didn't do it, then I expect you to be very helpful," Sakura said, putting her hands on her ample hips. When Orby nodded pathetically, she continued, "What have you discovered in your club meetings?"

"Nothing about *that,* I swear," said Orby. "It's mostly just seances. I promise. The next meeting is tomorrow night—you can come and see for yourself. I insist! Then you'll see. I don't know anything."

Sakura leveled a pointed look at him. "But if you hear anything . . ."

"You'll be the first person I tell! Promise!"

"Good." Abruptly, Sakura became sunny and cheerful again. "Have a nice night! See you at the meeting!"

As one, we turned and walked away. Once we were leaving the graveyard, Ryuko held his fist out to his sister. "He crumpled like a piece of paper. You ate him up."

"All in a day's work," Sakura agreed, laughing. She bumped her fist against his triumphantly.

"You two didn't even need me," I added.

"Yes we did," Sakura insisted, shading her eyes as she looked up at me. "Safety in numbers! More people means more perspectives. And more questions. Ryu, that was a good call about the friends, by the way."

Ryuko shrugged modestly. "Now we know for sure that the other two people from last night are in the club, too."

"Otto and Sloane," Sakura recalled. "Perfect. Now we also know our next step."

12

Cursed Love

"We are not spending all night investigating," I said as Sakura, Ryuko, and I walked back into town. "It's dangerous, remember?"

"We still have hours of daylight left," Sakura assured me. "Ryu, where should we go to find the other two?"

"Otto works at Lavender's," he answered, and looked across Sakura's head at me as he added, "feel like an early dinner?"

"That's a *great* idea," Sakura enthused.

The two of them now looked at me. I could read the writing in the air well enough. *If I don't go, I lose out on any chance to nip this terror in the bud,* I thought, and laughed. "At the rate you two go, we're going to have a lot to tell Officer Thorn."

"Where is she?" Sakura asked, scanning the shops and empty streets as though she might spot the errant police officer.

"Probably doing her best to make sure Miss Krinkle's safe," I said, more seriously. "And I wouldn't be surprised if she's setting up some kind of watch system, too. She's probably got Trent making a spell or something as we speak."

"Trent?" asked Sakura.

"Town Witch," Ryuko answered. "He's pretty chill. You'd probably like him. For once."

"Normal witches sometimes have a problem with the rest of us," Sakura explained to me. "This one must be pretty good, though. He's the one who was doing the magic scans last night, Ryu? Yep—that makes sense."

"Why?" I asked, curious.

"Because he could sense magic on Orby, even though there isn't much there," she answered matter-of-factly. "We'll have to wait and see about the other members of the club, but right now I would say Orby probably set it up because he wishes he had magic, but he doesn't. He's got a faint aura, but that's it."

"Hmm. Well, Trent *is* really good, as far as I can tell," I said. I was a little unnerved by what Sakura had said, but that was no reason not to give my friend his due.

"Speaking of," Ryuko muttered.

I looked up. We were just getting to the edge of Market Square. And there on the road before us was Trent.

"Oh, Ryuko, Red, it's just you," he said by way of greeting. "You'd never believe how paranoid Thorn is getting. She has me trying all kinds of stuff. I did an experimental spell this morning to see if I could tell if someone was talking about me, you know, like planning to make me the next victim or whatever, and it went off just now, and . . ."

Trent stopped talking, yawning, and stretching, which he had been doing all at once. He stared at Sakura.

"Hi!" she said brightly. "I'm Sakura."

"Hi. Hey. I mean, that's cool." Trent turned and focused on me as though he had laser vision. "Red, can I talk to you? *Right. Now.*"

Without any other social graces, Trent turned and stalked

off into the park. I shrugged at Ryuko and Sakura and went to follow him.

And found myself tugged behind a particularly large oak tree.

"Red," hissed Trent. "Who is she?"

"She's Ryuko's sister," I said, squirming away and brushing bark out of my hair. "Is there a reason we're hiding behind the tree like spies? I'm pretty sure she knows exactly where we are."

"*Red,*" Trent hissed again. "Shut up."

"Whoa, hey," I said, stepping back. "You asked *me* a question. What's going on here?"

Trent flailed and finally banged his fist against the oak tree, which promptly dropped an acorn on his head. The Witch sighed. "Remember last winter when you thought I might have a thing for Thorn and I said no because Witches do the true-love-one-partner-for-life thing and there's a whole ritual when we're in school where we can see the essence of the person who's going to be our true love so we don't have to go around guessing who it is?"

"Uh huh," I said, crossing my arms as I did my best to follow along.

"It's *her,*" Trent said.

"It's . . . oh." *Sakura.* The grin spread across my face like the rising sun over the horizon. "Trent, that's so—"

"But it's *not* her," Trent insisted, interrupting my joy.

I cocked my head. "I thought you said the whole point of the ritual was that you would *know?*"

"It is. I do. I do know," Trent said, hitting the tree again. "But it wasn't . . . she's not . . ."

I peeked around the tree at my waiting friends. Sakura

waved. Ryuko mimed checking a watch.

A glimmer of an idea took shape. I had a guess as to what Trent's problem was, and I decided to test it. "You said your ritual showed you the essence of someone?"

"Yeah."

"Not what they actually look like."

"Usually, those two things are pretty similar," Trent said. "Unless they're using a glamour. But the ritual wouldn't be fooled by that."

"So, I'm guessing you knew that Sakura does shadow magic?" I watched Trent's face as I spoke, and found all the confirmation I needed. "But you didn't expect all the pink and frills."

Trent leaned back against the tree trunk and sighed so forcefully it blew the hair off his forehead. "And I totally just blew it with her too, didn't I?"

"Well, you weren't exactly Prince Charming," I agreed.

"She probably thinks I hate her because she's not from Witch school," Trent lamented, rubbing his hand over his face. I had to put my own hand over my face to hide my smile. I'd never seen my young friend so dramatic. He went on, "But that's not it at all. I just don't get how someone could be . . . what I saw . . . and look like *that*."

"Why don't you ask her?" I suggested.

Trent looked at me like I'd told him to eat worms. "When? She won't want to talk to me now."

"I get the feeling she's very forgiving," I assured him. "Come on. We're headed to Lavender's to get a bite to eat and do a little investigating. You should tag along and get to know her better."

"Arrgh," said Trent.

I took that as a yes.

* * *

Lavender's tavern is an institution in Belville—some might say *the* institution. There are two rumors about the town's founding: first, that pixies had created it, and second, that Lavender's tavern created it. That is, that Lavender—yes, the same Lavender who lived and worked in town now—had built the tavern by a desolate alpine lake, and everyone else had built the town around it.

I wasn't sure which rumor to believe, personally. Lavender herself—though wonderfully warm and gregarious in most ways—wasn't confirming either way. It was enough for me that the rustic old tavern had great company, warm hearths, and delicious home-cooked food.

And a particularly fine spiced mead.

Ryuko, Sakura, myself, and Trent were squashed in a line along the bar. I'd tried to get Trent to stand next to Sakura, but he'd ducked me. The place was packed and noisy, full of locals swapping stories about mysterious wolf sightings and drinking pumpkin ale in between nervous glances out the front door to make sure the sun hadn't set yet. I was pretty sure that, busy as it was now, the tavern would be empty half an hour before nightfall.

That, or there'd be a rush to rent the rooms Lavender kept on the second floor.

"They said it'll be twenty minutes for a table to open up," Ryuko told us, casting an unfriendly glance at the patrons around us. Most of them were giving him equally unfriendly looks back. I was reminded of the urgency of clearing this whole ghost-story-come-to-life up.

"It's okay, Ryu," said Sakura, "we're happy with our drinks here. We'll take our chance to talk to Otto when it comes!"

Sakura's cheer was far from bright and flimsy—it had a solid backbone to it, an undercurrent that seemed to say, *I know this is an uncomfortable situation, but we'll get through it if we stay focused.* I admired her for that.

"How's the tea?" I had to lean down and yell to get my question across to her, even though we were standing shoulder to elbow.

"Probably nothing compared to yours," she answered, returning my smile.

I gestured at the mugs she and Ryuko held, both with bags of imported, pre-packaged tea sticking out of them. "I guess you can tell it's not a specialty of Lavender's. Her coffee is good, of course, but the tea is kind of an afterthought. It's like that all over Belville, actually. The bakery across the way does a passable chai, but it's pretty sweet. Sometimes I miss the café s of big cities."

Sakura's eyes lit. "Sounds like this town could use one! A café , I mean."

I watched her remove her tea bag with a deft hand, her earl gray perfectly steeped. A thought occurred to me, but before I could voice it, Ryuko harrumphed.

"They wouldn't know what to do with one," he said, practically leaning on top of his sister to get away from a nearby clump of fishermen.

Trent peered around my shoulder, as though feeling that it was safe to talk to Ryuko, if no one else. "Don't you *always* drink tea, Ryuko? I don't think I've ever seen you go for a pint."

"Sober three and a half years," Ryuko mumbled. His voice, lower than Trent's, passed under the ambient noise around us.

"Oh, wow, congratulations." *How many times has Ryuko told me he's trying to turn over a new leaf? And every time I doubt him,* I thought with a twinge of guilt.

Trent clearly felt the same. "I had no idea. I'm sorry about always asking you over to the tavern, then!"

"I don't care," Ryuko said, shrugging. "I don't care what anyone else is doing."

"But you have me. Solidarity," Sakura said, lifting her mug with a bright smile.

From Ryuko's quick smile back, it was pretty clear that he *did* care what some people did. And I could feel Trent goggling next to me at this act of companionship on Sakura's part. I elbowed him, wishing he would just say something to her already.

"Settling in, are you?" Lavender bustled around the bar, stopping in front of us. With long silver hair and sparkling purple eyes, more than ample around the waist, her mere presence was enough to cut through the noise. "And who's this?"

"I'm Sakura," said the shadow witch, leaning forward to shake Lavender's hand. "Ryuko's sister. Nice to meet you!"

"And you," said Lavender, a twinkle in her eye that brought truth to the words. "Only I'm sorry, honey, that you're not visiting at a better time here in town."

The person on Trent's other side slammed down their pint, sloshing foam onto the shiny bartop. "It's that *Marguerite,*" said the stranger. "She's completely mismanaged the town. If *I* were still mayor, things would be different!"

13

House of Wood

My first thought was *big talk for someone sitting at a bar at five in the afternoon.* But I didn't get a chance to voice it, because the tavern around us erupted.

"You ran out years ago, you keep your mouth shut about Miss Mayor!" half of the tavern seemed to be yelling.

"You're right, it's time for drastic changes around here!" the other half of the tavern shouted back.

"That's enough," snapped Lavender, and miraculously, the entire place went quiet. "You all know the rules. I don't tolerate talk like that here. Find something else to talk about or take it outside."

The room rumbled. Despite the mild autumn weather, no one wanted to go outside.

"Excuse me?" The host hovered over Ryuko's shoulder. "Your table's ready now."

* * *

"That was some announcement," I whispered to Trent as we followed Sakura and Ryuko to a table by the hearth.

"Yeah. Do you know that person?"

I glanced back at the rabble-rouser. *Definitely phoenix-kin,* I thought, noting the heavy red plume atop his head. *And definitely not Gloria.* "Nope. I haven't lived here much longer than you, remember. Although—he mentioned being mayor—could it be he's the new old mayor in town?"

"We'll have to ask Thorn," Trent said.

"Thorn?" Sakura asked with a smile as we sat.

Trent immediately reverted to being about five years old. "Nothing," he mumbled. But in his consternation, I managed to maneuver it so that he sat beside Sakura. He did so, glowering at me. He and Ryuko made excellent mirror images of each other across the table.

"Heya, I'm Otto," a tired voice announced.

As one, we perked up our ears and turned to our server with overbright smiles.

Otto, who turned out to be a harried-looking woman with brown hair and a penchant for leather bracelets, blinked back at us. "Uh . . . you ready to order?"

"Are we?" Sakura looked at me.

Okay, I guess I'm the leader. "Not quite yet. We got a bit distracted by the noise at the bar," I said, turning down the brightness of my smile to appear more sympathetic.

Otto snorted. "You might as well just ignore Peyton's ramblings. Trust me, nothing will come of it."

As she spoke I realized that, while I had only briefly noticed her at Lavender's before, I *did* recognize her voice. She'd been the decorations volunteer who was so judgmental the day before.

"Oh, is that who that was?" Sakura tilted her head. "Sorry, I'm new."

"Terrible time to come here," Otto said, glancing down at her. "Unless you practice dark magic."

"I do," Sakura said sweetly.

"Uh." Otto stared. "I—I'll be back in a minute for your order."

"*Saki.*" As our waitress retreated into the crowd, Ryuko beat me to reprimanding his sister—but only barely. "You shouldn't have told her that!"

"Why not?" Sakura batted long eyelashes. "It's true."

"But you don't want her to go spreading rumors about you and getting people to think you did it," Trent said.

Wouldn't William be proud—someone finally said it, I thought.

Sakura stared at the Witch. Not only had he *finally* broken his half-hour-long silence toward her, the desperation in his voice approached "drowning man in need of a life jacket" levels.

I coughed. "I agree with them, for the record, but what's done is done. Quickly, now, everyone tell me if you have any food allergies or aversions, so I can order for us when she comes back." Lavender's tavern was such an institution that there was no printed menu, and it was easier for one person in the know to make the order. "And does anyone have any ideas about getting her to open up?"

Trent gripped the table like it was his life raft. "All she's ever talked about when I've been here is how she grew up in a commune of harpies or something. Her great-grandmother was one, maybe?"

"Harpies?" Sakura looked interested. I personally wasn't— not in winged, ill-tempered people renowned for their fighting skills—but if it was true, maybe it explained Otto's unusual jewelry choices.

"It also explains her aura," Sakura said when I mentioned my thoughts aloud. She turned to Trent, one professional to another. "It's kind of like Orby's, don't you think? No wonder they were drawn to each other."

"Drawn . . . to . . . each other?" Trent literally gurgled, turning to me for support.

I sighed, and managed to explain Orby's "occult magic" club to him quickly.

"What a hypocrite," he murmured, fortunately under his breath. "Joining a club like that, and then looking at Sakura that way!"

I shushed him and ordered our food as Otto reappeared. "Four orders of shepherd's pie, please, and a cheesy garlic bread for the table—oh, and another round of drinks. Lavender will know what we've got. Say, didn't I see you yesterday, helping Officer Thorn with the decorations in the Square?"

In lieu of any suggested leads from the others, I'd had to draw on my own.

Fortunately, it worked—that is, Otto hunched up her shoulders and leaned away from me, but still, any reaction was useful at this point. Even a negative one.

"My friend got conned into it," she mumbled. "So I went along." And barely before she could finish saying "I'll go put in your order," she disappeared once more.

"That was good, Red," Saki enthused, draining her tea. Against the drab colors of the crowd around us, her white bob practically sparkled as she swung her head up and down. "I know exactly what we'll say next."

"'We,' huh?" her brother commented. From the way Sakura

grinned at him, I gathered this was a running joke.

And why not gather some information about Sakura as well as Otto, as long as we're here? I thought. "Does this sort of thing happen with Sakura a lot?" I asked Ryuko lightly.

"If you mean questioning people in taverns, then no," the woman in question answered. "But if you mean dark magic—"

"—or getting dragged into things that you didn't realize you were signing up for—" Ryuko added dryly.

"—but which always turn out to be very good for you, then yes," Sakura amended, seamlessly blending his comment into her own. I had to grin at her style. "It's okay, I know it's confusing to everyone."

"Confusing," Trent echoed, mostly into his glass as an efficient server replaced his drink.

Sakura paused, her blue eyes resting on Trent. I could have sworn that blue changed, just for a second. Did her eyes get darker, or did something else about her shine more brightly? Before I could figure it out, she turned to me and said more slowly, "Ryuko and I have been family since I was three. We were homeschooled together and everything. But I . . ." She paused, and smiled at her sullen brother as she said, "Well, obviously Ryuko is Ryuko, and the rest of our family—they're more like he is. I'm just a person, really, or at least, that's how I started out. Human, nothing more. But I always had an aptitude for magic—"

"Did you go?" Trent broke in abruptly. "To Witch school?"

Sakura looked at him again, and again I had that feeling like the rest of us had faded into the background. But this time she looked confused, even hesitant. "No," she said at last. "I never did. I studied with—well, I studied with someone else.

"And the whole point of my studies," she said, turning once

more to me and smiling again, "was that you *can't* be who you fully are unless you face the dark places inside yourself first."

"I'll drink to that," I said, returning her smile. In theory, what she said wasn't so different from alchemy. Breaking things down into basic truths and building them back up— that was exactly the sort of thing my old alchemical teacher was forever going on about.

Ryuko joined us in our toast, but as soon as his mug was back on the table, he squinted at Trent. "What's wrong with you today?"

"Ah . . ." Trent spluttered, and was saved from answering by the arrival of the garlic bread. Actually, it was Sakura, who immediately tried a piece and forced Ryuko to do the same, who saved him.

And Trent definitely noticed that fact.

My amusement at my companions was soon eclipsed by my hunger. But when Otto returned with our main course, it became clear that Saki was still at the top of her game—greasy fingers and garlic breath notwithstanding.

"I have friends who are supposed to be joining us tomorrow," she told Otto. "I was thinking about what you said, about it not being a good time. Have the other travelers been having trouble?"

"Haven't you heard?" Otto leaned back, and at first I thought she'd walk away again, but for some reason she stayed. As she talked, I realized that Sakura had played on her apparent loyalty to her own friends. "There've been attacks—theft. They say it's only a matter of time before it turns violent. The folks who *do* make it here do so without any of their silver."

"Silver?" Saki asked, eyebrow arched. I, too, wondered. That hadn't been on Ryuko's initial list of suspicious missing items, but it did seem like something I'd heard about in conjunction with magic wolves . . . or werewolves.

Meanwhile, Otto nodded. She had to speak loudly to be heard over the noise of the tavern, but her manner was conspiratorial. "Or copper, too. And of course any money they happened to have. Anything the thieves could sell."

"That's terrible," said Saki, "but I'm worried I won't be able to reach my friends in time. Is it safe here at the tavern, at least?"

"You mean to stay? Sure. I've got a friend who lives here," Otto said. I exchanged glances with Ryuko. Not only did this sound suspiciously like a joke, coming from our reluctant waiter, it also could lead us to another member of Orby's club.

"Must be nice," Saki laughed. "I guess they don't mind the noise."

"Nah. Sloane's up all night anyway."

Definitely our third club member, I thought.

"So much the better," laughed Saki. "But—is there enough room? I think my friends will want at least two rooms."

"Yeah, there's still plenty of space, from what I gather." Otto was turning to leave but stopped briefly when Saki turned to her brother.

Ryuko stirred. "The Rangers?"

Otto shrugged. "Everyone talks about 'em, but I haven't seen one yet. They're not staying here, I can tell you that. Someone at the bar said they're camping out in the woods so they can catch the criminal."

"Makes sense," Saki said, and went on, "Otto, do you—"

But her words were drowned out by a crash.

14

Toil and Trouble

Otto slipped away, but Sakura and Ryuko barely seemed to notice. Their eyes, like most of the others in the tavern, were glued on the figure standing on a chair by the fireplace.

"It's a tragedy," boomed the figure, whom—even in the increasing gloom—I recognized by his bright red plumage. Peyton, Otto had called him.

With a pint sloshing in one hand, Peyton went on, "Can we not even keep ourselves safe? Are we too busy celebrating and welcoming strangers that we can't tell who is a threat any more? In my day, things were different! We knew what was good for us and what was not. We held our heads high!"

I made a face. *He did say earlier that he'd been the mayor before Marguerite, and Ryuko said he's the one who got robbed at the beginning of this whole mess. Sounds like a personal grudge mixed with typical bitter political talk to me.*

But, I realized as I looked around, there definitely were some people in the audience who found it more palatable. Some heads were nodding, and others toasted their glasses;

some muttered in open contempt, and others stared blankly into the fire.

And one lone voice piped up in the smoky room. "Heads held high hide secrets in hearts," sang out Sakura.

This time *everyone* in the tavern, even Lavender, swiveled to stare at our table. I, too, stared at the shadow witch, my eyes wide and my mouth open like a gaping fish. *Where did that come from?* Her words were singsong, but even I—who'd known Sakura for all of an afternoon—could tell there was a sharp undertone in them, like she was nursing a grievance.

"How *dare* you," said Peyton, voicing the surprise awash in the crowd.

"It's a common expression where I'm from," Sakura said, quickly and brightly, too fast for Peyton to get another word out. "Maybe you've forgotten it. And there's more that you wish you could forget, isn't there?"

"You're a *stranger*," Peyton spat, as though this was a response that made sense. It didn't, not to my rational mind, but I could guess what he meant: something along the lines of *how could you know what I'd like to forget?*

And honestly, I was wondering that about Sakura myself.

"Yes, and you are drunk," Sakura said, her eyes glinting now less flirtatiously, more like steel. "And you're hiding something. But that never works as well as you think it will, does it?"

Peyton brought one hand up, like he had the perfect, powerful response. But the action seemed to imbalance him. The chair under his feet wobbled, and his drink went crashing to the floor. Finally, with a look of almost comic surprise, Peyton himself went tumbling down into the sticky puddle he'd created.

"You *hag*," he cried, hopping back up to point at Sakura. "You did that!"

As one, the room gasped. Even the folks who'd been stifling laughs choked them back. Previous mayor or not, Peyton's language was incredibly ignorant and crass. *He probably doesn't even know she's a witch,* I thought. *He just came up with the worst word he could call her.* In fairy tale terms, to call someone a "hag" was essentially saying "hey, I know nothing about you and I don't want to, but I'd like to be cursed, please!".

Ryuko rose to his feet with his fists raised, a sinuous movement that left me in no doubt that his shady past had involved more than one fight. Trent rose, too, pushing himself in front of Sakura, purple magic sparking around him. Members of the crowd were already reaching out to Peyton, trying to hold him back. I kept my gaze on Sakura, whose mouth had quirked back in one corner beneath an upraised eyebrow, almost as if . . .

. . . she was amused.

"That's enough of that." Lavender's voice rang loud and clear from behind the bar. "I'll have no such language in my place. Take it outside, or calm yourselves down. Now."

"But she did that! You saw it!" Peyton insisted, turning to Lavender like a frustrated child.

Lavender simply looked at the servers who flanked Peyton. Without a word, they seemed to understand their orders. They escorted the man outside.

"All that happened was he fell off his own chair because he's an excitable fool," Trent said, presumably to me, but loud enough to be heard across the room. "Why doesn't she just say that?"

"She" being Lavender or Sakura? I mused, still opting to keep

my mouth shut.

"Because to start an argument with someone so sloshed is to lose," Ryuko said quietly. He sounded more like a snake than ever, hissing ever so slightly on his "s"s.

Despite the vague aura of menace in his voice, he was right. Slowly, conversation resumed in the tavern. Even so, Ryuko and Trent remained standing.

"I think it's time to go," Ryuko added, looking down pointedly at his sister.

"You may be right," she said, rising. The primness and preciseness of her movements reminded me she had prosthetics to contend with—and even if they *were* magical and fairy-made, they probably weren't intended for fighting with very tall and angry phoenixkin. *Maybe that's why she wasn't upset that Ryuko and Trent leapt in,* I supposed. *She was probably planning on talking her way out of the fight, anyway.* I had a shrewd suspicion that Sakura, unlike many of my friends in Belville, did not start fights unless she knew she could end them.

". . . but that doesn't mean I agree with you," Sakura was saying, still to Ryuko. "He was wrong, and he should have been told as much. He's probably wrong a lot of the time, and he ought to get used to that feeling instead of hiding from it in drink."

"Is there something we should know about you and him?" Trent asked, his words a little strangled.

"No, there's nothing," said Sakura, smoothing back her silvery hair. "Nothing at all."

"Right. Well, if you think we're letting you walk out of here to find him and harangue him some more, you've got another think coming," Ryuko warned her.

Sakura scrunched up her nose at her older brother. "But *you* said it was time to go."

"Now I'm changing my mind," Ryuko growled.

"You're not the boss of me," Sakura quipped. "*I* think leaving is a great idea. Don't you, Trent?"

Trent gurgled.

"I think," I interjected, "that maybe we should ask around a little more about Sloane before we go. How's that?"

Ryuko sent me such a strange look that it took me a full minute to realize that he was actually smiling with *approval* at me for once. In the meantime, Trent was helping Sakura navigate the mess of chairs and fellow diners around us. Fortunately, now that the conversations were flowing once more, most people were at least pretending to ignore us.

Us, and more precisely the witch who just started a fight—and won it, I thought, glancing at Sakura from the corner of my eye once more. She was smiling up at Trent, saying something I couldn't hear.

"Back to the bar, then?" Ryuko said, mostly to me. Trent and Sakura were pretty clearly in their own little world.

"I think so. I guess I didn't exactly have anything in mind," I admitted. "I'm more used to chasing down mysteries in the lab—not with actual people involved."

Ryuko actually laughed, short and wry. "It's funny that you still say that after how many cases you've helped Thorn on."

I paused, genuinely taken aback by his comment.

"Speaking of Thorn," said Trent, rejoining the larger conversation, "she'll probably show up soon. I'd better hang back to talk to her."

"Good idea," Sakura said from his other side. "Come on, Ryu, it'll be easier to fit just three of us at the bar."

"Shouldn't Sakura be the one talking to Officer Thorn?" I mused aloud, to no avail. Trent just shrugged at me as he passed my shoulder on his way to the front door. He may as well have had little cartoon hearts circling his head. Sakura and her brother, meanwhile, had already found a piece of standing room along Lavender's bar.

"Here, Ryu, move over," said Sakura as I came up behind them. "Let Red do more talking. Actually—isn't that Otto in the corner?"

"Prob'ly on her break," Ryuko observed, as we all turned to look at our suspect sitting alone at a dark table tucked away to one side.

"You should go talk to her some more," Sakura said. "See if you can get any more information."

Ryuko looked at his sister, then looked at me—and then heaved a very heavy sigh. "I'll go, but don't get any ideas," he told Sakura. "I'll meet you back here."

"Sure thing!" Sakura waved him off, and then waited precisely two seconds after he'd left before turning to me and saying, "I already got Lavender to tell me which were the long term rooms. Why don't we just go upstairs and see if Sloane is home?"

"Wait," I said, bemused. "Didn't Ryuko say not to get any ideas about leaving without him?"

"Oh, that's not what he meant," Sakura assured me with a wave of one small, rounded hand. When I refused to look convinced, she laughed and explained, "He *meant* I shouldn't get any ideas about him and Otto. Remember when you were asking him if I always get him into situations over his head? Well, most of the time, it's because I'm playing matchmaker."

"Matchmaker?" I repeated, incredulous.

"Someone has to do it," said Sakura, very reasonably. "Because he hardly ever puts his best foot forward, now, does he? Not many of us do. Come on—I have a great idea for how we can get Sloane to talk."

15

House of Brick

"Hello," Sakura said brightly. "We just wanted to apologize for the noise downstairs and assure you Officer Thorn is coming to take care of it!"

She cheerfully repeated this not-quite-a-lie to everyone who answered her knock at the hall doors. And when we'd reached the one all the way in the back corner, we hit the jackpot.

"And why," asked the ghostly presence, "should I care?"

I recognized them at once—not only as the person Otto had alluded to, but as the third person who'd been on stage the night before. *And* in the town council. I thought they'd just been lingering to talk to Thorn!

This has *to be Sloane,* I thought. A quick look from Sakura confirmed that she agreed.

"Aren't you on town council?" I asked, surprised.

Sakura took that ball and ran with it. "Oh, we're very sorry to have disturbed you—you must be very busy!"

Sloane sighed, a long, wheezing sound. "I *am* on town council," they said, slowly and ponderously. "But I assure you the role is mostly ceremonial. It is little more than noise in the wind."

Sakura and I both stared at Sloane for a moment, uncertain what to make of this. Unlike Otto and even Orby, who cut very definite figures—for better or for worse—this third member of the occult magic group was incredibly vague in all senses of the word. They seemed tall, and slim, and remarkably staid, but a sort of hazy cloudiness blurred all those edges and made it hard to be sure. The gray see-throughness of Sloane's form reminded me a little of Jade, who had always described himself as a "shadow." In short, Sloane looked like a child's drawing of a ghost in a sheet, placed behind filmy, vintage glass.

"That was a joke," sighed Sloane. "Because I am a ghost."

They didn't say it with any particular pride or derision, but instead with a sense of regret.

"Wow," said Sakura. "You're a lot better-looking than most ghosts I've met."

I didn't want to be obviously incredulous, but I did risk sliding a glance at my partner-in-adjacency-to-crime. She looked sincere. I hadn't met many ghosts in my time—I usually made it a point to avoid them, actually—but I expected *some* of them must look better than hazy, gloomy Sloane.

"I have managed to give myself some form," said Sloane, rather stiffly.

"That's impressive," Sakura replied. "May I ask how?"

Sloane's gaze seemed to drift to me. "Why did you come up here, again?"

"To apologize," I said, clearing my throat.

"But we're really glad to have met you," Sakura added.

"Have we met?" Sloane asked, rather coldly. "I don't recall your names."

"Oh, sorry," Sakura returned at once. "I'm Sakura—I'm new in town. This is my friend, Red, who runs the alchemy shop. And she said you're on town council?"

"A matter of form only, such as that is," Sloane insisted once more—without properly introducing themselves, I noticed. I knew from hearing my mothers talk that some ghosts were amorphous because they'd lost connection to the physical world. But Sloane's voice and humor seemed quite distinct, which led me to believe that all their other vagueness was on purpose. Normally, there wouldn't have been anything suspicious about that choice; but after witnessing Peyton's rants and Otto and Orby's secret-keeping, I was a bit frustrated with all the hiding.

"I just happened to notice you there the other night, that's all," I explained.

Sloane shifted, with apparent effort, to look at me. Their toes skated over the wood floor. "And I saw you. One of the suspects, I believe."

"Well, I wouldn't go *that* far," I stuttered.

"That's actually what the noise downstairs was about," Sakura volunteered. "And Red's feeling bad now about potentially putting people off, which is why we wanted to apologize."

"And now you have," said Sloane. "Quite nearly enough for me, at least. Is there anything else?"

"Since we're talking about it, what did *you* think of the meeting?" asked Sakura, sweetly.

"If you're that interested," said Sloane, "I suggest you look up Leo. Good night."

And with a finality that belied Sloane's ghostly appearance, the wooden door clicked shut in our faces.

"Leo?" Sakura asked me in a whisper.

"Town reporter," I explained. Against my better judgment—because already, my head was filling with possible confrontations between the two colorful characters—I added, "You might want to find her tomorrow, actually. Her studio's above the art shop."

"I'll add that to the list," said Sakura. She took my arm and steered us back down the hall toward the stairs, saying as we went, "Sorry about that bit about you causing trouble. I didn't mean to throw you out to the wolves or anything—I was just trying to get Sloane to stop being so suspicious. That conversation certainly was the hardest of the three, wasn't it?"

"Definitely," I said, thinking of how Orby had caved immediately, and even Otto had warmed up over time. "And don't worry about it. I don't particularly care what Sloane thinks."

"I thought as much," said Sakura, beaming at me as we reached the stairs. "And good thing, too, because it seems Sloane doesn't think about much aside from *form*."

I stopped mid-stair. "Do you think that's important?"

"I think it's the best clue we got for our efforts," Sakura said thoughtfully. "In my experience, usually when someone's so hung up about some little detail like that—or so determined to make *jokes* about it—it's because they have a wound about it."

"A wound?" I asked, shifting to face Sakura.

"Shadow magic term," she explained, waving a hand. "What it means is, something that the person wants but doesn't have, or something they lost—some emotional or psychological pain they're carrying around. For Sloane, it's having a physical form."

"Interesting, considering that we're pretty sure magic of

some kind is at play," I mused.

"Plus it explains why a ghost would bother joining a club with two mortals," Sakura added.

"So," I said, turning to descend to the tavern, "do you think Sloane wishes they *had* a form? Or wishes they didn't?"

This time it was Sakura's turn to stop short. I turned back around at once, concerned, but she was beaming at me. "What an excellent question," she said, her eyes gleaming in the shadowy stairwell. "I knew I was going to like you, Red."

* * *

I have to admit, I admired Sakura's insights—and even her interviewing skills, even though Sloane *had* been a very tough nut to crack. And I was flattered she liked my question. *But still,* I reminded myself, as we rejoined the din that was Lavender's main floor, *she definitely has secrets of her own, and it might not be wise to trust her just yet.*

We found Ryuko at the bar, looking like he, too, was having second thoughts. "Nothing," he said, just as Sakura opened her mouth. "I barely even sat down before Otto was going on about how she's happily engaged."

"Is she? How nice." But if Ryuko had been hoping this would distract Sakura, he was about to be disappointed. She went on, "So you didn't get anything more than that?"

Ryuko shrugged. "Felt a bit silly hanging around to gossip about outlawed magic and summoning wolves when she was just talking about her betrothed."

Sakura rolled her eyes at her brother and smiled at me. "He's always thinking love and darkness don't go together," she said. "What an old gossips' tale. If you're going to be in love, you have to be willing to be honest about everything, even the dark stuff."

"Well, I'm not going to be in love with Otto," Ryuko said, draining his tea. "And you know I'm no good interviewing people without you. You probably just wanted me out of the way."

"You know me so well," beamed Sakura. To my surprise, Ryuko chuckled.

"'We *did* manage a little success," I told him. Briefly, Sakura and I filled him in on what he'd missed. When we were done, I asked, "What about Officer Thorn and Trent?"

Ryuko glanced down at his sister, and I wondered if he had suspicions about Trent's eagerness to run interference with Thorn. But, perhaps he was simply concerned for Sakura; after all, even at the crowded bar, patrons were giving her a respectable berth.

"Thorn was here and gone," he said at last, shrugging, like he really couldn't be interested in the comings and goings of the police. "Trent went with her. They might have been tracking down Peyton, but it could just as well be something else."

This seemed a bit less than helpful to me, but Sakura accepted it in stride. "If it's anything bad, I'm sure we'll hear about it," she observed. "In the meantime, how about we call it a night? We found out lots to think over, and it's probably twilight by now. Time to get Red back home."

"I'm fine," I insisted. I was, I realized, more than a little tired of people thinking I couldn't handle myself.

"Nevertheless," said Sakura, actually winking at me, "it's clear you have a way of attracting trouble."

16

Double, Double

It turned out I *had* attracted some trouble that night.

Sakura, Ryuko, and I made the trip from Lavender's Tavern to my shop uneventfully enough. Naturally, Sakura adored the pumpkin and ghost decorations strewn about the Square, and Ryuko was probably happy to be talking about anything but his love life. Overhead, the stars twinkled in the purple sky of nightfall; the world was almost peaceful, aside from a general feeling of menace in the air. I wasn't sure if it was because of the attacks, or perhaps because of Sakura herself. For all her prettiness, she wore an aura of darkness just as easily as breathing.

"Red," she asked, as we neared the corner, "who's that coming out from behind your shop?"

My ears pricked up immediately. I scanned the alley between my shop and Gloria's, expecting anything from a burglar to the undead . . .

Only to see a dark form in a black hood.

"Luca," I cried out, a little crossly because he'd given me a scare. *That's twice in one day!* "What were you doing in my backyard?"

"I wasn't *in* your backyard," he returned, petulant. "I was in your apartment."

"Why in Beyond would you be there?" I asked, honestly astounded. *If I wasn't home, what use would he have in being there,* I wondered, and immediately felt shallow and cross with myself for doing so.

"Hi," said Sakura. The four of us drew up on the sidewalk, and I have to admit I was glad for the distraction from my confusion. "I'm Sakura—Ryu's sister. You're Luca, I suppose?"

"The local bookseller," a new voice announced gruffly. For the second time, my heart leapt into my throat—but only just for a moment. William had followed Luca out, blending into the shadows of the alley.

"That's me," said Luca, smiling at Sakura in a way that made my eyebrows squish together. Did he always have to be so *friendly?* "What have you three been up to?"

"Nothing," said Ryuko.

"Investigating," said Sakura.

"Early dinner," I said, and when I realized that Sakura had let the secret out, I added, "But strictly unofficially—nothing you need to get involved in!"

Luca faltered a little as he looked at me. In fact, *everyone* looked at me, and it didn't feel like a positive reaction.

"What were *you* doing?" I asked quickly, trying to cover up my unreasonable shortness. After how kind Luca had been that afternoon, my own curtness stung even more than usual. And judging by the height of Sakura's pale eyebrows, the tone in my voice didn't quite hide it.

"Research," said William.

"But nothing," Luca added, "that we feel the need to share."

"Well, it looks like you two have a lot of not talking to do," Sakura declared breezily. "Ryu and I had better head home before it gets any darker. See everyone later, okay? Have a good night!"

"Have a good evening," I replied, still staring at Luca. *Since when has he ever refused to share anything?*

"Nice to meet you," Luca echoed, still staring at me.

Ryuko snorted as he and his sister shuffled off.

It was William who finally broke the face off. He plopped himself down on the sidewalk with an audible sigh and said, "*Luca* brought over tomes on hauntings in Belville and we looked over them together since *Red* was out gallivanting around with her new friends. That sums it up. *You,* stop being petulant," he said to Luca.

Exactly the word I was thinking, I thought. Not a little pleased with myself, I stuck my tongue out at Luca before thinking through what I was doing.

"And *you,*" continued William, rounding on me, "stop being childish. Now, is Luca going home, or is he going to stay the night?"

Suddenly I was glad it was dark. My cheeks felt like copper under the desert sun. "It's fine," I said, though I was uncertain what I meant.

"I—I—I didn't—well—that is—really," said Luca, even more incoherent than me.

"Do you *want* to stay the night?" I asked him. William *woof*ed, a sound that resembled laughter, and I hastened to add, "I mean, just for safety's sake. You know. You could stay on our couch."

"The couch is too small," William said unhelpfully.

"N-no, it's fine," Luca echoed my sentiment earlier. "I'll go home. I'll be *very* safe. I have protection spells from Trent and all the doors are locked and I have Frank!"

"Plus," rumbled William, "anyone who tries to attack you will probably get smashed under a pile of books first."

"The danger isn't *being* at home, it's *getting* home," I reminded everyone.

"I'm going," Luca declared. "I'll go right now! It's fine. I can literally hide in the shadows, remember? I'll be fine. It's two blocks. I was already on my way out."

He started walking down the street, just like that. But before he'd made it in front of Gloria's shop, something in me clicked.

"Wait," I called out.

He turned around, and in the light from the streetlamp I saw curiosity in his green eyes.

The only problem was, I had no idea how to voice what had made me call out.

"Just—definitely *do* be safe, okay?" I said at last. Luca looked at me, even opened his mouth to speak, but in an ill-advised rush I added, "This isn't anything you ought to be mixed up in!"

Luca's mouth snapped shut. "I *will* be safe," he replied. "Way more safe than *you*!"

* * *

William hustled me through the back door and up the stairs—otherwise who knows how long I might have stood there on the street corner, mad. Even after making myself a pot of chamomile tea and settling in front of my tiny fireplace at last, I was still fuming.

"You know," William said, panting happily in his window

seat, "he was just trying to be helpful."

"Bah!" I said.

"And our couch really is too small."

"That isn't the point," I said, even though I knew he was right. I was actually sitting on the rug with my head resting against the couch and my feet stretched out to the fire, because I liked having the extra space. And warmth. "The point is that Luca shouldn't get involved in this investigation at all. He should be home. All the time. *Safe.* I mean, for goddess' sake, Thorn didn't even want *me* getting involved at first!"

"Do you even hear yourself?" William asked, looking down at me from his special spot. "He's supposed to stay in his house literally all day? What are you going to do, put him under house arrest again?"

"Maybe we should," I grumped. "Since he won't stay put."

I was starting to sound exactly like Thorn, and I knew it. Frustrated, I blew bubbles in my tea cup.

"Maybe he thinks there's something more important about helping you than staying safe," William suggested.

Trying to help you feel at home, Luca had said. The words made my heart start racing again and I had to push them away.

Silence reigned as I tried to make sense of this. Well—not silence, exactly: the flames in front of me crackled along, and logs slumped into the hearth. As a desert child I wasn't a fan of cold weather on the whole, but I had to admit—if just to myself—I did *love* a good fire.

What I didn't love was my friends in danger. I shrugged off William's suggestions. "That doesn't make sense," I said, downing a scalding mouthful of tea.

"Fine," William rumbled. "But I thought you were supposed to be moving beyond your preconceptions. Not staying stuck behind them."

"I'm not stuck," I protested. "I know Luca's just trying to be nice. I know it's important to him to help his friends. But I'm just saying, that's not *as* important as not getting eaten or stolen or *dead* by some summoned demon or All Hallows monster, that's all!"

Rather than agree with me, William sneezed.

And the pit in my stomach told me I already knew what that meant. "Oh, great. Thorn really did ask you to help her, didn't she?"

"Huh?" William shook his floppy ears, but he knew he couldn't hide it from me. "Oh, that. Yes. I'm going out with her tonight, actually."

"Tonight?" I glanced at the clock above the fireplace, surprised. It wasn't unusual for William to go walking at night—he was a magical creature, after all, and he had to recharge his magic somehow. Exactly how to recharge depends on the creature or magic user in question, but for William, it always seemed to involve being alone under the stars. However, I was taken aback by Officer Thorn's sudden offensive move. "What are you going to do, patrol the roads?"

"Basically," he said, tail thumping against the window frame. "And try not to fight with Thorn. Much."

"Wow. I mean, she did mention to me that she'd sooner recruit you than me—probably she's just as worried about me as I am about Luca, I guess. You ought to be flattered she thinks you can handle yourself better than me, apparently. But still—she must really not trust the Rangers."

"That's part of what we're doing," William informed me. "Going to check on their camps and see what they're up to."

"That does make sense," I conceded. "But—*do* you feel like

you can handle yourself? I mean, I know you're magic and all, but I'm still worried for you."

Of course, I shouldn't have even bothered to ask the question. William snorted again. "I'll be fine," he said. I couldn't tell if he was making fun of Luca and me, or not. "I don't think the roads are as dangerous for people like you and me as you think. Thorn just wants someone who can sense magic, and she's hedging her bets by asking me instead of the Witch."

"The Witch is probably deeply asleep after everything else she's asked him to do," I observed sympathetically. *Asleep and dreaming of Sakura,* I added to myself. But my smile soon faded. "By 'people like you and me,' I suppose you mean anyone without stuff to steal? Like what Sir Rowan was saying?"

William nodded. "I think *that* part of the pattern is pretty clear, at least."

"Still," I said uneasily, "it doesn't hurt to be careful."

"It does when you make your—" William saw the look on my face and sighed. "Well, I'm just saying, there is such a thing as being too careful, that's all."

"And there's such a thing as being reckless," I pointed out. "Promise you'll run back here the moment you feel threatened?"

"I promise. Although I really don't think anything's going to come out of the woods with claws and teeth to attack me and a police officer who might as well have been carved out of stone."

"Be that as it may," I said, "there's no denying that *something* is out there in the woods."

17

Night Mares

After William left and I finally dragged myself to bed, I slept fitfully. It was the kind of sleep where I was never sure if I'd just been dreaming, sleeping, or laying in bed awake. So when a ghostly form appeared above me, I thought at first that I was dreaming about interviewing Sloane.

Or Jade.

But I was mad at Luca, so I slapped away those warm feelings. And when I rolled over and squished my arm and realized I was awake, I turned back to that spectral visage with a cascade of terror running down my spine.

"Whoareyouandwhatareyoudoinghere?" I croaked, scrambling to sit up.

"It's me," said the shadowy face floating in midair. When it grinned, I started to understand. "You know—Saki. I'm at the back door. Would you please let me in?"

Even if she introduced herself informally, I wasn't totally won over. "How in Beyond are you doing that? What about William's wards?"

"Yeah," said the spectral Sakura. "His handiwork is really good."

I stared at her, still wondering if possibly I was asleep.

"Do I have to say it?" she chuckled, wavering up and down. "I'm better!"

Good enough to have us all fooled? I wondered at first. Anyone powerful enough to get through William's protection spells—even if just to send in a ghostly image of themselves—was far more powerful than I could imagine.

But there's a lot of things you can't imagine, I could hear my mother telling me.

The memory brought down my last wall of distrust. I laughed and told Sakura, "You do have to spell those things out for me. I like practical—I don't do magic. Hold on, let me put on my slippers and I'll be down in a minute."

"But magic *is* practical!" ghost-Sakura sang out meanwhile.

I shook my head, smiling as I stuffed my toes into fuzzy teal slippers. *Something tells me that if Sakura was my teacher, I'd have a lot to learn.*

Clutching my robe around me, I made my way downstairs to let Sakura in. For just a brief moment, as I first saw her standing in her pajamas on my back doorstep, I wondered if I was doing the right thing. But then I decided that Sakura was far to honest to be a bloodthirsty murderer *and* to wear pastel flannel pajamas covered in flying sheep out in public.

"Thanks for letting me in," she said, and for a moment her blue eyes were kind and serious, as though she understood all my thoughts.

I blushed and waved her up the stairs. "Come on, no need to stand in the cold. Geez, it's freezing. So why are you out so late at night, anyway?"

"I wanted to see if you would help me with some scrying," Sakura said, climbing lightly up to the landing, and following me into the kitchen, where I lit a string of fairy lights and a lamp. I hated to disturb Sugar, who loved her beauty sleep, but it looked like Sakura and I would be up for a while.

"I'll help if I can, but I think I'm more suited to feeding you snacks while you do the work," I admitted. "Do you want anything?"

"Maybe just some tea, please. You *have* to have something better than at the tavern, right?"

"I have just the thing," I confirmed, pulling out my teapot and a bag of loose white tea.

"Perfect. And where is William? I had hoped to talk to him more."

"Now there's something that people don't often say about him," I grinned as I set the water to boil. "He's out with Officer Thorn, patrolling the forest."

"It looks like we're all having sleepless nights. I'm sorry to disturb you, by the way."

I looked up to meet Sakura's gaze across the kitchen island, and again I was struck by the depth of the sympathy in her clear eyes. "It's okay," I assured her. "I wasn't sleeping too well anyway. So, what is it you had in mind?"

"I want to do a stakeout," she declared, perching on a stool across from my workspace. "But from inside, not outside. And I didn't want to involve Ryu—he needs his rest, so I made sure he'll get some," she explained, with the sort of vagueness that left me wondering if she'd merely tucked him into bed or if she'd administered some kind of spell. *Maybe both? She is pretty resourceful.* I smiled to myself as I found that I was warming to Sakura, despite this air of mystery.

"So," I prompted as I set out our mugs and tea strainers, "can you really scry the whole town? 'Scrying' just means creating a mini image of it that you can watch from above, right?"

"Sort of, and not exactly," she admitted, selecting a delicate tea strainer shaped like a mermaid, another gift from my friends in Seaside. "I'm not familiar enough with Belville to envision all its streets and corners. But what I *can* do is set up a lure in the park outside your window!"

"A lure?" The idea was a little terrifying, but the way she said it had me biting back a laugh.

"Yep. Strictly magic—that part of it, at least. I'll anchor a spell in the park that draws anyone feeling strong greed or bloodlust, and we'll take turns keeping watch to see who comes by!"

I shuddered as she said *bloodlust,* but I had to admit that it did seem like the attacks were getting more and more bold. Seeing my distress, Sakura added, "If no one comes, then maybe the next night we can try a lure for secrecy, or power, or something. I'm not sure exactly what our criminal, or criminals, are after."

"But that's part of shadow magic, I suppose? Drawing people out based on their inner desires?" I asked, and Sakura nodded like a proud teacher as I began to pour out water for the tea. I added, "If you try the power one, I think we might get more than our robber."

Sakura immediately understood what I meant. "Unless Peyton *is* the robber," she observed.

"He was the first one attacked," I recalled, musing.

"The perfect cover, don't you think?"

I hesitated, taking the chance to ponder as I set away the teapot and pushed honey over the counter. *She seems to value being honest,* I reminded myself. *And that's important to me too.* So at last I said, "What was that, earlier, with Peyton? Do you know him?"

"Nope," Sakura chirped as she stirred her tea. "Why?"

"The way you were pushing him in the tavern . . . it seemed kind of like you had a personal grudge."

"I do." Sakura set down her tea spoon, and explained, "I don't know Peyton. Maybe I was being unfair. I just *hate* it when people won't confront their own emotions, and instead take them out on others. It's a pet peeve of mine, I guess you could say. Or a personal crusade."

I nodded slowly. "That, I think I can understand. And for what it's worth, I agree that he was being unreasonable. Sorry to pry."

"Oh, don't be sorry at all," Sakura beamed at me. "I can tell already that we are going to be the best of friends!"

* * *

We soon moved our tea into the living room, where Sakura stationed herself by the window and set up her lure. She insisted she could do her magic from inside, rather than in the park—and I must admit it was fascinating to watch. William's magic was blue, and Trent's was purple; Sakura's magic sparkled all around her hands and her head as she worked, bright flashes of black. It gave her pajamas an appropriately Halloweeny look.

Once she was done, I didn't see anything in the park to show for her chanting and hand-waving. But she insisted that that was how things were supposed to work. The lure was a feeling, an inexplicable draw, not an actual thing. It would work even though it was invisible.

And so, we settled in to wait.

"I'll take first or second watch, whatever you like," said Sakura. "I owe you, since you let me use your living room, and even made me tea!"

"It's no trouble," I said, settling on the couch with my mug. "For the moment, I'm wide awake, and I bet you are, too. It's actually kind of weird how quiet things are out on the Square."

"Is there normally business in Belville during the night time?" Sakura asked from her perch on one of my dining room chairs.

I nodded. "There's some. Not as much as there'd be in a city, of course. But we do have our share of nocturnal residents. Even William might count as one."

"I'm sure it's usually quite lovely here at night," Sakura said, smiling.

"It is. Hey," I asked, before I could think better of it, "did you pass the bookstore on your way here? Did you notice any lights on?"

"I don't know which building that is, sorry," Sakura replied. But then, with a slyness coming over her rounded features, she added, "If you're worried about him, maybe we should call . . . ?"

"Oh, no, I'm sure he's fine," I said hastily. "So, what did you think of Trent?"

Saki laughed. "I think the question is, what does he think of *me*! That was a strange meeting this afternoon, wasn't it?"

"Oh, you noticed?" I grinned along with her. "He was a bit surprised, is all. I don't think he was expecting . . . company, so soon."

"I know Witches do a love ritual in school," Saki said, reading my expression. "But that's pretty much all I know about it."

"So, you've never done one?"

Saki shrugged. "Nope. I suppose I didn't really feel the need. I was more focused on—well, dealing with my own past, and whatnot. Shadows."

"But the two go together," I said, reminding her of her comment to Ryuko earlier.

She laughed. "They do. It's true. Funny how easily we forget, right?"

"I think that's part of what surprised Trent," I said, cautiously. "Not put him off, obviously. But just . . . it *is* a little surprising, meeting you; you said as much yourself!"

"I know." Sakura shifted in her chair, setting down her tea. "Would you like to know, Red? About my magic, I mean."

I hadn't expected this openness—but maybe I should have. "Sure," I said at once. "I can't promise to understand it all, but I'm interested, definitely."

"I can say it so that you can understand," Saki said confidently. "Promise. You just have to think about it in context.

"What I do is called shadow magic, even though some people think of it as 'dangerous magic' or 'dark magic.' In that context, 'dangerous' and 'dark' are about things outside ourselves, right? Outside dangers. Shadows are about things inside ourselves. All the things we feel guilty about, or inadequate about, or sad or angry about. Shadow magic is about confronting those and letting them be part of your life, instead of hiding them.

"And it can be really hard," Saki added. "There's a reason not many people do it, not fully. Think about it like a journey. Maybe something happens to you that brings up all these emotions you don't want to have—a big loss, for example, or a trauma or an injury. That event becomes like a specter in your life. It's always hanging over you. You don't want it there, but you can't get away from it. So maybe you decide to burn it down—to be free of it. *That's* like dark magic. Destruction.

"But afterward . . . when you realize that there's a husk of that specter left, even after you tried to burn it down, and it's still right there with you and you can't get rid of it because *it is a part of you,* that is accepting your shadow. Once you're there, and you can be content being yourself, you're on your way to becoming a shadow witch."

"You were right," I chuckled. "You did put it really well. I think I get it."

"Told you," she beamed.

"Although," I added on a whim, teasingly, "I would have understood shadow magic even better if you had put it in alchemical terms. You know, we alchemists are forever breaking things down and then building them back up again."

"So I've heard, but I know nothing about alchemy," said Sakura, her eyes wide and rapturous, her elbow on the back of her chair and her chin in her hand. "Tell me *everything.*"

18

Everybody Scream

I didn't quite manage to tell Saki everything about alchemy. After all, it had taken me years to study it properly, and I still didn't know all there was to know. But we did stay up for quite a while talking.

Sometime deep into the night, a noise from Sakura woke me. I'd fallen asleep snuggled into a little ball on my couch, empty tea mug still in my hand. Sakura was still in her chair, although now she was sitting sideways in it, her hands and face pressed against the window.

"*Red!*" she whispered. "Did you hear that? Someone's out there!"

"I didn't hear anything," I mumbled as I tried to get my stiff spine into an upright position. "What was it? Was it William?"

"No." Sakura turned to me, her face troubled. "I thought I heard someone scream. I don't think it was a dream. But I—I don't see anyone outside!"

Clumsily, I shuffled off the couch and clambered into William's window seat for a better look. Knowing the lure Sakura had set up, and hearing the way she said *scream,* I had to swallow quite a few fears to do so. But despite her nerves, the shadow witch was staring avidly and bravely out the window, and I wasn't about to leave her on her own.

As I moved into place, I couldn't see anything but the darkness of night outside the window. But from somewhere off to the north end of town, I heard a heavy crash.

Sakura's head whipped to me, and I could tell she heard it too. "That one was definitely real," I said. "Does it have something to do with your lure?"

"I don't think so," she whispered. "The lure would just bring someone to it. It wouldn't make them act in any way. Unless it's someone feeling drawn to it, and fighting their attraction?"

"Could they do that?"

"They'd have to have a very strong will." Sakura smoothed back her hair. "I think I need to go out and look."

"You're not going alone," I told her. "But do you really think it's wise? It sounds like exactly the sort of thing I'd tell my friends *not* to do." *Or they'd be telling* me *not to*, I added, thinking of Thorn. Where were she and William when we needed them?

"We'll do our best to not be seen," Sakura said. She stood. Clearly, her decision had been made. "And if we *are* seen, I can use my magic to protect us."

"Let me grab my tool belt too, just in case," I said, mostly because I knew the familiar tools would calm my nerves rather than a thought that solidifying goo or weak acid would actually ward off a robber.

Sakura was already headed for the back door.

"Take one of my cloaks, at least," I called, stumbling up after her and following her to the door. I barely got one of my shorter, violet woolen cloaks over her head before she was down the stairs.

I admire the facing shadows thing, I thought as I struggled with my own vibrant orange cloak, *but I wonder if maybe it makes Sakura a little too reckless.*

From the kitchen, I saw a faint glimmer. *Sugar.* I took comfort knowing that if William came home while Sakura and I were out, the pixie would be able to tell him what had happened.

Without another thought, I trailed in Sakura's wake. When I got down to the back patio, I closed and locked my door as quietly as possible.

Sakura was standing at the far corner of the little yard. The night was inky and cloudy, and I could only make her out by the faint pale glow of her pajama legs and the shine of her uncovered hair. *Neither of us is looking very stealthy,* I thought with a sudden pang of regret. *But hopefully we won't have to be.* She turned and waved me over.

"I don't see or hear anyone," she whispered as I raced to her side. "But I see something in the road, off to the right—away from the Square."

"Toward the police station," I said automatically, my stomach dropping. "That way, there's just a few houses and then the police station, and then town limits."

Sakura's eyes roamed shrewdly over my goggles, which were askew in my messy hair. "Do you have good vision in the dark? I can only see as good as the average human."

"My dark vision is good," I replied, no longer concerned with things like hiding the traces of my mystic heritage. "And even better with these."

I tugged the goggles down over my eyes, fussing with stray strands of my hair as I did so. When I finally had everything in place, I blinked. The world was much more defined. It looked normal—just a little darker than usual. Not at all like the horrorscape I'd somehow been expecting.

Sakura pointed, and I leaned around the back fence to look down the road. I saw at once what she was worried about. A few blocks away, a large blocky shape sat at a strange angle. It would have blocked all traffic, had there been any traffic to block. Nothing around it moved.

And it was very near the police station.

Even though I *knew* that the shape must be a wagon, and that William and Officer Thorn hadn't had a wagon of any kind, and therefore it *couldn't* have anything to do with them, I leapt into action at once. My nerves made my feet itch to run. It was unthinkable to stay put in the yard after that.

In no more than two seconds, I was at the wagon. I circled it but saw no sign of movement. One wheel listed at a strange angle, broken, and the paneling along the sides was scraped and torn, as though it had been driven straight through a thicket. It was a rough wooden cart, the kind of thing farmers might use to bring produce into town, or some old-fashioned couriers used to transport mail between towns. A heavy, water-proofed tarp covered the cargo in the back.

Struck by an irrational, desperate curiosity, I began tugging at the rope that held the tarp down.

"Red," Sakura called softly as she caught up. "What are you doing?"

"Trying to see what's in here," I hissed back without looking. "It could be a clue. Or it could be important. Maybe it could tell us what happened or who was driving the cart—"

"Red," the shadow witch repeated, interrupting. Finally I paused and met her eyes—and noticed that she was glowing all over with those black sparks that indicated her magic. Simply *seeing* her, not even touching her, filled me with that sort of inevitable calm that you get from knowing that something is scary, but resolving to face it anyway.

"You don't need to do that," Sakura said firmly.

I immediately stopped fidgeting with the ties. "But why?"

"Because," she said, pointing to the front seat of the wagon, nearest to her, "From the looks of it, whatever was stolen was taken from up here. The tarp's all ripped up. And unfortunately, we know who was driving the wagon."

* * *

A quarter of an hour later, the night was no lighter, and Sakura and I sat on the front bench of the police station with our eyes on the abandoned wagon.

And its unfortunate driver.

"Sorry," I murmured to Sakura. "Believe it or not, I've actually encountered several murder victims before . . . it's never pleasant, but it doesn't usually leave me so jumpy I can't focus."

"You don't have anything to be sorry for," Sakura returned simply. "Clearly, the whole situation in town with the robberies and accusations has you keyed up. It could have that effect on anyone."

She kept talking—she'd been reassuring me for the past fifteen minutes straight. But I was starting to feel calmer, and my mind began to wander. What she'd said reminded me of what Luca had told me the previous afternoon. *We know this is hard for you.* Suddenly, I realized that as nice and perceptive as Sakura was, all I really wanted was to see Luca and feel his arms around me.

But the last thing he needs is to be dragged out here at this time of night, I told myself, shaking my head. *Focus, Cinnabar.* Using my mothers' name for me always helped me get a little perspective.

Next to me, Sakura stopped talking. She laid one soft hand on my shoulder. "Feeling better?"

"Feeling a little guilty for being so affected by all this," I admitted with a small, rueful smile. "But also very lucky to have such observant friends."

Saki cocked her head like she might ask a question, but instead she only said, "Birds of a feather."

"Right." I blew out a breath, collecting my thoughts once more. "Okay. So. What do we do? Can you get a hold of William somehow? He's with Officer Thorn. I have flares that I could use, but it might be more discreet if you did it."

The shadow witch grimaced. "I'm really not very good at communication spells. I know it's basic magic, but I never really learned it. I always preferred to write letters. And since I didn't go to school, there was no one to *make* me learn the spells, so . . ."

"I get it. Everyone has their stumbling block," I said sympathetically. "Good thing I brought my belt, then. Hold on a moment."

Sakura leaned back and gave me space as I located the flare on my tool belt and, moving carefully in the dark, set it off. With a red flash and a loud bang, it whizzed off into the forest. William had helped me make a whole series of flares, some that would go out to my friends, some that went straight to him, and some normal ones that would alert anyone nearby. I opted just to try to reach him rather than bring the whole town out to the crime scene.

"It should just take a moment," I told Saki, thinking, *the crime scene. And this one is in town . . . Officer Thorn was right about the attacks getting worse.* "They're both going to be pretty mad."

"They have right to be," she answered evenly. "But as far as the victim goes, it didn't seem like he was from town?"

"No, I didn't recognize him. I know sometimes the mail gets in super early, though, depending where it's coming from. I was thinking more that they'd be mad at *me* for being out at night."

I was proved right when Sakura's next words were cut off by a bark-like cry from the road.

"Cinnabar Sunset, why is it you're always doing the one thing you're not supposed to do?"

With a series of huffs and thuds and scrapes, William and Officer Thorn managed to come to a stop right before they slammed into Sakura and me—and the wall of the police station.

"Sorry, William," I said, and I meant it—though I was just a *little* bit amused, too. "It's a long story. You remember Sakura? Officer Thorn, this is Sakura, Ryuko's sister. She's visiting town."

"Nice to meet you," Sakura said politely. "If you like, I can create a light over the scene."

Officer Thorn glanced from us to William and back, still catching her breath. They'd clearly been running hard after they got my flare. "Cast a light over what? What was the emergency? Did you call us back here just to make introductions?"

"No," I said, squirming in my seat. "We, uh—we found someone who's been robbed, and, um, murdered, it looks like. Hit over the head while driving the mail wagon, maybe? They're out there—in the road."

"I told you," William growled as he and Officer Thorn turned to look. "I *told* you I sensed danger."

"And I thought I told *you* not to investigate," Thorn said, pausing to glare down at me. "But we'll discuss that later. Come on. I could use that light, after all."

The four of us surrounded the wagon. William sniffed the air as Sakura hummed to herself, chanting before she lifted her hands and a hazy white light bloomed over our heads. Officer Thorn turned to the victim at once.

For my part, I pulled my goggles back down over my head—I'd dislodged them in my anxiety following our initial discovery—and took a look at the front corner of the tarp. As Sakura had said earlier, it was clear that this was where the thief had got to work. The knots were still in place along the edges of the wagon, but the tarp had been sliced away with a series of sharp blades—probably much like claws, I had to admit. The destruction had created a triangular flap big enough to remove packages through. I found torn brown paper wrapping and frayed twine—clearly, the robber had been looking for something in particular. Mixed in with the mess were fragments of charcoal and tubes of loose paint. *Maybe this was supposed to be a delivery for the art store,* I thought sadly. My attention was caught by a reddish stain amid the paper.

In the meantime, Officer Thorn had pulled a notebook from her breast pocket and was working through a checklist. As she checked off the final item, she stepped back. "Looks like you were right, Red. The uniform's from the mail center down the mountain. We'll reach out to them, and have them ID the cart, too. But it looks pretty standard for a mail wagon—no animal or magitech hitched up; it was probably running on a spell controlled by the driver. Poor guy was hit over the head by something very heavy. Probably never knew what happened, is my guess."

I saw an opportunity to put that favor from the new doctor in town to good use. "I think I could get Doctor Goodberry to agree to take a look for you. He'll probably be a lot more helpful than I would about the cause of death."

"You may need a magical exam done, too," Sakura chipped in. "A medical doctor might not know how to spot faint traces of a spell . . . like if it was something *summoned* that did this."

"If the driver was hit over the head, then how'd the cart get here?" William asked. He sat a few feet away, near the rear of the cart. "Look at the state of it. There's pieces of wood all over the road, like breadcrumbs. And it smells like the forest."

"Could the attack have happened in the woods, and then the cart rolled?" I asked, eyeing the forest. The trees were a good block or so away from the police station, but the road was hilly.

"It could have," Officer Thorn decided, "but why? Our robber hasn't made this kind of mistake before. Why leave a wagon right out in front of the *station,* for goddess' sake? Why let it come out from under the cover of the trees?"

"Some kind of challenge?" William suggested.

"Or the robber was *afraid* of something in the trees," Sakura added.

"The robber is the scariest thing around here, aside from the law," Thorn retorted. "And it's the *Rangers* our robber should be challenging, not me. And why wouldn't they want to take their time with the robbery, since the driver wasn't able to put up a fight?"

"But wait," I interjected. "You're saying the driver didn't have a chance to fight, but look. Someone bled on the packages left in the wagon."

For the first time, Officer Thorn's controlled "investigation" face gave way and she looked startled. She stepped over and peered over my shoulder at once.

"You're right," she said, with a curse. "And I don't like any of this. Come on. We're going to get our victim into the station, and the cart into the alley, before sunrise. I don't know what's gone on here, but we need time to figure it out before everyone panics."

19

The Hunter in Black

After we'd helped Officer Thorn move all traces of the crime to the station for further investigation, William, Sakura, and I headed back to the shop. We left the officer to her lists and reports. Night was finally breaking, and after all our labor—not to mention the shock of the discovery—none of us quite felt like going to bed. Personally, I was very grateful not to have to perform any exams. Instead, we settled back into my living room with another round of tea.

William had opened his mouth and was no doubt about to give Sakura the fourth degree when the witch sat bolt upright on the couch. "Someone's out there!"

"We just *left* 'out there,'" William observed grumpily.

"Out by your lure, you mean?" I scrambled up, taking in the gray dawn light above the Square as I did so. "Are you sure it isn't just a farmer bringing things into the grocer's, or something?"

"I definitely felt something, as if they'd touched the spell," Saki answered tangentially. She climbed over the back of the couch and knelt beside a planter full of herbs, looking out the window. And in no time at all, she pointed out a strange figure underneath the trees outside.

I stood behind her at the window. To be fair, he wasn't exactly *strange*. Actually, that might have been the strangest thing about him. The man stood in a dark cape and boots, looking completely at home with the jack-o-lanterns, strewn leaves, and early morning shadows. He seemed to be about six feet tall and broad across the shoulders, but any other details were hard to determine. The Square was foggy so early in the morning, lending the stranger and all the All Hallows decorations a ghostly appearance.

As I took the sight in, I tried to take a sip from my mug, burned my tongue, and made a face. "Is he really wearing a velvet cape?"

Saki giggled next to me. "Is that all you can think? He might be our murderer!"

"I don't think I've ever seen him," I said, squinting harder as I tried to scan him for details. He was simply standing beneath the old oak, hands on his hips, looking around the Square almost as though *he* was trying to find *us*. "Can you tell if it was your lure that brought him here?"

"Not for sure," Saki admitted. "But it seems pretty suspicious, don't you think? Should we go down and meet him?"

"Meet him?" I hesitated. Dimly, I recognized this idea as yet another thing that I would emphatically warn Luca *against* doing.

"Yes," Saki said firmly. "We need more information. What's our excuse?"

"Excuse for what? Being out at the crack of dawn?" I looked at the stranger again, and yawned. Physically moving that mail cart had taken more of a toll than I'd thought. "We can say we're heading to the bakery. But I'm not even sure they are open yet."

"That's a great idea," said Sakura.

"In your pajamas?" William asked incredulously as she turned toward the door once more.

"No time," the witch answered, and for a moment she reminded me of Officer Thorn. "We have to confront him before he gets away!"

* * *

By the time I ran out of my apartment after Sakura, she'd already vanished into the alley. I followed, trying to move quickly despite still feeling a bit groggy, my feet scuffing through the fallen leaves. I managed to catch up with her just before she hit the Square—and the stranger. William was right behind me, though he didn't deign to say anything.

"Good morning," Sakura called brightly as we made our way across the grass.

The stranger hadn't moved; he still stood under the oak tree, hands on hips making him seem even bigger than he had through the apartment window. And we kept walking. Nerves fluttered in my stomach as we got closer and closer.

"Morning," he said at last, gruffly.

"Are you new in town?" Saki asked with impressive ease, given that she herself had arrived less than twenty-four hours before.

He shifted like maybe he wouldn't answer. Sakura came to a halt about four steps away from him, and I stood beside her. William sat just to my left. Finally, glancing between the three of us, the newcomer said reluctantly, "Here on business."

"Oh, it must be important, then," said Sakura. "We were just out to get to the bakery right as it opens. You should think about doing the same—their muffins are delicious!"

I resisted the urge to run my hands nervously through my hair, wondering how she'd known that.

"No time for muffins," came the reply. He still stood in the shadow of the tree trunk behind him, so I couldn't get a good read on his face. But William was intent next to me, so I hoped maybe he was getting a better picture than I was.

Meanwhile, Sakura blinked up at him innocently. "Really?"

"Maybe we should just leave you to it," I said, reaching out, ready to pull Sakura away. My feet itched fiercely.

But then the man changed my mind. He sighed, not huffily like William, but almost wistfully. "You really should, you know," he said. "It's dangerous out here."

"Isn't it dangerous for you, too?" Sakura asked, impervious to my nudging.

"No," he said, but he seemed a little self-conscious. "Actually, I—I seem to have lost the trail a bit. Have either of you seen a bloodthirsty witch about?"

As Sakura and I exchanged bemused glances, a new voice interrupted our conversation.

"You, there! Explain yourself at once!"

* * *

Earlier, as we moved the mail cart, William had confided to me that he and Officer Thorn had had a fruitless night. They'd spent hours walking and re-walking the same paths until they got my flare, and during that time, they hadn't seen a soul—not

143

a robber, not a Ranger, not a wolf, not anyone. This, I thought, seemed to help explain why Officer Thorn was starting to sound a bit frayed at the edges.

And the recent murder probably explained her immediate suspicions of the stranger in the cape.

"Who are you?" she continued yelling, as she strode in from the road to the station. *She must have finished her examination and been hoping to ask us about some detail or other,* I figured. Now, she glowered more than ever.

"No one," said the man in the cape, rather defensively.

"Then why are you here?" William added, speaking up for the first time. Blue magic crackled over his ears and tail as he stared the man down from my side.

"I was following a trail," the man in the cape said, sounding smaller and smaller by the moment. "I was contracted to be here."

"What kind of a trail?" Thorn persisted. "What are you doing?"

"Magic," he answered. His voice was now a mumble.

"Officer Thorn," I said, "I know a lot has happened tonight, but is this really how we greet newcomers these days?"

"It is when they show up in town and I don't know how, since I was on the road all night long," she informed me.

"Maybe he came in by the lake," Sakura chirped.

"I did," said the man, nodding quickly. "My boat's at the dock."

"I'll be checking that," said Thorn suspiciously.

"And you still haven't said your name," William reminded him, his tail wagging—but not in a friendly manner.

"What's all this, then?"

I nearly groaned aloud as *another* new voice joined the

chorus. Together, the five of us turned to see my new neighbor, the doctor, striding out from his office on the corner. "I heard the commotion and was hoping it was my mail," he explained as he came closer. "Is everything alright, Officer?"

"Of course it is," said Thorn. "Nothing to worry about, Dr Goodberry."

"Nice of you to come out and check on us, though," said Sakura, her blue eyes focused on the doctor.

"It's an old habit of mine to be a bit nosy," he said, nodding greetings around the group. "Please forgive an old man."

I studied him as he saluted me. *I thought doctors tried* not *to be nosy,* I thought to myself. But the sight of his shaky hands reminded me that he, too, had been a victim of the roadside attacks, and that he probably was feeling a little unsafe in town. I could certainly understand being curious in that case.

Too bad he probably won't be getting that mail, though, I thought, my mind flashing back to that torn tarp.

In the meantime, the man in the cape cleared his throat. "I really ought to be going."

"You really ought to be telling us who you are," William growled.

Again, the man sighed. But then he rallied himself and, drawing up, he said, "My name is Blake Bloodsworn, and I'm a witch hunter. I'm here in your town because the Rangers called me in to help, because—because there's evil magic here!"

20

Horror Show

"Nobody panic, though," Blake added. He looked rather uncertainly at the five of us, none of whom were panicked.

"Well, I see you have everything under control here," said Dr Goodberry to Thorn. "I'll be in my office if you need me." And with another genial nod, he walked off, leaning heavily on his cane.

"I'm feeling tired," Sakura announced with even more suddenness. "I think I'll go home and update Ryu. See you all later!" And with a cheery wave, she left.

"Of course there's magic here," said William, possibly the only one of us to remain focused on Blake. "Why else would the Rangers have called you in? Why else would people be getting attacked on the road?"

Blake bit his lip. "People are getting attacked on the roads? The brief only said something about a robbery."

Officer Thorn heaved the heaviest sigh of them all. "You, witch hunter. Go get yourself a room at the tavern, and breakfast while you're at it. I'll be by to talk to you in a bit.

You, Red, have some explaining to do about—everything. And William, isn't time you got some sleep?"

Blake hesitated, his gaze bouncing between us. Now that the sun had risen and my fear had totally dissipated, I took in more details about him: pale skin, brown hair, brown eyes, and a strong nose. Deep scars were scraped across his cheeks on both sides, one even nearing the corner of his left eye. Despite his impressive figure, though, he was still easily an inch or two shorter than Thorn. *And actually,* I thought to myself, *he seems like a nice guy, underneath the posturing.*

A nice guy who was apparently bent on hunting down my newest friend.

And had showed up in town the same night as a murder.

I still didn't really know what a witch hunter's job entailed, or what one would be prepared to do. But before I could venture to ask Blake a question, he apparently decided to respect Officer Thorn's authority. With one last glance at me, he turned and walked off to the tavern, following Thorn's gesture.

"You may as well go in, too," I said down to William, agreeing with Thorn's orders. "Sir Rowan will be in soon, and he'll be confused if no one's there to greet him."

William shook his ears—neither an agreement nor a disagreement—and trotted off toward the shop.

"That's *that* settled," said Thorn, and in her voice I could hear how spun up she'd been. *Was she really so worried about finding a stranger in the Square? Or was it something about the crime scene that got her so worked up?* I wondered. She went on, "All I want is a moment of quiet to get my head on—"

She paused, staring over my shoulder at the northwestern corner of the park.

I got a bad feeling that we weren't alone . . .

Again.

"That dratted drunk fool," Officer Thorn muttered under her breath. She continued cursing colorfully as she stomped straight past me. Something in her voice reassured me that we weren't facing a supernatural monster, but a more mortal threat. I fell into step behind her without another thought.

Although once I saw what she had, I almost wished I hadn't. Working his way around the park perimeter, Peyton was tying posters to trees and stuffing cards between jack-o-lanterns. A small crowd trailed after him, helpfully holding string and piles of paper.

Just goes to show that everyone, *even the wackiest among us, can drum up some followers,* I thought grimly.

And it was clear that Officer Thorn, after the escalation of the robberies and her all-night vigil, was similarly unimpressed.

"Who gave you permission to post bulletins in the park?" 'she called across the grass without preamble.

"The truth needs no permission!" Peyton cried back.

Thorn kept stomping straight for him. "Well, posters in public spaces *do*!"

"Just another sign of the current system trying to keep this information from us!" Peyton shouted back. "Do you deny that the robberies have happened in a predictable pattern? That, when plotted on a map, they create a specific shape which can tell us not only where the next attack will occur, but the epicenter itself, where the evil energy in the forest lives? The point from which Fenrir will be summoned?"

My head was spinning already. *Isn't it too early for this? How is he not hungover?*

"This is *serious*," Thorn said as she neared Peyton and his group. "People have been attacked. Lives are in danger. We *all* are working to find the culprit. This is a time to be safe, to look out for each other, and to *pay attention to the law.* This is *not* a time for politicking or ranting about epicenters!"

And with that, she ripped the nearest sign right off its tree, crumpled it up in her large hands, and tossed it directly into the nearest trash bin.

Peyton swayed in place as he watched this, and I realized, *Ah. He's not hungover because he's still drunk. Lovely.*

"She doesn't want you to know! She and the mayor! They're hiding it from you!" Peyton gurgled and spat at the small crowd behind him. "They'll be after your maps next! They're keeping information from us all! They don't want us to find the epicenter! They want us all to be *victims when the Day of the Wolf comes!"*

It occurred to me that for Peyton, it probably was a much more grandiose thing to be able to say he'd been the victim of evil geometric energy rather than run-of-the-mill roadside banditry. It also occurred to me that he might have bled on his tarp—the tarp Thorn had brought to me to test for evidence—himself. As a phoenixkin person, he probably did have somewhat magical blood.

I'd heard of Fenrir, of course—a legendary wolf said to be a harbinger of the end of the world. But I didn't see any reason to assume the thefts had been specifically to summon him. And personally, I didn't believe the geometry thing one bit. But from my scientific studies, I was familiar with the idea that certain shapes might aid in summoning—or revealing— demons. The pentagram was sometimes thought to be one such shape. That said, nothing had ever been proven, as far as I was concerned, and Peyton certainly wasn't winning me over.

"The only thing keeping *you* from a jail cell is the mayor's respect for your previous contributions to the town!" Officer Thorn roared back.

"You're part of the problem," Peyton slurred, pointing at Thorn.

This, understandably, was the last straw. Officer Thorn puffed up like an angry bear. "That's it. I'm done with this. All of you, leave the posters and go home. I'm confiscating everything. Go on! Get out of here! You shouldn't even be out so early!"

And ranting and rambling about public safety, she began literally running at Peyton and his followers.

People and posters scattered. Officer Thorn shouted and ran, waving her arms, which looked more and more like ill-proportioned wings with every crumpled piece of paper she snatched from a tree and held in her fist. Most of the townsfolk disappeared at once, but Peyton wasn't so quick on the uptake.

While Thorn and Peyton hashed it out, I couldn't help but wonder about the "maps" comment. *What in Beyond did he mean by that? Does he really plan on staking out some random spot in the forest?* I wandered in Thorn's wake, picking up pieces of posters and leftover cards. Everything was handwritten—apparently, Peyton hadn't been persuasive enough to get Leo to do his printing for him. Thanking the universe for small blessings, I turned over one of the cards in my palm and read it:

These attacks are not random the Geometry of them proves there is a Demon involved we can Predict where the next one will be you will be safe if you have the right Map the Information must be in your Hands

I rolled my eyes. I'd seen a poster campaign like this once before in Belville, during the previous winter. That one had very little result. I didn't expect this one to do any better. *Really,* I wondered, in my grumpy sleep-deprived state, *if they couldn't decide which words to capitalize consistently, how could they expect to make a cohesive argument?*

As I read, the yelling in the Square grew louder. I looked up to see that Officer Thorn had chased Peyton all the way across the park. They stood outside the salon arguing. And someone new had joined the scene—*Gloria!*

I ran over, half out of curiosity, half out of a neighborly duty to warn Gloria away from the scene. But as I came closer, I realized she probably had a better familiarity with Peyton and his theories than I did.

"Uncle," she was saying as I ran up, "you can't just show up and—"

"It wasn't my fault I left," Peyton panted. Running hadn't done him any favors. He leaned heavily on Gloria, one hand to his head, as he attempted to stare down Thorn. For her part, Gloria stood in her salon apron with a mop in one hand. Clearly, she'd been hoping to do some early morning cleaning, and had been interrupted by the noise. In the shadows of the salon door, I saw Johann, too. Gloria's assistant lived in the apartment above the shop, while she lived in a house at the edge of town. I made a mental note to ask Johann if he'd seen anything in the Square overnight. Between being part vampire and frequently on late night calls to his long-distance boyfriend, he was inclined to be more nocturnal than my other neighbors.

"I know all about you," Officer Thorn was saying gruffly to Peyton. "You and Owl were pals once, until he ran you out of town. But we aren't here to talk about that now. Right now, I need you to—"

"—not gotta do anything—" Peyton muttered, not listening.

Gloria glanced meaningfully at me, and I cleared my throat. "Maybe the *smart* thing to do would be to meet up later, when everyone has had a chance to think things over and clear their heads. And if you don't want to do so on your own, Peyton, then I'm sure Officer Thorn would help you to the police station."

"Naw," said Peyton, looking to Gloria for support.

"Yes," said Gloria, firmly. It warmed my heart to realize she was taking my side. "You're not yourself, Uncle. You're better than this. You need to leave and come back once you can think straight."

Peyton glared at Thorn, as if to dare her into an argument—into an excuse to stay. But the three of us stood silent, and so at last he pulled himself up straight—or, nearly straight—and stumbled off to Lavender's.

I watched him go, thinking, *My oh my. I wonder if Lavender's tavern is sturdy enough to hold all the strange characters it seems to be collecting these days?*

* * *

"At least we know one thing," Officer Thorn grouched. I'd managed to pull her up to my kitchen for a breather. Gloria and Johann had preferred to stay at the salon, which was just as well. The officer was a little too on edge for company. "Lavender won't sell him more booze this early, not when he's in that state."

"I'm sure she can handle him," I agreed, installing Thorn in one of the dining chairs by the front windows, and then bustling back to my pantry for some breakfast—and something stronger. I began pulling out ingredients to make my own, shall we say, *boosted* tea. Sometimes, it took more than caffeine to keep me running. As I rifled through the food-safe box I kept ingredients in, Sugar the pixie flittered over and took a seat on my head.

"And just what exactly were you and the little white-haired girl doing in the Square so early?" Thorn asked. The beauty— and downfall—of my studio apartment was that we could talk easily across the spaces.

"The 'white-haired girl' is named Sakura," I replied, busy with my tea pot and honey and goji berries. "Remember? I told you earlier. She's in town to visit Ryuko. They grew up together."

"Wrote that down in my notebook so I wouldn't have to remember. Knew there was a reason she seemed suspicious," Thorn muttered.

"You stop that," I said, waving a stirring spoon in her direction. "Saki's very nice, and actually, Ryuko's been helpful too."

"Helpful doing what? Almost becoming victims running around after a murderer at night?"

"Just looking into some things around town," I said, carefully. I pretended to focus on slicing and buttering some bread to make toast without dislodging Sugar. It was a strange feeling. I'd never had to defend my investigations to Thorn before. "We talked to Orby, and Otto, and even Sloane yesterday. *Before* hearing a noise and going out to find a crime scene.

There was never any running after murderers."

Thorn grunted. "And what, you just happened to be having a slumber party?"

Shoot, I *was* still in my pajamas. I glanced down at my flannel pants, pilly teal sweater, and oversized tank top. "Something like that."

"I can see why she'd rather stay here than in that hole Ryuko lives in," Thorn said, "but I get the feeling there's something more to all of this."

I hesitated, whipping up some almond butter and chia seeds. *She's in quite a mood this morning. Maybe we all are. And like Sakura said, we have reason to be.*

"That's why I was coming to find you," Officer Thorn pressed. "I never did get proper statements from you two. You ran off."

"We did not. We came home for tea after helping you set things up," I corrected, glancing over at her severely.

"Still," she insisted.

"Oh, fine," I said, doing my best to shake my head without dislodging Sugar. "Sakura showed up here last night and said she thought it'd be a good idea to keep a watch on the Square, in case anyone showed up. Since you and William were out, I figured it might be a good idea. But sometime in the middle of the night, we fell asleep. When I woke up, Sakura said she'd just heard a scream. Then we both heard a heavy *thunk,* or something like that. But we couldn't see anything happening, so we went out to investigate. As soon as we hit the road, we saw the wagon."

"You didn't hear the scream?" Officer Thorn asked.

"No," I said. Making the tea helped my mind settle into clarity. "But I was asleep and dreaming. I did definitely hear the *thunk*, though." I shivered as a thought occurred to me. "You don't think . . ."

"I don't," my friend confirmed. "I followed the trail of wood chips and torn leaves before I came out to get you. It went all the way back into the forest, a good five minutes' walk. There's signs there of the trap that broke the wagon wheel—William and I ran right past it. Off in the bushes, I found the tree branch."

"The murder weapon," I surmised. "But why use a branch when they seem to have claws?"

"Exactly," Thorn said, nodding. "And it wasn't cut—it was broken, roughly, like someone had been leaning on it and it split off from the tree. Seems almost like it was an accident."

"The murder, not the robbery?" I clarified.

Thorn nodded, settling back into her chair. "We knew all along it would escalate, of course. There's no doubt in my mind this was the work of the same robber that's plagued us. It just seems like they got sloppy."

"Bad time to be sloppy," I observed, wrinkling my nose. "Now that everyone's all up in arms."

"But that could also be why," she pointed out. "It could be that they were getting desperate, and nervous."

"Okay, so the murder was an accident, the robbery was on purpose," I summarized. "That still doesn't explain the blood, or how far the wagon traveled."

"The wagon traveling could have been part of the accident. The robber lost their head," Thorn theorized. "But I'll grant you that the blood is a problem. Especially because our mail carrier was some kind of banshee. I haven't had the doctor do the full exam yet, of course—we have to wait for permission. But his blood was definitely blue."

"Whereas I found red blood," I said, with another shiver.

"You see now I was right all along. This is *dangerous*," Thorn said. "Even more so with the Rangers and this Blake fellow and foolish rumors about Fenrir running about."

"I can agree with that," I said, as I assembled a breakfast tray. "But *you* should also see now that you can't be everywhere at once."

I leveled a stern look at her, only breaking eye contact when my tea kettle began whistling. She'd often used similar reasoning in the past to get me to help her solve mysteries. Now, I got to use it to make her accept help.

"I'll admit it," she said finally, turning toward the window as I mixed up our super-energy tea lattes. "Just this once."

"That's all I ask," I said, carrying two steaming mugs and a plate of toast over to the table. I left a tiny mug of honey on the counter for Sugar, who flew over to it with a glimmer which I knew meant excitement.

Officer Thorn took hers with what was almost a gracious smile, and then gulped rather than sipped. She sputtered. "What's in this thing?"

"You saw me mix it up," I answered, laughing.

"I thought you were making breakfast for Sugar, or something. That all went into this tea?" Officer Thorn glanced at her mug, then downed it. "I tell you, the true horror is you using your friends as experimental subjects."

"You say that now, but it works," I replied, still grinning. "Just wait and see."

21

Brraaaaii—*ahem* Maaaaapss

We'd just finished our breakfast and Officer Thorn had perked up considerably when William came bounding up the stairs.

"Sir Rowan and I opened the shop," he announced, as though Sir Rowan deserved an award for this exceptional example of doing his job. "There's no one out there though."

"Thank you," I said, ruffling the fur on top of his head. "Do you need to rest after last night?"

"No. I'm fine," William insisted, glowing a little just to prove it. "I got lots of starlight."

"We were certainly out there long enough," Officer Thorn said.

"And it was quiet as the grave," said William, wagging his tail. For a moment we both looked at him; I, for my part, was surprised that he'd beaten Officer Thorn to a punny quip. Basking in the attention, William took the opportunity to add, "Last night wasn't the hard part. The *real* work was trying to rein in the bookseller yesterday afternoon."

Thorn's brow lowered. "What's the bookseller up to now?"

"The bookseller has a name," I protested. "And he shouldn't be up to anything."

"Well he *is*," said William. "He's all fired up about researching ghosts and wolves, or something. He's color-coding the historical legends of Belville."

From the way Officer Thorn rose, I knew what was on her mind. I shot up out of my chair after her, saying, "There's nothing wrong with color-coding! As long as he's safe at home, what harm is in it?"

"I'm not going to get him into trouble," Thorn said. "Not yet, anyway. I just think it's time I asked him some questions."

I groaned. "That's what I was afraid of."

I couldn't tell her *I'm afraid because I don't want your questions to get him so involved in the investigation that he ends up in danger.* Saki probably would have called me on it immediately. But even after repeatedly hitting this wall, I still couldn't even admit it to myself; it was just a vague but insistent feeling of unease in my chest.

So instead of talking it over, I made Officer Thorn wait while I hurriedly washed up and changed into a thick yellow tunic, woolen floral tights, and high boots. Since the shop and the Square were still devoid of customers, I followed her out into the street.

I almost made a comment to her about that lack of business—it made the town feel creepy. But as we neared the bookstore, creepiness fell away, replaced by ominousness. Whereas everywhere else in town was quiet, I could hear voices coming from the bookstore all the way out in the street.

We almost didn't make it into the shop at all. Officer Thorn had to use her shoulder to push the door open.

"What is all this?" she asked, addressing the store in general.

"This" was far, far more crowded than usual. At first, that's all I could tell. Luca's bookstore was a haven for leaning bookshelves, piles of scrolls, and dust bunny colonies. The rows and aisles were entirely haphazard, and books stretched up to the ceiling, obscuring most of the light. The sales counter, really just a massive desk pressed up against one side of the door, looked like an impromptu barricade of paper and ink even at the best of times. And now, with the aisles full of just about everyone in town, Luca bobbed behind his barricade like a man desperate to keep his head above water.

"Luca," I called over the din, pressing my way past a family of dwarves, a fairy, and someone with rough, barklike skin— all heading for the door with their purchases. "Luca, what's going on?"

"I don't know," he called back, his normally bubbly voice now strained. "They were in line even before I opened!"

Luca and I might not have parted on the best of terms the night before, and I may have been frustrated enough to see red with him for investigating, but when I heard that note of desperation in his voice, there was nothing I wouldn't have done. Looking for the nearest opening, I vaulted behind the counter with him and swiped some change from his antique register.

"Everyone who wants to make a purchase, please form two lines," I shouted over the crowd. "Officer Thorn, you're in charge of returns and disputes!"

It was an optimistic order, because I doubted Officer Thorn knew enough about the bookstore to return merchandise to the correct place. I also doubted all the customers could hear me over the contained hurricane that was the bustle in the shop. But, fortunately, shoppers understood the physical process of getting in line automatically, even if they didn't hear the order themselves. After a moment or two, the endless crush of customers had divided into two even lines that crashed up against the counter in waves.

While Luca operated his register, a little *ring* sounding out with each purchase, I handled sales the old-fashioned way, with a handful of cash. I left Thorn to her business and focused on my task. My world collapsed to the expanse of the desk.

Two maps and a Belville biography. Cash, change.

Ring.

One ancient map, exact cash. A set of haunted Belville stories.

Ring.

Four maps, one of which didn't have a price penciled into the corner . . .

Ring. Ring.

"Showoff," I murmured to Luca as I counted out change.

"Well, it *is* my store," he whispered back. I could barely hear him. But the smile on his face spoke volumes.

I talked round a gnome who wanted to bargain, and finally made another sale.

"This may be your store, but I've been at this for *years*," I told Luca proudly, as the gnome walked off feeling equally proud but having paid me full price.

Luca chuckled as he rang up an encyclopedia. "If you're trying to make this a competition, you're on."

I lost track of what I sold after that. Everything became a blur of trying to count out change before Luca's cash register rang. I didn't even realize I was out of breath until I looked up, customer service smile in place, and found myself facing

Thorn.

"That's the last of 'em," she announced. "Except for some in the back corner I can't chase out."

"You don't have to chase them out," Luca said, sounding as breathless as me. "I'm okay with the business, I just didn't expect them. Why were they all here this morning? Does anyone know?"

"You mean you didn't notice?" Officer Thorn raised a dark eyebrow at the two of us. She waved a piece of paper in one hand—an old map, torn at one corner.

"Oh," said Luca, grinning sheepishly at me. "I guess I was more focused on—on speed. They were all buying maps? Of town?"

"This is the last one in the shop," Officer Thorn declared. "And Red knows why, don't you, Red?"

But I'd been busy looking over at Luca, trying to impress him with the wad of cash in my hand. "I do?"

"Peyton," said Thorn, as though I was about four years old. "Peyton and his cronies were putting up posters all over town this morning, spouting nonsense about maps and a demon wolf in the woods. They've been at it all night, I bet you. I heard the customers talking. They've created a panic. Word has already spread about the murder—you know how this town is. So everyone thinks they have to ward off demon attacks now. Because no one in town trusts the Rangers, and no one trusts *me!*"

"I can see why they might not trust the Rangers, since no one in town has even seen one," I said reasonably. "But as for you—"

"How could anyone not trust you?" Luca asked. "Thank you for helping get everything in order here, by the way."

"They don't trust me, and what's more, they're planning to venture out into the woods alone to do some sort of *exorcism!*" Officer Thorn continued as though we hadn't spoken.

Luca and I exchanged looks. Even though I *had* been paying less attention than I should have, I was fairly certain that Thorn was exaggerating. *Again.*

"No one would do that," said Luca. He winked at me as he said it.

"I'm calling an emergency meeting of the town council," said Thorn. "And then I'm putting together a team. We're going to scour those woods ourselves, in daylight, *before* Peyton and his ignorant cronies get to it. There's no such thing as a geometric summoning going on. I'm going to put a stop to this once and for all!"

"Officer Thorn," I said, shuffling beside Luca, "do you really think you're being safe and—"

"And you, Red," she spoke over me, "are coming too. Be ready to go, this afternoon."

Luca turned to me, gaping. But before he could find his words, the officer added, "What? Isn't this what you both wanted? To be involved in the investigation? Well, now you are. Congratulations. Now, someone ring me up. I'm buying this map."

22

Into the Dark, Dark Woods

I left Luca soon after Thorn marched out of the bookshop with her new purchase. But despite everything I had to think over, I paused on the doorstep.

"We never did decide who won," Luca remarked from the sales counter.

"Well . . ." I thought. "We both won, right? Because you made all those sales, and *I* was the faster seller."

"Hey!" Luca called after me as I made my exit, laughing.

But that laughter didn't last for long. I could tell that Officer Thorn meant business, and while I was glad she was asking—in her way—for help, finally, I wasn't super excited about a proactive charge into the forest. And the entire theory about maps and sacred geometry still seemed strange to me.

Not to mention that, for a town terrified of attacks on the road, we've got a lot of strangers hanging around, I thought as I paced the streets. *Sakura, of course, and then Peyton and now Blake . . .*

Officer Thorn had promised to talk to Blake, but I doubted she'd have time for more than a cursory visit now. I paused as I hit the Square. What would it hurt if, instead of going

163

straight to the shop, I swung by Lavender's and picked up some apple cider for William and Sir Rowan?

The Square was a little busier, now that the sun was fully up and the bookstore had emptied. I made my way to the tavern, waving and nodding at some of the folks I knew. The tavern itself was fairly empty—it was too early for lunch, and most people got their breakfast from the bakery or the small local diner, if they didn't eat at home.

"Hey, Lavender," I called out as I slid onto a stool at the bar. "Any news?"

"Nothing pressing, honey," she answered, busy cleaning tankards. "A few cuts and bruises among the patrons, and I'm sure you know why. But the new doctor got them patched up in no time. Handy having someone around to take care of those things, isn't it?"

"Oh, no, Peyton? He really was at it all night, then?"

"Just a few scuffles he stirred up amongst the regulars," Lavender said, sliding me a mug of cider without my having asked. "Nothing to worry over, dear. Though I do wonder if we ought to worry about your friend."

I was pretty sure she meant Sakura, but she glanced significantly over my shoulder as she spoke. I followed her gaze and saw Blake, the very man I had hoped to meet, sitting at a table in the corner.

"I'll take a quart of cider to go in a minute," I told her. "I'm going to go ask some questions first."

"Be my guest, love," Lavender said, chuckling, as I slipped from my stool.

I threaded my way through the empty tables and chairs, all clean and smelling of pine, ready for the afternoon crowd. When I reached Blake, I sat without asking—more than a year with Officer Thorn had rubbed off on me—and introduced myself again.

"I remember you," Blake said. Even in the gloom of the tavern, the scars on his cheeks looked livid. "Did you and your friend ever get your pastries, then?"

I looked him over closely. I would have assumed that a witch hunter could sense magic on people—especially if he had been drawn to town by a magic lure, as Blake seemed to have been. But did he really not know what Sakura was?

"In all the commotion, we forgot," I said honestly. Well, mostly honestly. "I suppose someone's explained to you what we've been dealing with in town?"

"Lavender did, and the officer stopped by for just a moment," Blake answered. He toyed with a penknife listlessly. "I guess I seem suspicious, to you."

"I guess you do," I agreed, taking a sip from my cider. "But you showed up after most of the attacks."

"Yeah, but I'm . . ." Blake waved at his face.

I didn't understand. *Does he mean his scars? Was he also attacked?*

"I'm a werewolf," he said at last, heaving a sigh. Seriously, this All Hallows season was turning out to be pretty morose.

And I still didn't understand. "You mean you think *we* think that you carried out the attacks? With your claws and teeth and—whatnot?"

"Don't you?" asked Blake.

"Well, I didn't until you mentioned it," I said blandly. This was met by sullen silence, and finally I asked, "Does being a werewolf help you as a witch hunter?"

Blake looked surprised. "I guess it does," he said, as though he'd never thought of it. When I waited patiently, he set down his knife and decided to talk. "It's actually *why* I accepted the commission," he said.

"From the police guild, right? You're like a special officer?" I strained to remember everything I knew about witch hunting. It wasn't much.

"The department's a joint effort between the Guild and the School of Witches," he explained, perking up a little. "To track down people who misuse magic or use it to harm people. I—well, I just got out of training a few months ago."

Ah. Perhaps that explains why he doesn't come across as a hardened tracker, I thought with a wry smile. "Congratulations, then. And how did you know to come here?"

"I have a magitech sensor for evil magic," he admitted. "I can't actually sense it myself. I'm still—to tell you the truth, I'm still new to the whole werewolf thing. I do have heightened senses, but they don't always make sense to me. If that makes sense."

"It does," I said, laughing despite myself. "Wait. If you're new to both being a werewolf and being a witch hunter . . ."

"I was cursed," Blake said, nodding along with where my question was leading. "At least, that's what I think must have happened. I'm not a hereditary werewolf, and I don't remember being bit, so what else could have happened? And now I just want to make sure no one else gets cursed like me," he added, leaning forward earnestly.

I smiled, and realized that I'd been right. Blake *was* a nice guy, cape and all. "I can get on board with that," I told him. "If you need any help while you're here, stop by the potions shop and let me know."

Of course, it didn't occur to me until *after* I'd collected my cider, paid my bill, and left that Blake might happen to turn up at the shop when Saki was there too.

* * *

"If I need any help," said Officer Thorn later, through gritted teeth, "I *won't* be turning to the Rangers."

"That's for sure," William grumped.

The two of them led the way as our little party of four hiked through the woods. I glanced to my left, toward Trent. He'd been too spacey to pay attention to conversation for most of the afternoon. We'd already been out for several hours, and I hadn't gotten any sense out of any of my companions.

We'd left shortly after lunch and had seen no one since we left the town limits behind. We'd even checked the old abandoned castle and every inch of the road.

"Maybe it only comes out at night?" I asked finally, thinking longingly of the tea at home.

"We were out all night and found nothing," William reminded me.

"Peyton and his cronies are convinced the attacks are predetermined by this geometry nonsense," Thorn repeated, squinting at the map from Luca's bookstore while she stomped straight through a log.

I sighed and let it drop, choosing instead to listen to the birds overhead and the crunchy leaves under our feet.

And then a thought occurred to me. "We could ask Sakura," I said, with a sly glance at Trent.

"We could? What? We could what?" he sputtered.

Officer Thorn and William ignored us, focused on finding deer trails in the forest. I laughed. "Just teasing. I mean, I do think she'd have insight about the map thing. What do you think about her?"

"I think, uh," said Trent, turning bright red. He reached out and swatted me, and almost got hit on the head by a low branch. "Come on, Red. You already know what I think."

"It's a romantic time of year, huh?" I teased him.

"You ought to know," Thorn called back.

I made a face. I hadn't thought she was listening. After the town council gave her the go-ahead on all things, she'd been even more focused than ever.

Fortunately, William was too subdued to notice. No matter what he said, I was sure he was tired from last night.

"Why should you know?" asked Trent, suddenly interested.

"No reason," I said. "Hey, why don't we check around the south side of town, by the lake?"

"But why attack people up here if their camp is down there?" Trent asked. "It's not like this has been the work of a lake monster."

"Well, what else can you think of?" I asked back.

"I dunno. I haven't actually given it much—"

"Wait!" I cut off Trent before he could admit he'd been spacey, which was probably for the best. "Look at that tree over there."

Across a small clearing, a tree with a thick, gnarled trunk rose, its own little island in the forest. That wasn't so unusual in itself. But the ground around the base of the trunk was trampled and disturbed, and some of the tree's lower branches were snapped off or broken, swinging at odd angles.

"It's a yew," I said, as I led my friends closer to it. I pulled my goggles down as I glanced around, but saw nothing out of the ordinary.

Officer Thorn had, however. "It's a campsite," she corrected, grunting as she scuffed at the bare dirt with her boot. "See? There's traces of a fire. Any sign of magic?"

"None," Trent said, glowing.

"It doesn't *smell* very much like a camp," William put in. "It must have been days ago when it was used last."

While they pondered the ground, I was more interested in the tree itself. Yew was poisonous, I knew that much, so I made sure my gloves were in place before getting closer. Despite what William said, sometimes one *couldn't* be too careful. I reached up into the low branches, running my hands along the wounded bark. Someone had cut branches away. *Was it for the camp? But why be so destructive? And why take a chance on a poisonous tree? If I remember right, it's the seeds that are most dangerous, but still.*

Behind me, William was talking. "Maybe if we get Luca out here—"

"What?" I immediately stepped down from half-climbing the tree and turned around.

"You might pay attention," he said, panting at me smugly. "We're ready to move on. Unless you found something?"

"No," I admitted. Something about the yew tree was pricking at the back of my mind, but I couldn't for the life of me remember what it was. *What's yew good for, again? There's something else besides the poison. I'll have to look it up when we get home.* "It's just strange. Maybe if we took a branch—" I reached out casually to pull on one of the nearly-severed branches, and noticed a stray gouge in the wood—like something made by a rough saw . . . or a claw.

Trent saw it too, and whistled.

"It's something," said Thorn, grimly. "I'll take it to the station. As for the rest of you, time to call it a day."

23

Out of the Dark, Dark Woods

Though my discovery had unsettled me, it seemed to have invigorated my friends. Officer Thorn led us back to the road with a pep in her step, and once we were there, we fanned out into a comfortable line. It became apparent to me that, unlike the focused (or unfocused) march of before, our walk home would be a time to talk.

Trent started things off. Leaning around my left shoulder to look at everyone, he said, "We don't *really* think this is all about a summoning, do we?"

I started, missing my footing on the dirt road. "If you don't, then why'd you do all those tests at the meeting a few days back?"

"We're keeping our minds open," Officer Thorn said, with a peculiar look at me. Between us, William sneezed, but before he could make any comment the officer went on. "Even if it isn't summoning spirit wolves or what have you, it's someone trying hard to make it look like that."

"But why do we actually think that?" I challenged her. "I mean, aside from what Ryuko said. And all the wolfsbane that was stolen, I guess."

"And he *would* be the expert," William grumbled.

"Not in magic," Trent said, rather hastily. I glanced at him, thinking that even though he and Ryuko were friends, he was probably a little more concerned for Sakura's reputation by association. I recalled what she had said about wolfsbane being used in shadow magic for protection, but decided against repeating it; even though I did believe she was trustworthy, I didn't know for sure if she'd been right. And besides, bringing up Sakura's name in conjunction with dark magic deities seemed like it would just make everything worse.

"But in criminal gangs," William replied.

"He always says he's left that behind," I reminded them.

"And so far as I can tell, he has," Officer Thorn admitted. She stared hard at the tree trunks around us as we walked. "But that doesn't change the fact that of everyone else in town, he probably *is* the expert in gang activity. Not that he's ever been forthcoming about it."

"You can hardly blame him," Trent insisted.

"I'm not saying I do," Thorn said. She shook her hair back and for just a moment, looked up at the sky—which threatened rain. She seemed to find it refreshing, but I found myself picking up my pace. "But as to your question, Red," she continued, "We think summoning might be at play because, thefts aside, now we have a missing body."

I skipped a step again—even though I had been the one to find the extra blood.

William nudged at me, and I knew he was reminding me to slow down. To Thorn, he said, "I didn't think you knew anything yet about that blood on the cart."

"We don't," Trent answered for her. "She had me over this

morning to try to trace it, but there wasn't enough there for me to get anything useful. But we know for sure the blood isn't from the victim."

"Normally, that'd mean it's from the murderer," Officer Thorn said in her best guild guidebook voice. "But if the murderer attacked from above and the victim died instantly, then why would the murderer be bleeding?"

"They could have made some mistake and injured themselves," I said uncertainly.

"Especially since they were already unfocused enough to lose control of the cart," William added.

But Officer Thorn shook her head. Above her, a flock of migrating ducks honked, and even though they probably had no interest in our problems, she lowered her voice. "This is the way I see it. The murderer was lying in wait, right along this road. We'll pass the very spot before we get to town. So, the mail carrier comes along, just like we're doing. The murderer, who's up in a tree, makes their move—but gets carried away. The tree branch breaks and kills the mail carrier, and the mail cart rolls right over it and down the hill into town. There's no one on board to operate the brakes. The murderer, desperate to cover their tracks and salvage some goods, jumps down— tosses the branch into the woods—and takes off running after the cart. They catch up with it outside the station. Seeing as there's no lights on, they decide to take a chance. They start their robbery—but then they're interrupted. So the question is, *who interrupted them?*"

"The question is also why you don't have better security outside your police station," William huffed.

"We can work on that," Trent intervened. "I have some obsidian that I can bury in the station yard to use as anchors for a spell. The kind of thing that might catch someone the, uh, the next time something like this happens. Or whatever may come up."

"Maybe you can get Saki to help you," I suggested, because I couldn't pass up the opportunity. I might not have been an older sister technically, but I had grown up in a very communal group where all the younger children felt like siblings, and Trent definitely brought out that familial feeling in me.

In response, Trent punched my shoulder.

"Are none of you listening? We may have two murderers on our hands," Officer Thorn said.

"Technically still just the one, since you think one of them might be dead," William said. No one paid much attention.

"Wait," Trent said, as he caught up with the conversation. "So you think someone found the robber, doing the robbery or something, and then that new someone decided to murder them? But why would they do that instead of just, I don't know, calling the police?"

"Saki did say she heard a scream," I mused.

Officer Thorn rounded on me from her position at the end of our little row. "And another thing. Don't think I haven't noticed that you're getting awfully familiar with a rogue witch. A rogue witch who likes to stay up at night looking for criminals!"

"She's a shadow witch. I'm not sure if that's the same thing as being rogue," I said, looking hesitantly at Trent. The besotted young Witch wasn't much help.

"You don't know anything about her. For all you know, she could have been outside doing the murder herself. Besides, you don't need any encouragement to go looking out for trouble," Thorn continued. "You're bad enough on your own."

"Says you!" I retorted. I wanted to protest about Sakura murdering anyone, but my logical brain had to admit that Officer Thorn was right: I'd been so sleepy that I couldn't *truly* account for Sakura's whereabouts before I woke up. *Maybe Sugar could?* I made a mental note to check, although I didn't like the feeling of investigating a friend.

"You're all helpless," William declared. "Dust and I are the only truly sane people in town."

"Hmph," was Officer Thorn's reply. Then, slyly, "What about Sir Rowan?"

"He lives out of town," William said airily. "I've been to his camp. He said maybe one day Daisy will let me see the Tree where she and the pixies live."

"Wait," Trent repeated from my other side. "We got distracted again. We think there's a murderer in town? Like, not just on the roads, but someone in town who killed the first criminal?"

"All we can say for sure is there's been a disappearance," Officer Thorn said firmly. "Whoever shed that blood—and it was fresh—has disappeared. Whether they were a clumsy murderer or a victim themselves remains to be seen."

"And anyway," William said, "just because the cart was in town doesn't mean that someone from the woods didn't come after it, the same way Thorn thinks the robber did. After all, it was barely in town."

"Don't tell me *you* think there's some kind of voracious demon in the woods, too," I told him, half teasing. *Hoping* that I was teasing, at least.

"The attacks *have* followed a pattern," he shot back.

Trent snorted. "Sure they have, because they've all been on

the road."

"Wouldn't you sense it if there was some kind of demon wolf running around?" I added.

"No one's senses are perfect," Officer Thorn interrupted. "That's why it's best to have a group of as-sense-tants."

Trent and I groaned. William took the opportunity to say, "I'm just saying, you have to be extra careful at this time of year. The veil is wearing thin."

"Everyone says that, but what does it actually mean?" I asked, looking to Trent for support.

The Witch flailed a bit, like his first instinct had been to shrug off the suggestion—but then he'd thought better of it.

"It means what he said," Officer Thorn said unexpectedly. "My grandma used to say it all the time, too, and so does my ma. It's an old Samhain tradition. That's All Hallows Eve to the rest of you," she clarified unnecessarily. I remembered how upset she'd been that her family couldn't join her for the holiday. "The night of Samhain is the one night of the year where the line between our world and *other* worlds is most vulnerable."

"Other worlds like the afterlife, or demonic realms, or whatever you believe in," Trent supplied.

"And 'vulnerable' meaning it's easiest for them to cross," William concluded.

"Right—that's why everyone dresses up and tells scary stories and all, to scare any interlopers off," I said. "I do remember that much, at least. But still—that doesn't mean we actually believe Peyton?"

"Of course not." Officer Thorn rolled her shoulders back, cracking her neck. "But even a broken clock is right twice a day."

"So you're saying you *do*," I argued.

"I'm saying we need to stay on the alert," she replied. "But now that the fight is officially on our turf, any criminal out there is going to be pushing up daisies. Metaphorically speaking," she added, grinning at us.

Once more, Trent and I groaned, and this time William joined us. We let the matter drop.

For a while we walked in silence. I'd puzzled so much over the case that I couldn't puzzle any more, so instead I watched the woods around us. Squirrels darted here and there, collecting nuts, and birds' nests were visible in the trees that had lost their leaves. Most of the trees were sturdy evergreens, though, and they filled the fall air with a piney scent. Even with the possibility of rain and the cloud of murder hanging over our heads, it was a lovely day.

As we neared town, Officer Thorn slowed.

"Here," she said at least, gesturing to a shallow hole and a set of scuffle marks in the road. "This is where it must have happened. The hole was meant to slow the wagon, or even stop it. Then the robber could strike."

"Is that how the robber always did it?" I asked, squatting down to look at the hole. "Seems like a lot of work to go around digging up the road each time, and then leaving all the evidence for the Rangers to find."

"Not that they *have* found anything," Thorn said, as William and Trent investigated the bushes where the murder weapon— a heavy branch—lay. "And neither have I."

"So this was a little different from the get-go," I mused. "I wonder if that means anything."

"I don't know yet, but we will soon," Thorn said grimly. "Last night, the criminal may have made their first mistakes.

But we'll make sure they're also their last."

24

Sheep's Clothing

The scene revealed little more than Officer Thorn's determination, and we were soon on our way once more. I was glad to be getting back to my shop. Though it was only four in the afternoon, the sun was already sinking low in the cloudy sky, and the chilly breeze was giving me the creeps.

William and I left Thorn and Trent—along with the yew sample I'd collected—at the police station and continued down the road. We cut in through the backyard and went through the lab. I was so exhausted—even having had my 'energy concoction,' as Thorn called it—that at first I felt like my day was starting all over again: entering the potions shop felt eerily similar to going in to Luca's bookstore that morning. Except that instead of finding a crowd of patrons and low roar as they gossiped, we came into a shop that had the feeling of *just* having hosted said crowd. Racks and baskets of merchandise were empty, the books in my reading nook were askew, the tea corner was littered with empty mugs, and dust swirled in the light from the chandelier. The only noise in the shop, aside from my footsteps, was a slight panting which I was shocked to discover came from Sir Rowan himself. He sat behind the counter with his head propped up in his hands.

"What happened?" William asked, bounding over to his side.

"Forgive me. I'll be myself in a moment," Sir Rowan answered, his normally polished voice trembling a little.

William looked over at me and whined.

I glanced around the shop for more clues. "Let me guess—there was a run of some kind?"

"On lightsticks, miss," Sir Rowan answered, pulling himself upright. "I regret to inform you that we have completely sold out."

"No problem, Sir Rowan," I assured him, stepping up to the front door and flipping the "closed" sign. "It's pretty close to the end of the day, anyway. So—what happened?"

With remarkable clarity for someone prone to saying things like *I regret to inform you,* Sir Rowan explained that right after lunch—in fact, shortly after William and I had left, thinking we were leaving Sir Rowan to a slow day—his luck had changed. First it was a few groups, then a large gaggle, then a steady rush of customers that hadn't let up until tea time. Mostly they'd been interested in lightsticks—something I found *extremely* disconcerting, seeing as no one was supposed to be out at night. There'd also been bulk orders for moonstone samples and sticky powder. Sticky powder made sense for people putting up last-minute decorations, but the moonstone put me even more on edge. I used it for sleep-aid potions, but I knew some magic practitioners believed it could enhance their powers of divination—and of summoning.

"Oh, boy," I said, as Sir Rowan finished. "First of all, I'm sorry we left you to face that alone."

"It was not your fault, miss. I'm sorry I let it get the better of me."

"None of that," I said, waving a hand. "I saw something similar at Luca's this morning—I should have known better. Now, moving forward, I think we're going to have to put a purchasing limit on moonstone. And we'll definitely aim to have two people in the shop at all times, at least until the party next week. Is there anything else you can think of that would help?"

"It might be prudent to consider putting a purchasing limit on the lightsticks, too, miss," Sir Rowan suggested. He was now more himself, and he was methodically petting William's furry head—for whose benefit, I couldn't tell.

"The lightsticks too, huh?" I pursed my lips. Those took time to make, and though I set them at a fair price during the autumn and winter months, they still weren't cheap. "How many were people buying at a time?"

"Most people bought only two or three," Sir Rowan said promptly. "But there were two customers in particular who bought a full dozen at a time. In fact, I see one of them now, miss."

"Really?" I turned, and saw a familiar face pressed to the glass of the front door. "Are you talking about Dusty?"

Without waiting for an answer, I strode to the door and let Dusty in. This in itself was strange, because Dusty often found his own way into the shop if he wanted to visit. Dusty, a gnome and the go-to tinkerer and plumber in town, functioned like a on-call fix-it service for most of the shops around the Square. In many cases, he knew more about the buildings than the shop owners did. Standing at two and a half feet tall, perpetually clad in baggy overalls and a floppy cap, Dusty cut the sort of figure that could immediately set people at ease. He was the last person I'd have suspected of running poor Sir Rowan ragged.

"Hiya, Red," Dusty said as he strolled in. "Woulda come around the back, but I'm here on business at the moment."

"Sir Rowan was just telling us about that," I replied, caught between amusement and censure. "Are you trying to create a lightstick shortage, Dusty?"

"Me? No, 'course not." Dusty ambled toward the back of the shop and hopped up to sit on the counter. Sir Rowan's face remained carefully bland at this show of impropriety. Pulling a handful of nuts from his pocket and pausing for a quick snack, Dusty explained, "It's for a job, see."

I leaned against a nearby shelf, my arms crossed and my eyebrow raised. "Someone hired you to buy lightsticks?"

"To deliver 'em, like," Dusty nodded.

William shimmied out from Sir Rowan's shadow to take an interest. Dusty was one of his great friends in town. In fact, with Dusty, myself, and Sir Rowan present, the shop probably contained all of William's favorite people at that moment.

"Who?" he asked the gnome.

Dusty scratched at the shaggy brown hair poking out from beneath his cap. "I guess I couldn't say for sure. I figured it was Lavender. I got the order on a note in my boxed lunch from the tavern, and when I left the lightsticks at the back door, there was another note asking for more."

"Does Lavender often do her business by note?" I asked. That hadn't been my experience; usually, she just mentioned something to me when I was in the tavern for food, or she'd send one of her servers over. But if she was already sending

Dusty a packed lunch, then maybe a note made sense. *Maybe she wants lightsticks for her guests?*

Meanwhile, Dusty shrugged. "Not often, but things've been strange 'round town now, after all, what with everyone being so suspicious. I'd be straight outta work if it weren't for everyone wanting new locks and tighter shutters. Why?" he asked, looking around at us. "Is something wrong?"

"We aren't sure." I said honestly. "William and I were out this afternoon, and we're just trying to put the pieces together. For now, though, I'm afraid we can't sell you any more lightsticks—we're all out. I'll start a new batch tonight, and they might be ready tomorrow afternoon if you still want some. How many did the note ask for?"

"Another dozen," Dusty answered. "Said the calculations of the first note were off."

William sneezed. "'Calculations?'"

"It does sound odd," I agreed, as Dusty shrugged.

Sir Rowan glanced up at me. "If you are ill at ease with it, miss, there is no need for you to fill the order."

"Yeah, I know. You're right." I tugged at my hair, thinking. "I'll just go and ask Lavender about it myself. You all hang tight—I'll be right back. In fact, Sir Rowan, why don't you put on a fresh pot of tea?"

"That, miss," he said, standing, "sounds like an excellent idea."

* * *

Of course, as with anything in Belville, my plan to nip out to the tavern and run back in fifteen minutes was disrupted by the appearance of a neighbor.

It was nice to have such friendly neighbors . . . wasn't it? I sighed, and tried my best to smile at Doctor Gavin Goodberry as he flagged me down from his front stoop.

"Red the alchemist," he said, smiling as I jogged over. "We seem to be running into each other quite a bit today, don't we?"

"It's been a long, busy day," I agreed. In the spirit of being friendly to the new person in town, I added, "How have things been going with your practice?"

"Well, thank you," he answered genially, "with the exception of my lost tools. But of course, I don't blame Belville for that. It seems to me that Officer Thorn more than has things covered in town."

"That she does," I agreed. "Although—I suppose you heard about the murder last night?"

"I did," said the doctor more seriously. "Officer Thorn suggested I might help with the examination of the body, once permission from the nearest relatives has been obtained. In fact, Red, that's why I flagged you down just now. It may seem old-fashioned, but . . . can you forgive a neighbor for being worried?"

I hesitated. It was a little strange to hear about Thorn asking someone else to help with the exam, even though I had been the one to suggest it. And Gavin really was much better suited to it than me. I was a little glad not to be going back to the station in the near future, actually. And—even though *everyone* in town was worried—it was admittedly nice to have someone worried in that solicitous way of a mentor.

"I completely understand," I assured him. "And I appreciate the impulse to be neighborly, I really do. I was just running out to check something with Lavender, that's all."

"Of course," Doctor Goodberry agreed. "Far be it from me to pry. Just make sure you watch out for yourself, and your friends, too. Especially Luca, hm? After all, if there really is an occult magician about, they might have special interest in both of your shops."

I had been about to walk away, but I stopped and turned back at that. "You really think so?"

"Just paranoia, I'm sure," he assured me, with a kind manner that must have served him well with patients. "But I can't imagine where else they might get their expertise, can you?"

"I guess I never thought of it like that," I admitted. "I assumed whoever was responsible already knew enough on their own. But don't worry, Doctor. Luca's much stronger than he looks. And William has put up great wards on the shop—some of the best in Belville, actually. Just don't tell Trent I said that," I added with a grin. I didn't mention how worried I was for Luca, myself.

"It'll be our little secret," the doctor agreed with an answering smile. "Alright, then, Red, go along your way. Be safe!"

"Will do," I replied, turning to run across the Square. As I did, I thought to myself, *Maybe this* is *a dark time in Belville, but dark times have a way of bringing out the light, too.*

25

Meet Me at Twilight

Once again, I made it only a few steps before I was interrupted. This time, instead of a meddlesome-yet-kindly doctor, I ran straight into a ghost.

At least, that's what I thought it was at first. But thanks to Luca, or more appropriately, Jade, I had experience with ghosts and shadows and things that aren't one hundred per cent tangible. In this case, though, I found myself tangled with something that felt very much like a sheet.

"Sorry," a voice behind me giggled. I recognized Saki's tones at once. When I turned, I saw that she'd come alone, and today she was wearing a feathered black fascinator and bright green dress with a flared skirt over striped orange and black tights. *She's certainly in the holiday spirit.* "I saw that decoration there and I couldn't resist a bit of light-hearted levitation! Here, let me put it back up. I think it was hanging from that tree . . ."

Her voice trailed off as she focused, waving a pale hand to direct black trails of magic which lifted the false ghost from my shoulders and back into place in the branches of the nearest oak.

185

"I guess I should feel proud that I get the Ryuko treatment," I observed wryly.

"Don't think I didn't notice how you helped yourself to my nickname. But it's quite alright," Saki assured me, the feathers in her hair waving as she smiled. "You're not in for the full treatment, not yet. We'll save the wails and wind for when we're *really* acquainted."

"Uh huh. Thanks." Momentarily distracted from my goal, I asked, "Is that part of the dark magic thing? Special affinity for ghosts and spooky winds?"

"*Shadow* magic, remember?" Saki corrected me with a grin. She finished putting up the ghost with a flourish. "And sort of, but not really. I mean, it's not like I find that ghost easier to levitate because it's a ghost. It's just fun. Part of shadow magic is real *magic,* after all."

"Right. You are still a witch. Just very different from Trent," I said, smiling, although truth be told I thought Trent and Saki were pretty similar—at least, with their goofy senses of humor, if not in what they actually did with their magic. "Listen, I'm really sorry, but I've got to run. I promised—"

"Did you forget?" Saki asked, so blithely that it didn't seem she realized she was interrupting.

I blinked. "Forget what?"

"The magic club meeting," she reminded me with an eye roll. "I can see that you *did* forget. You're just like Ryuko, really. Remember, Orby invited us to the next meeting of the three dark musketeers? It's tonight."

"Shoot. I do remember that now. Though I don't think that's what they call themselves," I pointed out.

Sakura waved a dismissive hand. "Oh, I know. Most practitioners of so-called 'dark arts' actually try to stay away from that term—so many outdated connotations. They feel it doesn't reflect who they are. Anyway, are you coming with me? Ryu bailed already, so I could really use someone."

"Geez, twist my arm, why don't you," I smiled as she put on her best pleading face. She laughed. I added, "I will come along, but hold on a minute. I have to warn William that we'll be out. Where was the meeting, again?"

"Just down the block," Saki said, gesturing with familiarity—as though she'd lived in the town for years. "The back room at the pizza parlor. Last night Orby left me a note at Ryuko's with a secret password and everything."

"Well, isn't this just going to be a hoot," I murmured. *Secret passwords and pretentious magic—what could be more fun?* I added dryly in my head. From the look Sakura gave me, she knew well enough what my feelings were. Still, she seemed amused, and happy enough to wait in the park while I ran home and told William my plans. He wasn't too pleased, naturally, but he was too deep into gossip with Dusty to really protest.

"It's funny," I said, as I rejoined Sakura. "The new doctor was just telling me to be careful. But here you are inviting me to secret twilight meetings."

"Even funnier," she said, with a twinkle in her eye as she gazed up at me, "is that your friend the scholar was just here, and *he* was talking about the doctor, too."

"Luca was here?" I scanned the Square as we began to walk, but couldn't see a black robe anywhere.

Sakura nodded. "He left just as you were coming—said he had to get dinner for Frank. That's a mink, I take it? Anyway, he only stopped because he had something on his mind. I take it he's been having bad luck with his friends," she said, with a meaningful glance at me that made my cheeks hot. "Apparently he and the doctor had some kind of falling out just now. He wouldn't say why, exactly, but it sounds like they *had* been getting along swimmingly—until the doctor started to treat him a bit resentfully. I told him it might have something to do with his heritage and well-established roots in Belville, which a newcomer might be jealous of," she concluded.

"Wow," I couldn't help but say. "You got all of that, on top of the usual pleasantries, in a five minute conversation?"

"Oh, I'm not much of one for the usual pleasantries," Saki said with a sly wink. "And like I said, it was clear something was bothering Luca . . . but he didn't want to talk about *you*."

"I'm sure everything will turn out fine," I hedged. "Even if the doctor does have a—a wound about jealousy."

"Look at you, using the lingo," she laughed.

"Gavin was telling me how his wounds, metaphorical and otherwise, make him a better doctor," I continued, smiling now too. "If only Peyton could take a lesson from that."

"If only," Saki agreed, more thoughtfully this time. "Sometimes it's so easy to deceive ourselves."

Deceive ourselves, indeed, I thought, as we reached the pizza place, optimistically named the Third Slice, and I held open the door for Sakura to go inside first. *And William and Thorn think I'm bad for being reckless—here Saki's diving into every mystery in town!*

As I followed Sakura, I was hit by a wave of cheesy, tomatoey warmth. The pizza parlor was cozy, probably half the size of my own shop, with an open kitchen along the left side and wooden booths lining the right. I had never spent much time in the shop itself—occasionally I'd get takeout to bring to Luca or Thorn, usually during an investigation, but if I wanted a sit-down meal I usually opted for Lavender's. Still, I knew the Third Slice was often jammed full and popular, especially with Belville's younger residents.

Jammed full, that is, on any week *but* that week leading up to All Hallow's Eve. Sakura led the way past empty booths. It seemed like a laughable precaution when she whispered the password to a server and then pointed to me, assuring him, "she's with me."

With an unnecessarily furtive look, the server opened a nondescript door and let us into a back room I hadn't realized existed.

It looked much the same as the front half of the shop—brick walls, wooden furniture, tile floor. But crowded around a round table in the middle were Otto, and Sloane. And both of them were staring at us.

"Hi," said Sakura brightly. "Orby invited us yesterday. Isn't he here yet?"

Otto shifted uneasily, and Sloane wavered in midair.

"We're very interested," Saki continued in the silence. "Right, Red?"

"Hold on," I said. I was watching Otto, and there was something in the way she avoided my gaze that set off alarm bells in my head. "Where *is* Orby?"

"It is likely that he will not be present," said Sloane stiffly.

Sakura seemed to catch on to what I'd noticed, too. "It's 'likely'?"

"What happened?" I pressed.

"What *happened*," Otto echoed, mocking me. As she rose from her chair, she said, "What happened is *her!* She's too dangerous to be out. The very nerve, showing up like this!"

She pointed directly at Sakura, like she was expecting the

shadow witch to melt away under the accusation. But Sakura stood strong, indignant, and I was only more confused.

"I would have thought he wanted to see Sakura again," I mused aloud.

"Oh, I bet he did," Otto agreed. Her eyes flashed, but she didn't come even a tiny step closer to Sakura and me. "I bet that's how you did it, didn't you? You *wiled* him. You charmed him! You knew how much this meant to him, and you went and stole everything!"

"I haven't done anything," Sakura protested. "What are you talking about?"

"I'm talking about the fact that Orby is *missing!*" Otto wailed.

"Presumed dead," said Sloane, quite coolly.

I tugged at my ponytail. "Why would you presume that?"

But even as I asked the question, I realized that I already knew the answer . . .

The blood on the wagon, that didn't belong to the cart driver.

"Everyone knows," Otto was saying. "The cart was right here in town. The goods were gone. He never would have done that! He wouldn't have run off like that. We're all in this together. That's what we promised. We take turns, and we pool our resources, and we share the claw. That's why it has to mean someone else interfered. Someone else like *you!*"

She ended by pointing at Sakura again, but it was clear at this point that she was far too afraid of the shadow witch to actually come close.

"Back up," I said, my head spinning. "*Orby* was behind the robberies? Or—no—all *three* of you were, weren't you? And you used the same claw-weapon to make it look cohesive. But still, that's why sometimes the robber seemed quick and ghostlike . . . and at other times, the robber made mistakes or dug holes in the road . . ."

Otto and Sloane were silent, but it was clicking into place. Sakura had said that Orby left a note for her at Ryuko's—so we knew he'd been out last night. Despite the fear in town. And he *had* seemed a bit twitchy and desperate when we'd interviewed him—even the fact that we interviewed him probably made him more nervous! No wonder he hadn't conducted the robbery the way Thorn had expected—not only was he one of *three* robbers, he also hadn't been as confident as before.

At my side, Sakura was clearly thinking this through, too. "Then, this meeting was actually to transfer stolen goods?"

"Of course not," Sloane said.

Otto, by far the more forthcoming one, burst, "He should have been by the tavern *this morning*! I was on the early shift looking out for him, but he never came. You can quit it with the act. We all know what you are and what you've done!"

"You don't know anything about me," Sakura retorted.

"So, was Ryuko right all along?" I asked, still puzzling over it. "You were stealing things like bloodstone and herbs and copper and—and graphite out of pencils," I realized, thinking of the stolen box of art supplies. "Those things are *conductive*. What exactly are you trying to do?"

Sloane shimmered. "Nothing can be proven."

But no matter what defense Sloane wanted to maintain, Otto had apparently decided that admitting to crimes was a necessary step in accusing Sakura of murder. Perhaps, without Orby, they'd lost all cohesion in the group. Otto declared, "We weren't doing anything with conductive-ness or whatever. We were just exploring the dark arts. We were just going to help Sloane."

"And the wolfsbane?" Sakura asked, an arch tone in her voice.

"You mean *monkshood*. For protection when connecting with spirits who've passed on," said Otto, adding, "I wish it worked against *you!*"

Using wolfsbane—or monkshood, which I dimly recognized as another name for the same plant—for protection tracked with what Sakura had said at the beginning about Hecate. *Perhaps I should have trusted her then, and not let everyone get me all spun up about a wolf.* But I had other things on my mind. "Did you also buy up all my moonstone?" I asked, wondering if I ought to feel glad they paid for it, at least.

Otto wiped furiously at her eyes. "I was just trying to find him! He didn't deserve this. We weren't going to hurt anyone!"

"But you did," I pointed out, my hands shifting to my hips.

"*No,*" Otto insisted. "That was *her!* She killed the mail carrier, and Orby, too! Maybe she sacrificed their souls to the demon in the woods for more evil magic!"

This was quickly dissolving into nonsense. Rather than argue with Otto about Sakura—or even about whether or not robbery was, in fact, a way to hurt people—I decided that the best thing to do would be to get Officer Thorn. I turned to tell Saki, but apparently the shadow witch had other ideas.

Sakura had drawn herself up. "Am I hearing you correctly? You think *I'm* responsible for murder?" Otto grimaced and Sloane said nothing, and when Saki turned to me, I thought I saw a tear in her eye. The momentary shine was soon replaced by fierceness, though. "You're wrong about that, but you are right about one thing. I *am* too dangerous for your club. Because *I* am not a sycophant who's going to tell you things you want to hear. You want to know the truth? I do have magical power. I have more than you'll ever dream of. And even if Orby were here, none of you would ever get what you want—not by whining about it and using someone else's made-up rituals in the back of a two-bit restaurant for the rest of your lives!"

And with that, she stormed out. It was such an exit that all that was left for me to do was to stand, glare at the people who'd made such accusations and hurt her feelings, then trail out in her wake.

* * *

When Sakura and I spilled out into the Square, the sun had only just finished setting. Around the park, jack-o-lanterns glowed. It was a sad sight, because normally children should have been there, laughing and enjoying the spooks. Instead, Saki and I were alone on the sidewalk. I put my hand on her shoulder, about to say that we should track down Thorn and then have some tea and real dinner at home, when we were interrupted. It turned out, we weren't as alone as I thought.

"Red, I'm glad I caught you," Gloria called, her voice furtive. She gestured at me from the door of the salon, a few shopfronts away. "Come over here. Come in. You should know—"

"Ah-HA!" cried another voice across the Square. My heart sank as I recognized Peyton and a gaggle of followers spilling out from the tavern. "There she is! *She's* the one who is summoning the dread beast Fenrir—there can be no doubt. And she's already taken at least one life! But here she is out in the open, like she has a right to be here!"

Saki's lower lip protruded. It was so obvious that Peyton

had singled her out; he was headed right for her, pointing in a manner that was almost obscene. I'd just watched her tell off a room full of people in the pizza parlor, but it seemed like this was the last straw for Sakura's nerve. She didn't seem as resolute as before, so I stepped up in front of her as Peyton and his cronies came near.

"Nothing you just said has been proven, or even makes sense. She *does* have a right to be here," I said, loud and clear. "We all do. Except you and your hate-mongering speech!"

The tiny crowd wavered just like Sloane, and I realized in that moment that I was officially throwing my lot in with Saki's, for better or for worse. *Well, so be it,* I thought. *Better her than them—at least she's honest about how she feels!*

"*You* don't have any right to say that," Peyton spat at me. I couldn't help but wonder if 'drunk' was his natural state. "Who are you, anyway? You're nobody! You don't know anything about the End of Days! I don't remember you being in town when *I* was mayor!"

"Red isn't nobody. She has far more sense and morals than you do, Uncle." As Gloria spoke, I turned, baffled, to see her striding up to take my part. Standing next to me, she asked more quietly, "Do you really trust her?"

I looked back at Sakura just briefly. And just briefly, all of Otto's accusations rang again in my mind. "Yes," I decided.

"Then so do I." Gloria lifted her chin. "Go back to the tavern, Uncle. Or better yet, go home. You need Father to look after you. You haven't been the same since Owl tried to blackmail you, and you know it. You can't fix your reputation by bringing down my friends."

Peyton reeled like he'd been hit on the chin. The crowd behind him murmured uncertainly. They were all Belville locals—I thought I spied the grocer amongst them—so they must have known what Gloria was referring to. I, for one, was unfamiliar with the history but beyond impressed to hear my friend speak up like that.

"You're ungrateful," Peyton began, addressing Gloria.

"You're being childish," she interrupted, looming taller, her red plume shining in the night. "And everyone here ought to know it. Please, Uncle, just go home. Stop this nonsense."

"You're . . . you're . . . you'll regret this, that's all I have to say," Peyton mumbled, stepping back. He fell back into his little crowd, and from there, retreated to the tavern. "You'll be sorry when the wolf comes to end the world!"

"Lavender really needs to cut him off," I murmured.

Gloria turned to me, pulling a face. "He stood up for her while he was mayor, so I think she feels like she *has* to serve him. He wasn't like this then, with all the Fenrir stuff. It was all years ago, though, just when Owl was really getting started. When Uncle Peyton left, Owl used to joke that there was only room in town for one bird of prey in town."

"Gross," I said, wrinkling my nose. "I really think that's enough prejudice and shallowness for one night. We have plenty to tell Officer Thorn, that's for sure. What do you say, Sakura?"

Together, Gloria and I turned back to the shadow witch—only to catch her with tears streaming down her reddened face.

"Thank you so much," she sobbed, "both of you. That was so—so beautiful. I never . . . Not in any town I've been . . ."

"I know," Gloria said, not unkindly. "Nowhere else is quite like here. It's Red's fault. So you should stay here, and be her friend—that's what I've done."

26

Pillow Fights

For the record, I don't really think I can take credit for making Belville a place where friends stand up for each other. But in the moment, I couldn't really contradict Gloria properly, because I was too busy blushing up a storm.

Just like I was helpless to protest when, after we'd all given lengthy statements to Thorn and sent her after Otto and Sloane, Saki suggested that we set up another overnight trap and invite Gloria to the party to catch the *real* murderer.

"I guess I could help you keep a lookout," said Gloria slowly. We still stood in a close triad on the sidewalk next to my shop. We kept our voices low; even though part of me wanted to sing from the rooftops about the news of Otto and Sloane's confessions and the *absence* of a spectral wolf in their plans, I knew we ought to wait until Officer Thorn had done her bit. Still, I was really hoping that this new break in the case would calm down all the rumors about Fenrir . . . though I had a bad feeling that the town was too far gone for that. Especially since there *was* still a murderer and potential thief

196

on the loose.

"Of course you can help," Sakura enthused. Her hair, dress, and tights seemed to glow eerily in the twilight. "And more importantly, this evening you just took a big stand against your uncle—I could tell. You shouldn't go home and be alone after that. We should celebrate!"

"By attempting to catch a murderer?" I asked, with a desperate sort of humor.

"Of course," said Saki, her sapphire eyes now shining with excitement rather than tears. "What could be better?"

Setting her up with Trent *might be better,* a distant, particularly clever part of myself thought. The smile grew on my face as I hatched my plan.

Meanwhile, Gloria caved and agreed to the sleepover, which both surprised and delighted me. She stopped off at her salon to pick up some things while I went ahead inside, where I found William waiting.

"Listen," I whispered to him, as though Saki might overhear. I explained our confrontations earlier, and then the trap and the party to him, adding, "Do you think you could go get Trent and convince him to come?"

"Trent?" William cocked one furry ear at me. "Not Luca?"

"Luca?" The suggestion pierced right through my heart. *Maybe all the accusations tonight have got me riled up.* "No—not tonight," I decided, albeit uncertainly. "One thing at a time. I really want to get Sakura and Trent together. Plus, it might be helpful to have him around."

"Suit yourself," William shrugged. He leapt up and ran out the front door just as Sakura and Gloria came in.

"What was that all about?" Sakura asked brightly.

"Oh, just a thought William had," I said, almost honestly.

"You'll see . . ."

* * *

Several hours later, surrounded by devastated plates of nachos and half-drunk mugs of cider, Gloria and I exchanged glances from the ends of my couch.

William was pretending to sleep in the window seat.

And Sakura and Trent were entrenched around the dinner table like it was the last scrap of land in an all-out war.

"I'm just saying," said Trent, with that air of someone who's saying much more than what they appear to be, "that there's a lot more to herbs than I thought."

"And my point," Sakura volleyed back, "is that just because you didn't think there was much to herbs doesn't mean there actually isn't anything there!"

Trent's elbow came down on the table. "I'm not disagreeing with you, though."

Sakura's hands flew about her face. "You aren't hearing all of my point, either!"

"Whose idea was this, again?" Gloria murmured dryly to me, taking another sip of her cider.

I laughed—or I tried to, but then interrupted myself with a wince as Trent began referencing school textbooks. "Sorry," I said to Gloria, underneath the sounds of Sakura's indignation. "I thought it was time they got in the same room and talked."

"And how well has that worked out for you?" Gloria asked.

"What, you mean, tonight? Well, we did still get the lure set up and everything. And I thought dinner went pretty well, considering two of you had never even thought of making nachos before."

"No," Gloria said, rolling her eyes so hard her plume wavered over her head. "I meant, in your *own* relationship."

"Which relationship?" I asked, blushing. "Say, what do you think of Sakura's choice to do a lure for secrecy tonight, rather than greed or bloodlust?"

"I wasn't here last night, so I couldn't really say," Gloria observed. She eyed me with a particularly piercing gaze, as though to let me know she knew exactly what I was up to.

Sakura, meanwhile, had heard her name. "I know it's a little strange, because we wouldn't normally think of someone having an all-consuming desire for secrecy," she called across the room. "But if you think about it, that's probably at the top of the murderer's mind. Because the last thing they want is to get caught."

"That's assuming the murder was on purpose," William piped up. Apparently he wasn't so asleep after all.

"I think it was," Trent said. "I mean, I agree with Thorn that whoever killed the mail carrier—probably Orby—did that by accident. But I think Orby was found and killed on purpose. I think Sakura's on the right track."

"So there's someone *worse* than Otto's club running around?" Gloria pointed out as Sakura glowed.

Trent shrugged and downed his cider. "I don't know about worse, but they're *smart*. They hid their tracks around the wagon really well."

"But then again, maybe they were just being opportunistic," Sakura pointed out. "They discovered Orby in the middle of his robbery, and decided to step in. You didn't think of it that way, did you?"

This set my teeth on edge for round two of the argument, but Saki's tone was actually very playful. And Trent grinned back at her. *Maybe this was a good thing,* I decided. *At least letting them argue means that Trent can actually talk to Sakura without tripping over himself now.*

"Maybe," he agreed. "But who would have been out just by accident?"

"I guess we'll see," Sakura beamed. "Who wants first watch? We should probably try to get some real sleep tonight, after how last night went!"

This, we all had to admit, was entirely reasonable. We ended up drawing straws, and mine was first. As my friends settled in on the couch, the hearthrug, and the bed, I hummed softly to myself as I began to clean. I kept one eye on the window the whole time, of course. But my watch was as quiet as the graveyard outside of town.

* * *

I dreamed of howling wolves and Blake the witch hunter trying to explain to me that Sloane was evil. Or was he saying Sakura? I couldn't focus because the howling was so loud. In fact, when I woke up, for a moment I was angry that someone had let such noisy wolves into Belville.

Then I realized the howling was actually William baying to wake us all up.

"Someone's in the Square, someone's in the Square," he barked, as we all mumbled and groaned from our various sleeping positions. "Someone's in the Square—and it looks like Thorn!"

That was the *last* name I'd expected to hear. I was up and out of bed in a minute, reaching immediately for my warmest cloak. Trent was right behind me. We tumbled down the stairs like disjointed springs. Before I could unlock the back door, though, Gloria caught the hood of my cloak.

"Could you please *try* not to run into danger unarmed?" she hissed.

"Armed?" I got the door open but paused, confused.

"Here." She stuffed a walking stick over my shoulder and waited until I took it. "I've got a frying pan, and Trent and Sakura have magic. Okay, *now* you can run out into the middle of the night."

I wasn't so sure that a walking stick would do me much good, since I wasn't trained in martial arts. But I carried it along rather than argue. William was panting behind us on the stairs, clearly eager to get out there. I flung the door open, and the five of us swarmed around the corner and up the alley.

By the time I hit the Square, I was running, walking stick tucked under my elbow like a ram. I knew that Saki's lure might attract someone, but it wouldn't hold them—after all, Blake had been free to move around yesterday morning (though that was assuming that he'd been attracted by the lure and not just some vague notion of dark magic). I think I half thought Officer Thorn was in danger. Maybe she'd been chasing a suspect, or had an encounter out at the police station and was running into town for help.

Whatever the case was, whether she was in danger or not, it was pretty clear from Officer Thorn's face that when she turned around and saw us coming, she felt threatened. A person with a stick in a cape, another tall person wielding a pan, two sparkling witches, and a glowing dog at their heels—who *wouldn't* have been surprised?

"Whoa, whoa, whoa!" Officer Thorn called out, spreading her hands. "Steady! What is this, Samhain dress-up?"

"We aren't in costume," I panted, skidding to a halt next to her. "We were worried about you. William saw you from the window."

"You were keeping watch out of a darkened house?" Officer Thorn's eyes narrowed as she looked at the rest of the party, which was stopping about as gracefully as I had in a tight-knit circle. "Trent? Gloria? Why are you here?"

"It's a long story," I answered. "Why are *you* here?"

Thorn paused with a look which even in the dark said *I'm going to talk to you about this later,* and she said, "Someone just threw this rock through a window at the station. Or they tried to, anyway. I chased them up here, but I lost them when I got to the Square."

She held out the rock for us all to see. With the aid of starlight, I could clearly see a geometric shape and a message in red paint: *hunt them down or they'll hunt you.*

* * *

"Right here," Thorn said, as our little party trooped up to the station. She'd insisted on showing us the scene of the crime, since we were up and asking her so many questions. Now, just a few blocks off Market Square, she pointed at the dusty yard of Belville's police station. Dawn was starting to light up the sky, and some scuff marks were visible in the dirt beneath one of the station's windows.

"They tried to throw it through the window," Thorn added. "But there's a protection spell on the glass that made the rock bounce off. Then it set off an alarm that woke me up."

"Hum." I glanced over Thorn as Trent and Sakura went to examine the yard. The officer seemed just as proper as ever;

her hair was perhaps a little mussed, but that was it. *How'd she get ready so fast? Does she sleep in her uniform?*

"It seems like whoever it was stood in the yard for a little bit," Sakura observed. "Maybe they weren't pleased with the window protections."

"Even so," said Trent, his gaze glowing purple as he studied the station, "they didn't leave any magical trace."

"Nothing *you* can sense," William pointed out.

I nudged him. "Can you sense anything?"

He sneezed, which we all took as a no.

"In that case," said Gloria, "there's no point in us all standing around outside. Can we at least go in where it's warm if we're going to talk about this?"

"Come on," said Thorn, leading the way up the path to the station's front door.

As we streamed in and arranged chairs around the station's bare front desk, Sakura was already talking. "Well, we know it was someone referencing those fliers around town from Peyton. But Peyton and his followers were just using those ideas to rile people up—they weren't making threats. Who would actually threaten Officer Thorn?"

"Or maybe want to keep her safe," William observed, glowing with blue magic as he held the rock aloft to look it over. He sat on the ground beside my chair, making it easy for me to look too. "After all, it doesn't say *we* will hunt you. It says *they* will hunt you."

"So there's disagreement within the group?" Trent suggested.

Gloria shrugged as we shared a perplexed glance. I ventured, "We *were* just talking earlier about whether the murderer acted by chance or not. I think we just don't know enough, still."

"The geometry stuff *could* actually go along with summonings," Sakura said thoughtfully. "Otto said they weren't using their herbs to summon anything, but that doesn't mean she was telling the truth. Or that someone *else* didn't steal the club's stuff and decide to use it."

"Wait," Trent protested, clearly picking up on the ominous emphasis of the words "someone else." "You all really think that Peyton is behind *all* of this? I really don't think he's that powerful."

Sakura turned to focus on him. "He's staying at the inn where Sloane lives, right? So he could have access, depending on where they kept their stolen goods. Was he at that meeting where you did the scans? Have you had a chance to examine him?"

"He wasn't, I mean, I haven't exactly . . ." Trent looked to Officer Thorn.

And so did we. Officer Thorn leaned forward over the desk. "I may as well tell you now. That whole test was really just mining the town for people who might know about dark magic. I told Trent myself, I didn't expect our suspect to be there."

"So that was actually you picking people you might want to *help* you?" I asked, aghast, thinking of Orby and Otto and Sloane. "After you told me to stay out?"

"For all the good it did," Officer Thorn said, smirking.

"And it's not like Ryuko had a *bad* idea," Trent said hastily, focusing on Saki. "It's just—we couldn't exactly do what he wanted—but we could do *something* . . ."

"I can't believe I didn't realize that before," Sakura said, straightening in her perch on the desk. "You were trying to figure out who could help you without getting flooded with incredible tips. I love it!"

Trent blinked. "You do?"

"Of course. What a good way to catch people in an unexpected moment of honesty," she said, clapping her hands. "Don't worry, I'll be the one to tell Ryu. He won't be mad a bit."

"Well, that's one mystery solved," said Thorn, watching as Trent sagged in obvious relief. "Now I know why you've been making such spooks of yourselves."

"But," I said, heading her off before she could complain further, "we still don't know who threw the brick. What other suspects do we have?"

"Still Peyton, or any of his pawns," said Sakura, promptly.

"There's that new guy, Blake," Gloria pointed out.

"And I don't think Ryuko should be totally ruled out," Thorn insisted. "Brother or no, he's hiding something."

"Oh, he's always doing that," said Sakura blithely. "What we're looking for is someone who only recently started acting suspicious."

"Or recently showed up in town," I reasoned slowly. "Like Blake, I suppose, although technically he arrived after the attacks started. Same thing with Gavin. Though that could have been a front."

"Doctor Goodberry's been very helpful," Thorn interjected. "He did the exam on the victim. The approval came through this afternoon. Offered to examine the mystery blood, too."

Oh did he? I thought, wondering suddenly, *What is my role here going to be as we move forward, then?*

"Besides," William was saying, "the doctor's too hoity-toity to murder someone. We need a person who's *desperate*."

"There's someone you're all overlooking," said Officer

Thorn. "A group of someones. A group which might have disorganization and dissent!"

"Who?" Trent voiced the puzzled look on all our faces.

Officer Thorn smiled grimly. "The Rangers."

27

Pitchforks and Ash

Soon after Thorn's revelation, I invited everyone back to the shop. William's early morning spotting worked out well for me: while Gloria and Sakura cooked breakfast upstairs, Trent and Thorn helped me put together a new batch of lightsticks.

Naturally, for the entire time we were trying to convince her not to go after the Rangers . . . but it didn't work.

Especially when she started to make sense.

"Think about it," she said, brandishing an empty lightstick bottle. "We haven't even seen one of them. Not one! They could be any manner of people!"

"They could have big claws and teeth, you mean?" I asked dryly, thanking my lucky stars that William had decided to patrol the town. If he'd been present, he'd either have been making fun of Thorn—something sure to rile her up—or completely in agreement with her, and ready to search the forest again.

"That, and ruthless," Thorn said.

Trent continued meticulously laying out caps. It was kind of cute, actually: he was so intimidated by the idea of science that he was treating everything, even little pieces of cork, like it might explode if he did something wrong. "I thought you said the claw thing was something the club cooked up. Besides, didn't the Rangers have to introduce themselves to you, or anything?"

"Usually they would, but this was an emergency case," said Thorn. "They got special orders from the guild."

"So did Blake," I remembered suddenly, looking up from stirring the lightstick solution. "Have you talked to him more?"

"No," she admitted. "He's on my list too."

Trent chuckled. "Your list must be miles long."

"Don't you laugh," Thorn said menacingly, pointing glass at him. "You're going to be helping me shorten it."

"After the lack of sleep we got last night?" Trent grimaced.

"That's why I've come down to get Red," Sakura's voice floated in from the doorway. "Red, can you come up and make some more of that energy drink you were talking about yesterday?"

"That stuff?" For a moment, Officer Thorn looked alarmed—but then she grinned. "Actually, good idea. Make *lots* of it. We're going to have a busy day."

I went up the stairs after Sakura, muttering.

"I don't think it's responsible of me at this point to be giving them any more energy," I explained to Gloria when she raised her eyebrows from her post at the kitchen sink.

"Oh, that. Yeah, it's probably not. But," she added, while washing a truly worrying amount of mixing bowls, "it's only a few more days until Samhain."

"I'd forgotten that," I admitted as I began preparing the tea.

"I guess I've lost track of time. No wonder Thorn is feeling the pressure."

"We all are feeling it, whether or not we realize it," Saki said. She'd taken a seat at the stools around the kitchen island; a little turtle timer in front of her indicated to me that she and Gloria were waiting for something to finish baking. She'd also managed to change her outfit already—she must have come over last night prepared. Over a vibrant orange and purple patterned swing dress, she wore one of my stained flowered aprons. She went on, "Samhain is traditionally a time of ghost stories, and we're dealing with a real live ghostly attacker. Doesn't it seem natural to make the connection that something especially bad might happen on the big night? I know *I've* felt worried, and I'm new to all this."

"Yikes." My hands went still over my mixing. "I think you're right—that's been in the back of my mind this whole time, for sure."

Saki nodded. "So, we need to—"

"We need to do something," William barked as he ran in from the stairwell. "Peyton is calling for an emergency election, saying Otto and Sloane's confession was made up. He's making a big to-do about 'standing up for victims.' He wants to drive anyone with connections to dark magic out of town, and he says he'll have Trent do it. It's not just Sakura he's after—it's Ryuko, too, and Otto and Sloane, and *you*, Red!"

* * *

"It has nothing to do with me, I swear," said Trent for the third time. "He never even talked to me. I don't even know him."

We sat around my hearth—the table was too small. Despite

209

the cozy setting, the air was tense. Saki and Gloria's breakfast harvest casserole, which was truly delicious, disappeared off plates in almost vicious bites.

"And he also wants to bring in the Rangers," William said. He wasn't even pretending to eat. He sat nearest the door, as though waiting for someone unwelcome to trudge up the stairs.

"The *Rangers*." Thorn looked fit to burst. "I'll give that good-for-nothing old mayor a piece of my—"

Gloria cleared her throat, and when that didn't work, Saki clattered her fork against her plate. When Thorn glanced at her askance, the shadow witch looked innocently at Gloria.

"I was just thinking," Gloria said, "that at this stage, I don't think talking to my uncle will help."

"Then we'll do something," Thorn said, and she seemed to relish this even more. "If we catch the Rangers red-handed before Peyton can force this ridiculous election, then the whole thing is moot."

"True," I agreed, "but—"

"Come on, Trent," said Thorn, standing. "Red, you don't mind if we take our mugs to go, right?"

"No," I sighed, knowing it would be impossible to stop her. Case in point: she'd already started stomping down the stairs.

Trent wavered in her wake. "You know I didn't mean for this," he said, directly to Sakura.

For what seemed like a full minute, she just looked at him. Then she said softly, "I know, Trent. Just go, and look after your friend."

And then it was William, Gloria, Sakura, and me. We looked at each other glumly.

Gloria was the first to break. "I'm going to see if I can go talk to him, anyway," she said, standing and grabbing her discarded plate.

"Do you want company?" I asked.

"No, thanks. I think I'd better try it alone." Gloria tossed her fiery plume, then smiled down at me briefly. "I'll be by later this morning, probably. I still have to open the salon, after all. Johann's been making progress, but he's still too much of a law student to actually give creative hair cuts."

"We'll keep an eye out," I promised, then turned to William as she left. "We should probably open the shop. I don't know what business will be like, but I need to work on the lightsticks, anyway, and Sir Rowan's not in until the afternoon."

"Can I stay with you?" Sakura asked.

"Sure," I said, a little surprised. "But what about Ryuko?"

"He'll be okay at the apartment," she said. "But I have to do something—after all, this is partly my fault. I did provoke Peyton, back at the tavern."

William growled. "He would have done something like this eventually, regardless. Why else would he have come back to town?"

"Maybe he really does believe Belville is next to an 'epicenter for summoning,' or whatever it was he said," I mused.

None of us could think of a response to that, so we went about cleaning up and putting away leftovers. After cleaning up and changing, I brought my mug downstairs. Because of our early wake up call, I was still ahead of time for opening.

But it turned out, I needn't have hurried anyway. In fact, we might as well have stayed upstairs and taken naps.

"No one's even stopping on the sidewalk," William complained from his post at the sales counter. We'd been open an hour—long enough that the rest of town should have been awake.

"Guess more people that I hoped are listening to Peyton," I murmured to Saki. She sat beside me at my lab bench in an oversized green lab coat, not touching anything, not doing anything in particular. But it was, I realized, extremely helpful to have her there. Just her presence helped remind me to check my racing heart.

"And most of them will turn on him just as easily as they believed him," she assured me. "It isn't even really belief. It's just that they're scared and grasping at anything that might help."

"I know, I get it," I replied, trying my best to keep the irritation out of my voice. "But still."

"He clearly has history in the town," Saki added. "It's not like he's a stranger that's taken over."

"It feels like it," I admitted. "But that's just because I never knew him as mayor, I guess. And Trent wouldn't have, either."

"I know," Sakura said easily. "He's too young, like me—he wouldn't have been the official Witch ten years ago when Peyton was around. I know what you're getting at, Red."

Something in her voice made me smile, despite the tension between my shoulder blades. I lifted my head from my work and looked at her. "So? What do you think?"

Sakura laughed. "I think you're the least subtle matchmaker ever. You can't just come out and ask someone how they feel about someone they might fall in love with."

"Why not?" I asked, grinning crookedly.

"Because they never answer honestly!"

"But you do."

"I know—you've put me in a tough spot," she said, still chuckling. "I'm not sure what to say. I know Trent means well. He's actually a really thoughtful, really earnest person, and those are things I really like. But . . . it's awfully fast, and with him being a Witch and me being basically an outcast . . ."

"Trent wouldn't care," I said, confidently.

"Of course not," Sakura agreed. "But still, sometimes it's a lot harder to let someone love you than it is to love. Don't you think?"

I wanted to say I had no idea what she meant, but the words died in my throat.

And at just that moment, the bell on the front door rang out, and through my lab window I saw Luca enter the shop.

"Hi, William—hi Red!" he said, spotting me over William's shoulder. "Good morning, Sakura. It *is* Sakura, right? Sorry— I'm not always good with names. How are things going, Red? Are you doing okay?"

"Luca, who's in charge of your shop?" I asked, my brain blanking out and focusing on the practical things.

"Frank," said Luca, as though having an ancient three-legged mink with no magic look after a bookstore made perfect sense. "I just wanted to pop over here quickly. I need, um, I really need some . . ." he glanced around, his hood ruffling as he looked up and down the shelves. "I don't have any candles," he said triumphantly, seeing my display of seasonal scents. "I definitely need lots of these, for All Hallow's Eve. Do you want to come over and trade scary stories that night? I mean, after the party, if everything goes well. I think I need like four or maybe five of these, for sure."

Luca picked out a whole section of apple cider- and pumpkin spice-scented candles, and carried them over to the sales counter, where they rolled and tumbled and got lost in his loose sleeves. It ended up being an even half dozen; I watched

William count them out numbly. Normally I left candle selling to Lumi, Belville's resident candlemaker, but these candles had some additions—like sparkle powder—that I'd wanted to test out.

"That's so very sweet of you," said Sakura at my side. "And such a good idea!"

"You could come too," Luca said, smiling over at her. "We could bring everyone. I decorated the back room of the bookstore and it has a fireplace and everything, so it's really nice."

"Never mind the fact that booksellers shouldn't be allowed to have open flames," William said, as he rang up the candles. Even if it might be hastening a disaster, William wouldn't say no to a sale.

"Really," I managed at last, "thank you, Luca. And I love that idea, too. I can make something to bring along?"

"Oh, no, you don't need to, Red. I know you're really busy—"

"But Luca, I can't just leave all the work to you," I protested, growing vaguely desperate.

"But I'm happy to," he returned.

"But—but you shouldn't have to," I insisted.

"Why not?" Luca blinked his green eyes at me.

"Because—" for the second time, my brain went blank. I sputtered out the worst thing I could have. "Well, because if we want it to work out, like, without endangering the bookstore, like what William was saying about the flames—"

"You don't think I can do this?" Luca snatched up his candles, spilling one back on to the counter and snatching it up with a fierce glare. "Just like the investigation. Like I can't even defend myself. You don't think I can do anything, do you? You're still treating me like I'm just Owl's apprentice."

"I would never," I blurted, horrified by the very idea of Luca reverting back to his life under Owl.

Luca, however, was not having it. "Then maybe you should think about what you've been doing now!" he declared, making a sweeping exit with his candles in tow.

"Oh no," I said numbly, wincing as the shop door slammed closed. "Did I just . . ."

"Yeah," William said. "Even for you, Red, that was pretty bad."

28

A Forlorn Fog

For once, William hadn't exaggerated something.

I stared down at my lightstick fluid, oblivious to my friends. My thoughts were on a loop—an unhelpful one, at that. When I could finally think real sentences and not just *oh my goodness oh my goddess oh my god,* I became even more glum.

How could I have ever let Luca feel that way? Like he isn't useful and can't handle himself? He's so incredibly smart and more capable than he ever lets on—even before, when he and Jade were separated, he was that way. He was only ever confused, that's all. He was always such a good friend—how could I have let this happen?

I was so incredibly disappointed in myself. Particularly because, the more I thought about it, the more I knew that Luca was right.

As much as I hated Owl and everything he'd done to Luca . . .

. . . . For the past week or more, I *had* treated Luca in a similar fashion. Because I'd been so scared of losing him.

"Miss Red." Sir Rowan's genteel, but very firm, voice coming from somewhere above my shoulder interrupted my thoughts. "I admit I am no expert, but I believe you are in danger of spoiling your new lightsticks."

"O—oh." I shook myself a little as I surfaced from my sorrow. "What—?"

"Miss Sakura left shortly after I arrived," Sir Rowan went on helpfully, "precisely one half hour ago. She said something to the effect that it would be beneficial to leave you to your thoughts. However, I am of the opinion that lightstick fluid is not supposed to be brown . . . ?"

"Hm. You're right, it's not," I agreed with a sad attempt at a chuckle. "I'm going to have to start over. Sorry about that. Have I seriously been ignoring all of you for that long?"

"We were apprehensive about interrupting you," Sir Rowan said.

"You really put your foot in it," William added through the lab window.

My attempts at humor vanished as I frowned at him. He whined. "Well, it's true. And frankly, I'm glad he called you out on it. Otherwise I would've had to do it."

"You mean you've noticed too?" I realized, miserable. For Sir Rowan's sake, I added, "'He' is Luca. He was in earlier. Oh—we need to stock more candles."

William snorted. "Why bother?"

I glared at him again but chose to ignore his pessimism, instead focusing on Sir Rowan. The knight held out his gloved hands, taking the pot of fluid from me as I removed it from the burner. As he carried it to the sink built into my workbench a few steps away, he said quite noncommittally, "I did have some idea that was the case, miss. Miss Sakura indicated that the trouble was, perhaps, an affair of the heart. Now that I have your attention, I wonder if you would consider a brief respite from town. Perhaps you might like to come and stay with my lady on the mountain. She would certainly welcome you, and a change of scene may be what you need."

"Really?" I pulled off my gloves and leaned my elbow on the table, then my head in my hand, staring at Sir Rowan. Archaic as he seemed sometimes, he'd been a stalwart presence around the potions shop for the past year, and I respected his opinion. Plus, given that he had a dragon lady he could in good conscience refer to as "his," he was clearly better at relationships than me. "Do you really think that's what I should do? It feels kind of like . . . running away."

My feet itched in my boots. They liked the idea of running from Belville and *all* its problems very much.

"I merely offer it as a suggestion," Sir Rowan said as he continued washing out the pot. "'Time heals all wounds,' as they say."

"That's true, but talking to him might help too," William said from the empty shop, in a rare example of disagreement with Sir Rowan.

I glanced over at him. "You sound suspiciously like Saki. And anyway, what do I even say to make up for that? For how I made him feel? It must be awful for him. I was supposed to be his friend, and support him, and instead . . ."

I couldn't bear to say it aloud.

Sir Rowan and William exchanged a glance. "Perhaps," said the knight, "'friends' is not what you were supposed to be."

The mere suggestion struck new terror in my heart and made me feel even worse.

"I'm going over to Lavender's," I declared on impulse. "I

have to check with her about the lightsticks. I never did get around to it yesterday. I'll make more when I come back. It'll just take a minute—I just need to clear my head."

* * *

Unfortunately, Lavender didn't offer me the reassurance I sought.

"Lightsticks?" she asked, barely looking up from wiping down the bar. "No, honey, I haven't sent out any orders for them. Do you have some extra? Because I might buy them from you if you do. Everyone's up in arms, and who can blame them?"

"But are you sure?" I protested, with the creeping feeling that I was watching my whole world turn upside down. "It would have been yesterday morning?"

Lavender looked up sympathetically. "I'm sure, love. Nothing from me yesterday. Is this something to do with Peyton and all that end of days wolf trouble?"

"I don't know," I said, more miserable than ever. "And at this point, I'm not sure I should find out."

"Red, honey," Lavender said, setting her rag aside. "Sit. When was the last time you ate something?"

"I dunno. A while ago," I admitted. "We got up really early. And also stayed up really late."

Lavender bustled about behind the bar, shaking her head. "You need your sleep, dear, and you need to eat. Look at the state of you! I bet you haven't even been keeping hydrated."

In mere moments, I had a steaming mug of spiced cider in my hand, and a grilled cheese sandwich sliced neatly on a plate in front of me. Lavender leaned against her side of the bar as she watched me eat.

"There, that's better," she said approvingly. "I don't know what you've gotten yourself into this time, but you can't forget to look after yourself. You, of all people, dear! Usually you're the last person I have to worry about," she added with a little laugh.

I looked up at her guiltily—but I did feel lighter, and the melted gouda was delicious. "You worry about us? Everyone in town, I guess?"

"Innkeeper's prerogative," she affirmed with a small smile. "It's an old habit, dear. And don't you do a fair bit of worrying, yourself?"

I wrinkled my nose. "Usually I prefer to think of it as being practical," I protested, but even as I did so, I laughed at myself. "But yes, you're right. I guess I let it get the better of me today."

"There's still daylight left," Lavender remarked enigmatically. "Get back out there and back at it, love. We're counting on you."

29

Bloodsworn

When I left Lavender's, my belly was full and I felt a little bit better about the world. But that didn't change the fact that I was as confused as ever about the lightsticks—and I had to patch things up with Luca somehow.

And, of course, there was still Peyton.

As I walked out into the Square and noticed a crowd gathering in the corner nearest my shop, I figured at first that Peyton was behind it. A full-on protest of my store wouldn't have surprised me at that point. *What I was always afraid of,* I thought. *Here it is.* But I kept walking toward it anyway, a little curious. Facing Peyton was a lot less scary than hurting Luca, and since I'd already done that, I think I figured I was fearless.

And in any case, it turned out I wasn't quite on the mark. The crowd wasn't gathered around Peyton or one of his hateful posters—instead, it was *Blake* everyone had circled.

And at the witch hunter's feet was a wounded elf.

I was about to run up and see what had happened, but the

nearest tree grabbed me. I whipped around and faced Sakura and Ryuko, both partially hidden behind the tree's trunk.

"Just wait," Saki said, pulling me over to stand with them. To her orange and purple outfit she'd added a black beret, giving her more of a spy feel than ever. "Just watch. We saw him come into town as we were heading to your shop. He just came in from the forest, carrying that person."

"That elf," Ryuko grunted. "It's a Ranger."

"Seriously?" I leaned around the tree for a better look.

". . . needs help," Blake was saying. "Where is the doctor in town?"

"Here!" called Doctor Goodberry, emerging from his office right on cue. He moved toward Blake as quickly as his stiff legs could carry him, his cane in one hand and a tool bag in the other. "I'm here. What happened?"

"I was patrolling on the mountain when I found them," Blake said, gesturing to the elf leaning against the light post beside his feet. "They're one of the Rangers tasked with keeping the town safe—the ones who asked for my assistance."

I bit my cheek and scanned the crowd. Fortunately, Officer Thorn wasn't there yet to protest against Blake's descriptions.

"I think they've been attacked," Blake continued. "They're barely conscious."

"You did right to bring them here so quickly, then," said Gavin. Carefully, he knelt down on the cobblestones and got to work examining the patient. As I watched him—as the entire crowd watched him—it seemed all of Belville was holding its breath.

And, of course, into that respectful and anticipatory silence, Peyton emerged.

He seemed almost to come from nowhere. Maybe I'd been

too focused on Gavin to see him. One moment we were all waiting together, and in the next moment, Peyton was clapping a hand on Blake's back, and the townsfolk nearby were shifting uneasily, preparing to take sides again.

"A very brave thing to do," Peyton announced, as though he was already mayor once more. "And one that will be very helpful to our investigation, too! I have no doubt that when this Ranger wakes up, we'll get a full description of whoever—or *what*ever—attacked them."

"It may be some time," Gavin broke in, speaking in the clipped tones of a professional who resents their practice being sensationalized. "These are some severe slashes across the shoulder. I'll need to stitch the wounds. It would be for the best if we kept the patient asleep."

I shivered, suddenly glad I couldn't see the Ranger very well.

"Slashes," Peyton repeated, and he didn't sound at all sorry. "Did you hear that, everyone? Maybe we don't need to disturb the patient at all. That seems like pretty conclusive evidence of a demonic wolf attack to me! So something *has* been summoned!"

Blake shifted uncomfortably, as if he'd realized he was standing too close to Peyton. In that moment, I felt bad for Blake: not only had the Rangers sought to use his expertise, now Peyton was trading on it, as well. And it hadn't been so long ago, in the grand scheme of things, that werewolves might have been considered a kind of "demonic wolf" too.

"We have to take everything into account," Blake began saying. "We can't say—"

"Yes, that account from the Ranger will be very enlightening, when we do finally get it!" Peyton interrupted. He actually rubbed his hands together. "I have no doubt that the Ranger will tell us that it was a demon—a wolf-demon summoned and controlled by the shadow witch!"

Next to me, behind the tree, Ryuko stiffened. Sakura had gone very still.

"We can't make accusations," Blake insisted.

"But when we have testimony, then we can finally move to make the town safe again!" Peyton cried triumphantly.

And I have no doubt, I thought, *to use one of Peyton's own phrases, that when that poor Ranger wakes, anything they say will be twisted into exactly what Peyton needs.*

Our chances of actually restoring peace or even celebrating All Hallow's Eve were looking very slim indeed.

"I must have them moved," Gavin said, cutting through the posturing with a no-nonsense practicality. "I'll need to do the stitching in my office. Who can help?"

Several members of the crowd stepped up at once. Unsurprisingly, despite his grand gestures, Peyton didn't actually end up helping to lift the unconscious Ranger. And when Blake moved forward to assist, Peyton held him back by one arm and continued talking loudly.

"What else did you find at the scene of the crime?" the former mayor asked.

"I—I have all their effects with me," Blake answered, looking around the crowd with a little confusion, as though he wasn't quite sure what his role was any more. "They were simply on the trail above town. I think maybe they were trying to get back to their camp, but I didn't go that far."

"But you must have found *evidence,*" Peyton pressed, as the Ranger was carried away. "Evil magic leaves its marks!"

"I—I did find something in the Ranger's hand," Blake admitted. "A list. It seems to be a list of anyone who might have known anything about what was going on."

Ryuko jerked again, and Sakura laid her hand on his back—a reminder to keep quiet.

"But they aren't suspects," continued Blake, before Peyton could speak. Perhaps he'd become used to everyone staring at him; he certainly stood a little straighter, and spoke with more confidence. "In fact, I think there's just one person behind the attacks. The strategy is too concise. It'd be too risky for more than one person to be in on the secret."

"What are you saying?" asked a voice from the crowd.

"I think the murderer is trying to mislead the town," Blake answered.

Peyton took a step away from him, but still said, "Of course! Trying to hide their dark magic and nefarious alchemy!"

"Actually my theory right now is that they're just pretending to be some kind of creature or demon," Blake said in a rush. "Just to make people more afraid!"

At this, everyone in the street stopped. Even the doctor, who was holding open his office door for the folks carrying the Ranger, looked up in surprise.

"What?" It was Peyton who spoke. Even from twenty paces away, half hidden behind a tree, I could see the outrage growing on his face.

But Blake was not about to be intimidated. My esteem for him rose as he said, "I know it may come as a surprise, but this is how the hunt is evolving. I was trained for this—I know the difference between real demons and a disguise!"

At this moment, naturally, Officer Thorn came up. And as everyone turned to her, I noticed that William and Sir Rowan were watching too, standing on the front steps of the shop.

And Blake was staring at them, not Thorn.

This made my stomach turn, but I didn't have much time to think about it. As Peyton and the crowd faded, and Officer Thorn made Blake tell his story all over again, Sakura tugged on my sleeve.

"That list he mentioned," she reminded me. "A list of people 'in the know.' It would probably include Luca, right? Who else in town but the historian would know something dangerous?"

My stomach went from turning to doing cartwheels. "You stay here and watch what's going on," I told her and Ryuko, who had a grim 'I told you so' look on his scaly face. "I'm going to go warn Luca right now."

30

Eye of Newt and Leg of Frog

I didn't even notice if there was anyone else in the book shop. I strode right in and put my hands down on the desk, not giving myself time to feel nerves or doubts.

"Luca," I said, "I know I've been terrible lately and we have to hash that out. And I know it's especially bad since you were just trying to be so nice. You have every right to be mad at me. But I came over now because there's something I have to tell you. Blake, the witch hunter, is in town and he found someone injured and it looks like you might be in danger. *Directly* in danger, because of the person behind the attacks. They might be after you."

Luca leaned back on his stool, his face shifting from uncertainty to surprise to shock as he listened. "Even if they are," he said, "I'm not reckless. Like I keep saying. I have spells from Trent and new locks and everything, and Frank knows everything that's going on, too. We look out for each other."

I took a moment to glare at the mink, who was curled up in a ball at the edge of the desk, ignoring me.

"I'm not *saying* you're reckless," I insisted to Luca, pressing my hands into the desk for emphasis. "Honestly at this point what you are is *annoying.* No—what I mean is," I ran on, holding up a hand for silence, "what I mean is the way danger seems to be attracted to you is really frustrating right now, because if any creature came in and tried to get you—if anyone tried to lure you out—basically, if *anything* happened to you, then *I* would be the most dangerous thing in town.

"Which really wouldn't help my case," I added, panting slightly, in the reeling silence. "I mean, with trying to run a shop and not get run out of town by Peyton, and all."

Luca stared at me for another long moment.

"Do you understand?" I asked, pleading.

He cocked his head, looking at my face, and then slowly, he nodded. And smiled. "Yeah, I think I get it, Red—I really think I do."

"So you're going to be safe?" I threatened more than asked. "Stay in here, only let in people you absolutely trust? Tell me or Thorn the moment anything happens?"

Luca nodded. "But only as long as you also will—"

But I didn't hear the rest of it, because in my relief and embarrassment, I took that moment to run out the door.

* * *

When I got back to the Square, most of the excitement had died down. Officer Thorn had chased off the onlookers, and the injured Ranger had long since been safely carried into the doctor's office. Blake, too, had disappeared—probably hauled into the station for thorough questioning, was my bet. I was a little disappointed I wouldn't be able to sneak a closer look at his list, but I knew there were bigger risks at hand.

And, fortunately, Ryuko and Sakura were still standing beside their maple tree, talking grimly. Saki waved as I approached.

"We were just talking about you," she said. "Good timing!"

"You missed the end of the show," Ryuko added more gruffly.

"Yeah, I noticed," I replied, looking around at the emptied park. "I had to make sure Luca would be safe. But I have to admit, I'm a little frustrated we don't know yet who else might be on that list Blake found."

"Oh, we do," said Sakura, a large smile on her face belying the serious nature of our predicament. "While Officer Thorn was talking to Peyton and answering people's silly questions about sacred geometry, I happened to notice that Blake was . . . shall we say, distracted?"

"He was staring at your shop," Ryuko told me.

I blanched. So I hadn't imagined that. And William and Sir Rowan had been right there on the front step! "He didn't threaten anyone, right? He didn't say they were also on the list?"

"That wasn't why he was interested," Sakura laughed. She added, "I went up to him and started a conversation, and guess what he asked me? If the knight, your assistant, was seeing anyone. I guess he made quite an impression!"

I sighed, untensing a little as I grinned back at Saki. *Trust her to be talking to someone for two seconds and get them to confess their interest in someone,* I thought, recalling her account of her conversation with Luca the day before.

"So of course I told him that Sir Rowan happens to be *very* involved with someone, seeing as I've only exchanged three sentences with the man, and he mentioned Daisy in two of the three," Sakura added, still beaming. "But I can totally understand why Blake was interested. Rowan *does* cut a dashing figure in his cloak."

"Alright, alright," I said, chuckling along. "Enough about Sir Rowan. What else did Blake say?"

"Not much," Sakura said. "He bemoaned his bad luck, of course. If you ask me, *I* think his luck could benefit from a little shift in his mindset. He's clearly far too hard on himself about the whole werewolf thing. And—"

"And," Ryuko broke in, clearly familiar with his sister's rambles, "anyway, while Saki was talking to him, I picked his pocket."

"You *what?* You stole an important piece of evidence?" I gaped. I was certainly interested and relieved, but still, I gaped. *There'll never be any chance of reconciliation between Thorn and Ryuko now!*

"Of course not," Saki giggled. "We gave it back. It's an old trick. You know, the 'oh, I think you dropped this'?"

She looked positively angelic as she said it. But from Ryuko's unruffled expression, I intuited that this was a common con between the two of them.

I shook my head. "Oh boy. I can't believe Thorn hasn't conscripted you two for her force. Okay, so I'm guessing one of you has a really good memory?"

Sakura nudged her brother in the ribs. He nodded, albeit reluctantly. "I got a good look at it," he said. Then, staring up into the maple's bare branches, he recited, "*Monster wants people in the know. Geometry, forest, graveyard. Mayor. Police Officer. Doctor. Werewolf. Someone's meddling. Witch?*

"Exactly like that," he added, as I stared at him. "'Witch' had a question mark at the end. And 'geometry' and 'forest' were crossed out—or maybe underlined. Whoever wrote it was writing fast, and their aim was bad. The whole thing was just scrawled on the back of a piece of notepaper."

"Whoa. You got all that from one quick look?" I raised my eyebrow, thinking, *well, I guess that solves the question of 'what exactly did Ryuko do in his former life that made him so useful to thieves and underworld gangs.' For him to be so good with handwriting and notes, I bet he was some kind of forger.*

"Also," said Ryuko, ignoring my question and turning to his sister, "I think it's bad news they included Officer Thorn on the list. Anyone going after her'd have to be desperate."

"And Blake, too, don't forget—if that's what they mean by 'werewolf,'" Sakura agreed thoughtfully. "They'd been watching us all. Which isn't good, when you think that none of us has ever seen the Ranger camp all those times everyone's been out in the forest."

"Blake is a bit touchy still about the werewolf thing, and probably wouldn't have told anyone," I said, unsure if I'd ever shared that with Sakura or not. *How did she know he's a werewolf? Seems a little unfair that she knows so much about him, and he can't tell she's a witch.* I also noted with interest that someone—most likely Trent—had been telling her about our trips into the woods. "He only told me because I went and talked to him at the tavern, and he was worried I suspected him somehow. This was after we met him yesterday," I added to Ryuko. He nodded and stuck his hands in the pockets of his long, drab trench coat.

"So that's another reason he was protective of that list," Sakura said, still musing. "But it doesn't explain any of the *whys*, like why the mayor was on there too."

"Or which mayor," I pointed out. "The old one or the current one."

We glanced at Ryuko, as though for confirmation, and he shrugged. "There wasn't any indication on the note. Both of them could've made the murderer mad, though."

"Mayor Marguerite by starting the search, and Peyton by stirring people up," I agreed, thinking it through. "Hmm. I don't know if the note is helpful, or just more confusing. And I should probably get back to my shop and make sure William and Sir Rowan are okay."

"Are you really worried?" Sakura asked, curiosity shining in her big eyes. "I just wonder because Sir Rowan is a *knight*, after all."

"A knight who prefers mixing drinks to slinging swords," I responded dryly. "But no, I'm not exactly worried about them having been attacked yet or anything. Just—things are tense right now."

"That makes sense." Sakura nodded like I'd passed a test. "Listen, I have an idea. Why don't you and William—and Sir Rowan if he wants to—come over after work for dinner? I'll make something at Ryuko's place, since you're always hosting us."

"That's kind of you," I said. "Should we invite the doctor too? He might have something to report. He still kind of owes me a favor, unless Officer Thorn called that in already."

"We can try, but he might be busy," Sakura reminded me. "Besides, I still think all this—the investigation—might be a bit out of the usual medical practitioner's depth. It's beyond any one of us, really. We need to talk it all over and make a plan."

"Make a plan for what?" A new voice asked. Gloria sauntered up to us from the direction of the tavern.

"Did you have any luck talking to your uncle?" I asked,

distracted.

She shrugged one shoulder. "About as much as I expected. We can talk about it if you're making plans."

Ryuko shifted. "You want to be involved in all of this too?"

"Yeah, I want to," said Gloria, staring him down. "In fact, I'm already involved in it, and there's nothing you can do about that."

Ryuko lifted his hands in a "okay, I'll back off" gesture. Sakura glanced around at us and beamed.

"Well, that settles it, then," she declared. "Everyone come to Ryuko's as soon as you can, and we'll figure this out once and for all."

31

With this Curse

Naturally, as closing time came, it began to rain.

Sir Rowan politely declined Sakura's offer when I relayed it, saying he had to get home to Daisy—which, honestly, is exactly what I had expected him to say. As he stepped out the front door and headed up the mountain, William and I stepped out to head further into town.

After the first few steps, we picked up Gloria, her bright red plumes dulled somewhat by the drizzle.

"I've never been a fan of Ryuko," she confided to me as we walked the darkening, quiet streets. "He kind of reminded me of Owl for a while. But if you're going to be facing danger, then I'm coming along."

"My thoughts exactly," William woofed. "Plus, Sakura isn't so bad."

"A far cry from what you thought of her at the beginning! You just like her now because she stirs things up," I chuckled, ruffling his dewy head. Though I carried an umbrella, William was rarely under it. "I think both of them have been right on the money and invaluable this whole time. So let's hear what they have to say with open ears."

For the rest of the walk, the only sound was the plodding and splashing of Gloria's boots beside mine.

I couldn't help but feel the weight pressing down on us as All Hallow's Eve drew closer.

But Sakura, of course, was an exceedingly competent host. She bustled away our glum looks with the same ease she used to direct Ryuko to take our wet coats.

"Hi, everyone! You're just in time, as always. I made chili. You don't mind stew, do you? I thought it would be good and warming and filling, and if I'm honest with you, it's really the only thing I can make well," she confided with her habitual smile. "I'm a total novice cook. But it's the thought that counts, right? Plus, I got the cornbread recipe from a friend of mine who's a great baker, so I'm sure that couldn't have failed us! Come on, come sit down. We may as well start eating right away, right?"

"Sure," I agreed, my stomach growling as I followed her lead. She and Ryuko had clearly been busy that afternoon: the apartment was far less cobwebby than I remembered, and there was an actual table with plenty of chairs. Mismatched chairs, but still, it was nice not to have to cram into my little corner dining room.

"And we've got a lot to talk about," Sakura continued, waving us to our seats and passing around bowls. "Gloria, I'm *so* curious about how your meeting with your uncle went."

Gloria sipped at her chili, made an appreciative face at that, and then made a disapproving face—presumably about Peyton. "If you could even call it a meeting," she answered. "It was mostly just me trying to force water down his throat. I don't think he's been sober in years."

"Is this whole, uh," I waved my spoon, trying to express the thought delicately. "The whole deal with geometry and Mayor Marguerite, and wolves and all. Is that a recurring problem, then? You said the Fenrir stuff was new?"

"Kind of," Gloria said, taking another bite as she thought it over. "He's always been a little bit obsessive, ever since Owl ran him out of town, at least. It didn't start out being specifically about Marguerite or anyone in particular, I don't think. He was just angry. And embarrassed, which was probably even worse."

"And to add to that, he was without a proper outlet for his anger, it sounds like," Sakura commented. "Since he couldn't face Owl directly, what with being exiled."

Gloria nodded, though she added a caveat. "It's not like he was ever great at confronting the truth anyway. That's why Owl got the better of him back then."

"So you think he's made everything up?" William asked. With strings of starry blue magic, he lifted a second and third piece of cornbread from the bowl in the center of the table.

Gloria's mouth was full. In her place, I said, "There *is* such a thing as sacred geometry—Peyton didn't invent that. Same goes for myths about Fenrir. But as to how important those things are in the attacks . . ."

"That, I think he totally made up," Gloria said, pointing at me. "He's so drunk he can hardly walk in a straight line, much less draw one on a map. It's all just him getting carried away and not wanting to admit he was robbed by a totally average thief. I heard at the tavern that Officer Thorn's put Otto and Sloane on house arrest, and confiscated most of the stolen goods, by the way. Except some missing herbs and art supplies."

As Sakura and I exchanged gratified glances, Gloria paused for another bite.

"Did he say why he was actually in town in the first place?" Ryuko asked quietly.

"No, but I figured it out," Gloria answered. "I called up my dad. Turns out, Peyton got kicked out a few weeks ago and had nowhere to go but here. They had some kind of argument about death, of all things."

"Death?" Sakura looked interested. To be honest, I was, too. Since phoenixes were immortal, I wasn't sure how long phoenixkin like Gloria and her father and uncle lived. And it was all starting to sound very close to Peyton's 'end of days' talk . . .

"Dad said Peyton was being morbid," Gloria said. "Whatever that means. Look," she added, setting down her spoon as we continued to stare at her. "I wouldn't be half surprised myself if we found out Peyton was behind all this . . . but I don't think he's actually the one doing the attacks."

"You're worried he really has called in some kind of creature," Sakura guessed.

Gloria nodded but said nothing.

In the silence, William whined. "We won't know for sure unless we catch it."

"Or *one* of them. There could be multiple creatures," Ryuko corrected—a startling reminder.

"But we haven't had any luck with the lures," I pointed out.

"I was thinking about that," Sakura said, smiling at me. "Ryu and I were talking about it earlier. I think our problem is that Market Square is too busy—even these days, when everyone's mostly hiding inside. It's too likely that someone will come in by accident, like Officer Thorn. So we need a place that is less frequented—a place where we can *know* we've caught the right person."

"But a place that also has cover," Ryuko added quickly. "For us. Or whoever's waiting."

"Which should be all of us," Gloria said, frowning at Ryuko. "There's safety in numbers."

"The graveyard," I blurted. *That* got everyone's attention. I explained, "It was on that list Blake found, right? So it could be an important spot already. And we know our way around it pretty well, since we went there to visit Orby. *And* the chances of catching the wrong person or getting them involved in any kind of confrontation would be pretty low."

"Good enough for me," said William, in a rare display of loyalty. "None of the rest of you are scared of ghosts, are you?"

"Oh, most hauntings are in far more emotionally-charged places than graveyards," Sakura said blithely. "I think Red's right, too. And I also think there's one more person we should get, assuming we're going to leave Officer Thorn to her own investigations with Blake and the Rangers. I think," she said, taking in a breath and looking directly at me, "that we ought to bring along Trent."

The reason for this rather dramatic pronouncement was lost on everyone else, but it wasn't lost on me.

Sakura's willing to involve Trent, I thought. *More than that— she's okay with asking for his help. And I haven't once suggested we go to Luca tonight . . .*

But that list had struck a terror like none other in me, and my last few meetings with Luca had been pretty mortifying, on top of that. So I held my tongue.

And in the absence of any other comments or concerns,

the plan began to take shape. William left to collect Trent, and as Sakura and Ryuko cleared up the dinner plates, Gloria scoured the apartment for weapons.

"You'd think a shady character like Ryuko would have tons," she muttered to me as she upended a couch cushion.

"What are you going to do, bash someone over the head with a pillow?" I returned, batting the thing back into place. "Be nice. You're as bad as William sometimes."

"Or maybe he's as bad as me," Gloria shot back, smirking. "I just think we need to be prepared."

"Are you worried?"

"No. I mean, I think this whole plan is foolhardy. But then, foolhardy is what gets stuff done," she said, alighting finally on a walking stick from behind the front door. "That's what Johann tells me, at least."

I had to admit, I agreed with her. My feet were itching to get the entire encounter over with.

On the way across town, Trent and William caught up with us, and I stopped in at my shop for a few things. By the time we arrived at the graveyard, night had fallen, and we were two witches, one magic familiar, one reformed crook with a net, one angry lady with a big stick, and one alchemist armed with slime and flash powder strong.

"I really think it's going to work this time," Sakura said, beaming at us as we formed a small circle in the clearest patch of grass.

"In that case, I *really* think we should have told Thorn," Trent said. "I mean, come on, Red. You know she'll be mad."

"I do," I agreed. "But it's a bit late now, and she's probably still with Blake—otherwise I bet she would've stopped by the shop. So does anyone feel like looking for her before we start?"

There was a silence—and then Ryuko sighed. He stepped up and handed me his net. "I'll do it," he said, sounding more like a gloomy donkey than ever. "If we do it now, then at least she won't be able to say we didn't try."

With this enigmatic remark, he set out before anyone could protest.

"Don't worry," chirped Sakura. "He's a really fast runner. And a lot better at fighting hand-to-hand than you might think. Okay, so with that done . . . I'm going to set up the lure. Everyone, get into position behind the stones!"

William bounded to a headstone lying on its side near the front gate. I found a good spot behind an old marble monument which allowed me to see the entrance and Sakura at the same time. Gloria found cover behind a gnarled tree opposite me, and Trent slid in to share my hiding spot.

"Isn't she just incredible?" he whispered as he watched Sakura sparkle with magic in the clearing.

"Two seconds ago you were arguing with her about this whole plan," I said, amused.

"Not about the whole thing," he protested. "It's because she's so powerful that I worry. Someone has to think of the details, right?"

"Yeah," I agreed, caught between a chuckle and a deep feeling of missing out. "Someone has to, for sure."

"I'm going to set up a containment spell while we wait," Trent said a moment later, as Sakura finished her work and headed for an old stump to hide behind. "I should've thought of it earlier. If I just lay down a perimeter, it'll help keep someone from getting away."

"If you want help with it, flag down William," I said, stepping aside as Trent crouched to put his hands on the earth. He already seemed lost in his spell. As he chanted, I glanced over at William, just in case.

And that was how I happened to be looking in exactly the right direction when the caped figure appeared.

32

I Thee Bind

The next part of the night happened incredibly quickly. The stranger entered the graveyard gates at a run. A cape billowed behind the figure, and their footsteps were loud on the muddy path. In the darkness, I could only see shadowy suggestions of color—but I very clearly saw the blue sparkle of William's movements. Like a shooting star, William set out on a collision course with the newcomer. And from across the clearing, Gloria emerged, stick held high.

She never had to use it, though. William collided headlong with his target and the two went down right in the center of our circle, where Sakura had set her magic lure.

"Get off! Get off!" cried the person roughly.

"Caught him," William announced smugly.

"Who is it?" Gloria wanted to know, advancing with her weapon held high.

"Wait!" Sakura cried belatedly, emerging from her stump. "That isn't who we want!"

"Who could it be?" Trent asked me, his voice betraying some frustration—perhaps at Sakura's compassion for someone new, or perhaps because his spell had been interrupted. I looked at him askance and moved out into the clearing.

"William, let him talk normally," I said as I neared the scene. "I'm pretty sure that's Blake. We've caught him once before."

"You caught him and you let him go?" asked Gloria of me.

"You know this guy?" Trent asked Sakura.

"There's dark magic here!" wailed Blake.

"We know," the rest of us replied.

A moment of silence ensued.

And apparently, since I wasn't locked in a stare with my beloved or wielding a weapon, that made me the voice of reason. I sighed. "Blake, we've been using dark magic snares to try to catch the necromancer."

"Ohhh," said a muffled voice from under William's rump. "That makes sense, actually. Wait, so every time I thought I was close to catching the bad guy, I was actually just catching *you?*"

"I don't know about every time," I said, reasonably. "But definitely the first time you came into town."

"But which one of you set the snare?" Blake asked. He tried to lift his head, but William wasn't moving, and Blake was covered in dirt. "Are you sure they're not the rogue practitioner?"

"Of course we're sure," snapped Trent.

"It's Sakura," said Gloria, more dryly.

"It's who?" asked Blake.

"Listen," I said generally to the group. "This conversation would be much easier to have if Blake's face wasn't in the mud. William, won't you let him sit up, at least?"

"How do we know he wasn't the summoner all along?" my loyal companion replied.

I exchanged a look with Gloria, since Sakura and Trent were making eyes at each other again. "I guess we don't."

"I'm not," Blake called.

"That's what a summoner would say," William answered.

This conversation could have gone on all night, and probably would have, had it not been for the arrival of a new person on the scene. I didn't notice him until he was almost upon us.

"Red, William, Gloria!" called Dr Goodberry, limping into the clearing. "I saw Blake running through the Square from the police station, and I followed him here. I had a feeling something was wrong."

"Something *is* wrong!" Blake called.

"Oh dear," said the doctor, looking at the poor witch hunter stuck under a glowy dog. "I'd better see to him. What's going on? Has there been some kind of fight?"

"You could say that," I admitted. "William, let the doctor take a look."

Reluctantly, *finally,* William shuffled off of Blake—who remained on the ground. Gavin carefully knelt beside him, asking what had happened.

"I fell," said Blake, rather tactfully, I thought. "I think I twisted my ankle, here . . ."

"Yes, it seems so," said the doctor. "The ground out here is very uneven. It can certainly catch you off guard. Trent, my boy, would you give me a hand?"

As Trent moved forward, I caught a glimpse of Sakura to my right. She seemed to be flashing at me. At first, though, I assumed it was something she and Trent had been doing with magic—perhaps resetting the lure?

"Yes, indeed," the doctor continued meanwhile. "A great many of my patients come in because of similar slips or mistakes . . ."

Something in his voice sent a cold shiver down my spine. "How *are* your patients, Doctor? What about the Ranger?"

"Not so good," said the doctor.

"Then why'd you leave them?" asked Gloria, picking up on my concern.

He could have said anything. He could have blamed it on some nameless desire, and we would have believed him, like Blake. Well, I would have. Saki had already taken a step toward him at that point, and the flashing had become a swirling mass of shadows.

"You know, all this started because I was trying to do a good deed." Doctor Gavin Goodberry looked up and smiled grimly in the darkness. "But at least at this rate, I'll be able to do all the experiments I want."

* * *

If time sped up when Blake burst into the graveyard, it seemed to slow after Gavin's announcement.

Trent leapt back at once, and even Blake scrambled away. William stood beside the witch hunter, growling. And carefully, quietly, the doctor rose to his feet. He thrust one hand in the air, and the magic lights around us winked off of a strange medallion in his hand.

And as the medallion went up, the graveyard wasn't quiet any more.

While the rest of us were still wrapping our heads around this turn of events, a crashing, groaning sound emerged from the woods.

My first thought was *Fenrir,* and my second thought was

zombies, but I realized quickly that neither were the case. The groaning wasn't the sound of demonic wolves or mindless monsters—it was the sound of magitech joints in motion. And the medallion, rather than being some dark magic amulet, was instead a sort of remote control. As though called, three strangely jerky shapes converged upon us. They were like robotic puppets.

No wonder Gavin was so interested in whether I did any tinkering.

The largest puppet seemed to have been made with pieces from a magitech train. It was easily five feet tall and moved heavily over the wet ground. William leapt for it furiously. I cried out and launched myself at the doctor, who was clearly controlling the puppets' movement. The world sped up.

Trent shot fireballs straight past me, at the two smaller puppets closing in from the graveyard gate. The graveyard lit up with streaks of yellow and orange, and filled with roars and cries of rage. Sakura was throwing spells, too, dark balls almost like slime, which sailed over my head. But at the last moment, the doctor dodged them. He feinted toward Gloria, who was running in with her stick raised—she could have got him—but at that moment William barked in alarm, and Gloria swung round at the last instant. With her momentum, the stick she held knocked the big puppet away from where William had slipped on a headstone.

I had a clear shot, but Ryuko's net was too big. I fumbled it at the last moment. The doctor used his cane against me, much as Gloria had used her walking stick against the puppet; I saw it and avoided tripping, but I missed my chance to hit the doctor himself. Instead, I spied Blake, still on the ground.

"Come on, we've got to get you out of here," I told him,

reaching down to grab him by the arms.

"I thought I was done for," he kept saying, clutching at me.

I dragged Blake several yards away, to the cover of Sakura's spell casting.

"Help Trent!" Sakura yelled at me.

I stood and turned to see the two small puppets, both rather worse for wear, collapsing on Trent. Without thinking I grabbed the vials of slime from my belt and hurled them. Fortunately, all the criminal-catching I'd been doing with Thorn paid off: my aim was true. The vials smashed across both puppets and the slime held them in place as it solidified.

"It won't hold forever," I yelled to Trent, warning him.

He nodded without looking back. Strands of his purple magic wound around a vine and pulled it down from a nearby tree, winding it around the prone forms.

"So *you* will take hostages too, will you?" the doctor shrieked, seeing this.

The moment I heard "hostages," all I could think of was Luca. At once, I was seeing red. I charged straight for the doctor, leaping over Blake's legs and past Sakura's spells.

It wasn't until I reached him that I realized he'd actually been talking about Gloria. Doctor Goodberry swung around at the last minute, shielding himself with Gloria, his scarf around her neck. I collided with them both, sending them flying. I managed to stay on my feet, but my feeling of triumph was shattered as I watched Gloria collapse. She was still in danger.

I was just gearing up to charge the doctor again when another of Sakura's spells went right by my nose. This time, her aim was true. It collided squarely with the doctor's chest . . .

. . . and bounced right off of him.

33

From Bad to Worse

"**M**agic repelling charm!" Sakura cried helpfully. Of course, this wasn't much help to *me*—I was as confused as ever. But Trent went into action at once.

The spell Sakura had sent rebounded straight for her, leaving her bound. In the background, I saw William knock down the final puppet for good. Trent had finished wrapping his up, but as soon as Sakura called out, he ran for her—much as I had done a moment ago. I turned to watch him as he went straight for her and began trying spells to get her free.

"Red!" Blake called. "He's getting away!"

I turned to look where the witch hunter pointed, but I was still slow and confused. I saw the doctor running in an ungainly fashion back toward town, but I was too worried to leave Sakura and Gloria behind.

"Looks like the lure worked," William announced, panting.

"Told you weapons would come in handy," Gloria added as she struggled to her feet. Both of them seemed winded but otherwise no worse for the wear.

"We've got to go after him and get Thorn," I said, thinking aloud. "But first, he's done something to Saki—"

"I got it!" Trent cried. Then, before we could celebrate, he said, "or not. Curse it. Why does her magic have to be so strong?"

We all hesitated for a long moment, watching Trent's magic spark as he struggled.

"I'll stay here and guard him while he works on it, just in case," Gloria decided finally. "You two follow the doctor."

"Hey, witch hunter!" William barked. "Have you got anything to help Sakura?"

"Um—uh—I have a curse-breaking amulet," Blake called back, scrambling up. "But nothing for binding. I think that's what she did. It's really advanced."

"In that case, come with us," I suggested impatiently. "As long as your ankle can stand it?"

"I'll be fine," Blake declared. "Lead the way!"

* * *

Our decision-making took less than ten minutes, but it was still enough to give the doctor a head start.

Clearly, he knew the town well.

But I was certain I knew where he was going. Where else could his lair be, after all? I led my friends down the road, headed straight for the doctor's office.

As the three of us barreled into town—well, barreled as fast as we could go, given how Blake was feeling—we hit the northwestern corner of Market Square. Two large shadows were coming for us. At first my blood went cold and I feared it was more magitech, but then I realized that the forms were leaping over Halloween decorations much more agilely than the doctor's creations would. And besides, the two shapes were familiar.

"Officer Thorn! Ryuko!" I called out, waving to get their attention.

The pair skidded to a stop right in front of us. "Where have you three been?" snapped Thorn.

"We were at the graveyard—didn't Ryuko tell you?" I panted.

"I *did*," said Ryuko, glaring at Thorn. "She didn't believe me until Blake got all twitchy and left the station. And even then she thought I wasn't telling her everything."

"I did believe you. I was hedging my bets," Thorn replied. "Besides, I know Red and William and Gloria could handle themselves as long as they were together and knew what they were in for. Is that Blake there?"

"Here," the man in question said. "But we don't have time—"

"We ran into the doctor at the graveyard," I said, thinking too fast to get the right words out properly.

"We ran into him a few moments ago," Thorn said, shrugging. "I was going to escort Luca to the station, to take a look at that note, but then he and the doctor went off. The doctor said he needed help with some elf thing."

"No!" I took off without any further discussion.

Vaguely, behind me, I heard William explaining things to Thorn. I heard Ryuko shout, and Thorn order him to come along with us rather than run back to the graveyard and Sakura, which struck me as odd. But after that, four sets of footsteps sounded behind me. If I hadn't been so worried, I might have grinned. It was nice, I decided, to have backup.

And maybe Thorn had a point, I realized, out of the blue. *Even though she was worried about us originally getting accused by the*

Rangers, she could at least recognize our strength now, when we stand together.

The way I should have done for Luca. If I had, he might not be in danger like this . . .

Setting this aside for later, I ran straight into the door of the doctor's office. "Locked. Of course it's locked . . ." I began fiddling in my toolbelt for acid or picks.

"Watch out," William called from behind me. "I've got it, I've got it!"

A ray of blue sparks showered by me as William's magic entwined around the door. There was a flash of blue, and then the door swung open.

"Sub-par wards," William remarked, tail wagging.

I stepped over the threshold. The front room was quiet and empty. "I think we're going to have to search."

"The three of us will stick together," declared Thorn. "Blake, you stand watch here. Shout if anything happens. Ryuko, you'll be the rear guard once we're in."

"On it," Blake called from somewhere behind us.

Thorn strode sideways through the door, as though she meant to take the lead. In any other circumstance, I would have let her. But with Luca on the line, I wasn't having it. I slipped past her and into the front room.

Very little had changed since I'd been in to talk with Gavin days before. *Clearly in his time of not being open, he also hasn't been decorating,* I thought vaguely. Behind the counter there was one door square in the center of the back wall, which I immediately went to. William, with his magic, opened it as I neared it.

Behind us, Ryuko cleared his throat. He'd followed Officer Thorn in, but had paused beside some framed certificates on the wall. "These are forged. If it helps."

"What?" Officer Thorn screeched to a halt, and so did I.

"Forgeries," he repeated, waving a hand at the doctor's diplomas. "Good ones, but still. You can tell by a glance the wax if you know what to look for. Also, what was he burning?"

I guess it makes sense a forger would also be interested in documents that might be gotten rid of in a fire, I thought. Normally I would have been just as interested as Ryuko in investigating the office, but my feet were itching so fiercely I was hardly touching the ground any more.

"Wood," Officer Thorn grunted at first. But then she added, "It's that funny wood you found in the forest, Red. The bark looks the same as the sample I have in the station."

Yew. My stomach plummeted about a yard down under the topsoil beneath us as I finally recalled what I'd forgotten about yew. *Not only is it poisonous, its leaves and ash are sometimes used for magic or experiments—ones that have to do with the dead.*

When I stammered this aloud, Ryuko nodded like it made sense. "It's like opposites attract," he said. "Make the lie the opposite of the truth."

Officer Thorn seemed like she might question this further, but I wasn't about to waste that time. My recollection only added a layer of desperation to my need to find Luca. I turned once more to the door, leaving them to their conversation.

The interior door opened into a hallway with two rooms on either side. I chose one, and William peered into the other. We found nothing. But a series of bumps and thumps drew me to the end of the hall, where a rug had been thrown out of place.

"I'm getting tired of this door opening stuff," William panted, shouldering his way up next to me. "My powers're getting a bit thin."

"Do you need to go outside?" I asked, as I pulled my goggles over my face and began scouring the ground for clues.

"No," growled William.

Together, we pulled back the rug the rest of the way to reveal a trap door.

And trapped in one corner of the frame as a scrap of black fabric—black as the robes Luca wore.

"If you don't want to magic it, we could smash it," Thorn suggested, as she and Ryuko caught up.

Another bump vibrated the wooden floor.

"Let's do it," I decided. "All together. Let's go!"

34

Haunted Lair

Right before Thorn and I could throw our weight on the door, it flew open. The space beneath it was gloomy, lit by flickering lantern light, and full of shouting.

"Red! Red!" Luca was calling.

"Stop! No! Come back!" Doctor Goodberry was yelling.

I was down the staircase in a flash. It was a rickety, wooden thing, hastily built, and it led down into an old stone cellar. As I went down, it was the smell of moss and cleaning fluids that hit me first. Then the strange shadows gave me pause, just for an instant.

Dr Goodberry was standing in the center of the room, surrounded by two large tables. Trunks and instruments lined the walls and filled the corners. It was a classic underground scientist's laboratory—except for the fact that there were lightsticks and bottles moving on their own. *My* lightsticks. *So that's where those big orders went.*

Luca's okay, I thought simultaneously, smiling for the first time all evening. I saw at once what had happened. Dr

Goodberry had lured him down there thinking he was dealing with a mild-mannered scholar who would make a good hostage. But then, Luca had gone ghostly on him. Drawing on the power of the curse in his blood, Luca had made himself into a shadow, and he was evading the doctor's grasp—frustrating him, in fact, by disrupting his plans.

There wasn't anyone else in the lab. Apparently, the doctor had exhausted his supply of puppets, and no zombies or living lackeys or spooky wolves were in evidence. *Good,* I thought briefly, and instantly made a leap for him. Officer Thorn and William were right behind me.

"Stop what you're doing! Belville police!" Thorn thundered, effectively halting all other conversation.

"Officer Thorn, at last," Gavin said, turning and trying to arrange his face into an honest expression. It didn't work. In fact, as I watched him, I saw exactly how he had been acting the entire time he'd been in town. Just acting—that was all. Hiding his real thoughts behind an impassive mask—"hoity-toity," as William had called it.

But now those thoughts shone in his face. Frustration, and rage, and exertion had reddened his cheeks, and his eyes were sharp and cold.

"There is a man in here harassing me," the doctor went on. "He tried to trap me—he's destroying my lab!"

"Stuff it," barked William. "We know you tried to get Luca. You've been after him since you got here. Was it Cairn's old documents that gave you the idea?"

"What idea? I had no idea," protested the doctor, falling back as I approached him with Ryuko's net in both hands.

"The secret lab says otherwise," I said, glaring daggers at him.

"As does our missing person and the stolen packages," Officer Thorn added behind me. "Time to give yourself up, Goodberry. Is that even your real name?"

"Of—of—" the doctor stared around at us. As I glanced behind him, looking for where Luca might be hiding, I noticed a hatch that must have led out to the road. It looked to be firmly shut, but I saw at once how the magitech puppets might have entered and exited through there, and I made a note of it in case we needed another escape.

"Of course it isn't," Gavin burst at last. "Curse you, you backwater fools. This was supposed to be a quiet town! A safe haven for me to continue my work—work none of you could possibly understand—"

"*I* understand," Ryuko said.

He'd slid down the staircase after Thorn, so quietly none of us had noticed. He stood now in the middle of the room, off to the left, beside a table heaped with magitech bits and pieces—and, I couldn't help but notice, one makeshift glove with claws on its ends. *Probably stolen from Orby*. Ryuko wasn't holding any kind of weapon, but his voice had gone strangely soft and he was elongating his "*s*"s again, and that was enough to stop me in my tracks.

"I know what you are," Ryuko continued, addressing the false doctor. "You're a confidence trickster. A con man. I know the type. I used to work with countless fools like you. You know it, don't you? You *are* a fool, but you can't help it. It's like an addiction. It makes you feel safe. You can't live the truth any more—you need the lie."

"It isn't a lie," not-Gavin protested, but his voice was strangled. I knew at once that Ryuko was right. Briefly, I remembered my first meeting with Gavin, when he'd been so interested in costumes . . . so interested in a chance to be someone else.

"And then it wasn't enough," Ryuko continued. "You saw a chance for more, and you had to take it, didn't you?"

"I—I was doing you a favor," the false doctor said, turning wildly to Thorn. "He was a murderer. A robber. I *saw* him at it."

Of course, I thought, drawing in a sharp breath. *Because the mail cart, being next to the station—and to my shop—was also next to this building, too. And he said earlier that he thought he was doing a good deed!*

And, I realized, thinking again of that trap door to the street outside, *Saki and I heard a dull crash . . .*

My stomach turned. But none of us spoke: mesmerized, we let the con man and Ryuko continue their strange dance.

"You could have done the honest thing," Ryuko said softly, drawing out the *s* in *honest.*

"There isn't any such thing as honesty," un-Gavin snapped. "Just the bare facts. He was a murderer and he needed to be stopped. So I did. And when I saw what I had done . . . such a perfect corpse . . ."

Blegh, I nearly said aloud, physically recoiling. I could tell that Officer Thorn beside me had the same reaction. But then I remembered: Orby, the "murderer," as Gavin viewed him, was a dark elf. And—*gods and goddesses, please no*—Luca was an elf too, underneath his glamoured hood.

And Gavin was half elf, but he wanted to be something else . . .

"Ssso," said Ryuko, his voice a whisper in a room that was deadly silent. He glanced wryly at me. "From the beginning, I was wrong about the wolves. It was necromancy after all."

Necromancy, the study of bringing the dead back to life. That's even worse *than demonic wolves. But—the yew,* I realized, rooted to the ground in horror. *The conductive materials. Electricity. Corpses . . .*

"I wasn't going to bring him back to life," Gavin protested. "I don't want a minion or a zombie. All my work—it's all been to improve *myself.* Only myself. I never hurt anyone else. Never before! But there he was—I couldn't pass up the chance—I could have a new body—I could do what's never been done—I could finally fix it all, and start over, and live *perfectly*—"

His words ended with a *thud* as a heavy microscope collided with his head.

"Sorry," said Luca, materializing behind the doctor. "It's just, he's been going on like that ever since we got down here, and I'm really tired of hearing it. That was enough, wasn't it, Officer Thorn?"

"More than," said Thorn gruffly. She'd gotten down on one knee to check the doctor's pulse. "He's fine, and this way, we'll get him into a cell much more quietly."

I opened my mouth, but footsteps above silenced me. I glanced to the staircase to see Blake's face.

"I heard yelling," he said, "while I was watching the door. Is everything alright?"

"Perfectly," Thorn answered, getting up. "This time, witch hunter, we didn't need any special forces."

35

Dawn Breaks

Of course, Thorn's bravado wasn't strictly true. After all, we wouldn't have lured the doctor out at all if it weren't for Sakura.

Officer Thorn carried the doctor to the police station, with Blake in tow for support and some medical assistance to finally see to his ankle. William ran off to see what had happened with Trent and Sakura, not to mention Gloria. Though his blue sparkles were faint, he could still bound along quickly enough. And besides, I wasn't about to leave Luca—who wasn't about to leave me, apparently.

The two of us stood awkwardly with Ryuko in the Square, saying things like "probably should have seen that coming" and "did you really fight magitech puppets?" and "this has been the wildest Samhain ever."

When William returned, he had a glowy purple silhouette in his wake. But the purple shadow wasn't of *one* person—it was two. Trent was carrying Sakura, with Gloria close behind.

"What happened?" Ryuko asked, barely beating me to the punch.

"She's fine," Trent said. "She's just tired. You know that binding spell that she was going to put on Goodberry, that bounced off him and onto her? We only just got it off. She was fighting it from the inside while I was trying to take it down from the outside."

"Sounds like you're both tired, then," I said.

William came up and nudged me. "One of them more so than the other."

I couldn't help it: I grinned at him. Then I said, "Trent, if you're still playing caretaker, how about you bring Sakura up to my apartment? I have potions, at least, and we'll start a fire. Ryuko, you can come too. I know you're worried about your sister. Everyone can come. It's closer than the Hut, at least."

"Yes," Trent said at once. "Thank you."

Of course, it wasn't just Trent who accepted the offer and tramped up the stairs to my place—it was *everyone*, all seven of us in total. We nearly sent Sugar into a tailspin as we streamed into the kitchen and living room. But many hands made light work: while Trent and I tended to Sakura as best as we could, Gloria and William found a batch of leftover peanut butter cookies and a set of plates, and Luca finally got to make his "famous" hot chocolate. Even Ryuko made himself useful, pulling the dining room table out from the corner and arranging extra stools around it.

"I put in one for Thorn," he told me gruffly as I came over. "Figured she'll be here eventually."

"True," I said, surveying the little forest of chairs and stools and table. "Although it's not like she doesn't have her *own* station for conducting meetings in. This is getting to be a bit much."

"You love it, Red," William informed me as he bustled

over from the kitchen, carrying a platter of plates balanced carefully on his nose. Before I could worry or grab them from him, he tipped them onto the table and claimed a seat. Truth was, he was right. Especially after the revelations of the evening, I really appreciated the warmth and company of friends. I shivered, thinking again about Gavin.

"Better here than in the station with *him* there," Gloria agreed, carrying over the cookies.

"Although given how hard I hit him, he might be better company than usual for a while," Luca said, tugging bashfully at his hood. He was still in the kitchen, putting the finishing touches on a small army of steaming mugs.

"About that," said Ryuko. He slid into a seat beside William and glanced around at all of us. "We're sure we tied all the loose ends up?"

Everyone looked at me—even Luca, who nearly tripped as he carried over a tray laden with his creations. Trent, it seemed, wasn't leaving Sakura's side to join the conversation.

I bit my lip. "Well, let's try to put things in order. First of all, from his lab and the puppets that attacked us, it was pretty clear that he *was* interested in experimenting with the limits of life. But I don't think he had any magic."

"He didn't," called Trent. "Not any."

"Okay," I nodded. "But still, overall, I think you were right, Ryuko. Originally, the thieves were Orby, Otto, and Sloane, who *were* trying to do dark magic—or whatever they might have called it—as part of their club. And then Doctor Goodberry—although he admitted that wasn't his real name— he came in and was using some of the things they'd stolen, like graphite from art pencils, doing similar experiments, just with science instead of magic. The only thing is, it wasn't about summoning wolves—it was about . . ." I hesitated to say what Ryuko had said so easily: *necromancy.* But everyone at the table clearly understood.

"It's never actually about wolves," William remarked sagely through a mouthful of cookie.

"Good point. Still, he totally fooled me at first," Luca agreed as he set the tray down on the table. "When Gavin came to town, he was really nice to me . . . but then he started getting a little strange. I thought he might be jealous," he confessed, looking briefly at me.

"He probably was," William grunted. "Because you can hide your curse."

Luca looked surprised, but I understood what William meant. "His injury to his leg," I said, for the others' benefit. "He told us when he first arrived that it made him more sympathetic to others. But I wonder if that's what he wished he could change about himself."

"He said the same thing about being half elf," Luca agreed, plopping into a chair after having passed out mugs. "It sounded like he had a hard time growing up—really felt like he was stuck between two worlds."

Ryuko stirred. "Sakura would say that he'd internalized the prejudice of the adults around him, or something like that."

"Which also sounds like the kind of thing she'd say a person ought to face head-on inside themselves, instead of with weird science," Gloria added.

"It does very much sound like a 'Peyton vs Sakura' moment," I observed. For a moment I was so tired, thinking of everything that had happened in the past few days—but looking over at William, seeing him eating cookies and Gloria and Luca with chocolate mustaches and even Ryuko leaning safely in the corner, I was suddenly overwhelmed with gratitude. I smiled before going on. "I think all that makes sense. Because all that stuff he had in his lab had to be collected over years. Same thing with those magitech puppets. This is something he's been working on a long time. And he said it himself—he came to Belville because it was quiet. He probably thought he could do as much experimenting in his basement as he liked."

"But I don't think his experiments always had to do with *people*," Luca piped up. "I think he was telling the truth about that. Because at first he was just asking me about scientific references. Just chemistry—nothing like anatomy, or something like that. But—Orby's body *was* in the basement. He hadn't done anything yet, but it was there, in the corner," he added quietly.

"He still had prep work to do, I guess," I mused with a shudder. " I don't actually know what's involved in scientific resurrection."

"And that's why we don't run you out of town," said a new voice—Officer Thorn. She'd let herself in and now came straight for the table, swiping an extra mug of hot chocolate on her way. Glancing at the horrified expression on my face, she added, "Oh, don't be a chicken, Red. No one's ever running you out of this town. They'd have to go through me first."

"And me," Gloria said firmly.

"And me," said Ryuko, unexpectedly.

"And me," said Luca softly, looking directly at me.

I flushed. "Well . . . thank you. All of you. And . . . anyway . . . did he wake up? Did he have anything to say for himself?"

"He did," she said, nodding as she licked peanut butter cookie crumbs from her fingers. "Couldn't get anything out of him *but* talk of himself, actually. The way I see it, he strangled Orby in the street using his scarf and his cane, and then from there on out, he was just trying to cover his tracks. As soon as I revived him in his cell, he was ranting about the 'flawed nature' of all us small-town folk and how we should have been grateful he saved us from Orby, and how he had one of his puppets toss that brick through my window for my own good. Insists that all along he was being helpful, and in return we interrupted him creating the perfect being."

"Ew," said Gloria, wrinkling her nose. I couldn't help but recall that he'd also tried to use that scarf on her. "Is he out of his mind, or something?"

Ryuko spoke up first. "No. Anyone can get a little obsessive or short-sighted in the wrong situation. We're all 'not normal' at times. But some people are something else. They're convinced they're alone."

"It's often a lack of empathy, or dangerously narrow focus on a single goal," Luca chipped in. "That's what most of the literature suggests. When I was putting together the Samhain display, I came across a really interesting book about what are sometimes called 'Frankensteinian' monsters. The people who create them are often trying to use science or magic to find something that they're missing within themselves. At least, that's what this one scholar was arguing."

"Well, our Doctor 'Goodberry' can find whatever he's missing after he's sentenced by the court next month," Thorn declared.

What we're missing. The phrase echoed in my mind as I looked at Luca. He'd clearly known a lot about Gavin—in fact he'd had as much part in putting together the truth as I had. I'd told William days ago that I wanted to work on my preconceptions, because I wanted to see the truth. Then I'd spent days trying to control everyone's movements, like it was all a big experiment. Truthfully, wasn't I also trying to fill voids in my life—things I couldn't predict—with scientific thought?

It's never actually about wolves. William's words rang in my mind. Maybe my determination to stick to facts hadn't been entirely about "good practice," either. Maybe I'd just been avoiding embracing the truth.

"Trent," Thorn called, looking over at the couch. "You going to let your sleeping beauty get some rest?"

"I wasn't—I mean—yeah," Trent said finally, standing with a sigh. "I guess I should. I think I've done everything I can, for now. She should be fine."

"'Should be'?" Ryuko repeated, his eyes sharp.

"She will be," Trent corrected hastily. "I promise. But we should probably get her some new clothes and that fairy dust she uses for her legs, for when she wakes up. Which will be soon," he added hastily, still bearing up Ryuko's brotherly glare. "Probably tomorrow morning. She used up a lot of energy."

"I believe it," Thorn said, slurping happily at her hot chocolate. "You know, Trent, I believe you'd make a fine doctor yourself. Much better than the one I've got in the station, anyway."

Trent blushed right to the roots of his dark hair as he joined us at the table. "I dunno . . ."

"So you caught him in the graveyard, and then chased him into his lair in town," Ryuko clarified, uninterested in hearing Trent's thoughts. "But what about the witch hunter?"

"Oh, yeah." Thorn turned and yelled down the stairs. "Come

on up, Blake!"

I gaped at her. "You just left him standing down there this whole time?"

"He wanted to," she said. I didn't believe her. Sure, the night time outside wasn't quite as dangerous as it had been, but it was still chilly and dark.

"I wanted to give you all a moment alone," the witch hunter explained for me. He wore a shy smile and a new ankle wrap as he limped into the kitchen, leaning on the walking stick Gloria had had earlier. "I know this has been a lot."

"It was Blake here who recognized our murderer," Thorn informed us.

"I saw his picture during training," Blake told us modestly. "I never spent enough time with him in town to place him, until I really looked at him in the station. His real name is Garth Meretti. He's known to be a con artist—no real background in medicine at all. I should have noticed him . . . but I didn't know what to look for. This is the first time he's killed anyone."

"First and last," said Thorn, draining her hot chocolate. "The wolf in sheep's clothing's been caught in a pen."

* * *

Eventually, some—only some!—of my guests went home. Trent, of course, was not leaving Sakura, but Gloria and Thorn did at least see the use in going home for a change of clothes and a quick nap.

"But I'm coming back here," Thorn warned me, "as soon as I get up, for one more of your energy drinks."

"I'll make a whole batch," I promised, as heads around the

room nodded.

"And then," said Blake, still a bit shy, "can I take you all out to breakfast?"

"*All* of us?" Luca said doubtfully, looking around the crowded apartment.

"All of you," Blake affirmed. "I think there's more I have to learn around here. If it wasn't for you, I might have really messed up my first case. And don't worry about the money, really. Before I went into the guild, I worked at a bank. We did pretty well."

So saying, he left, with Officer thorn and Ryuko close behind him.

In their wake William muttered, "Well, no wonder he never did figure out how to rush the right person. He's too used to sitting behind a desk."

"*William,*" I reprimanded. "Blake was actually one of the bravest of us, I think, given that he was attacked at least twice. Once by you!"

"And he was the only one of us who actually found a Ranger," Luca added.

"That's right," Gloria recalled, thinking. "That whole thing with the Rangers is still weird, isn't it?"

"I have a feeling we'll be hearing about it tomorrow," I assured her. "For now, let's try and get some rest."

And rest we did . . . although William stuck to my side like a barnacle, not giving me much time to talk to Luca one-on-one. I knew I needed to, and every moment that passed before I got the chance made me feel more and more guilty.

Still, guilty or not, I needed to sleep. And for the first time since the whole affair began, I actually slept deeply.

The next morning found us all bright-eyed and somewhat

bushy-tailed, or at least, clutching mugs of energy tea which we *hoped* would make us bushy-tailed, at a large table on Lavender's patio. We had a lovely view of the Square. The same old pumpkins and red falling leaves and bare branches looked festive, for once, rather than sinister.

"Here's to working together," said Blake, at the head of the table. He lifted his own mug, and in sequence, Thorn and Ryuko, Trent and Sakura, Gloria and Luca, then William and I saluted too.

"And to facing the darkness!" Sakura chipped in. She had dark circles under her eyes, but her smile was bright as ever as she looked across the table at Trent.

"What we need to know now is," said Thorn, pausing for effect and looking down the table at Gloria, "what's the deal with your uncle?"

"I actually went and visited him before I came here," said Gloria coolly, like she never had needed a wink of sleep in the first place. She sipped her tea and set it aside. "He's going back home. *Finally.* When I told him about what happened last night, he admitted he'd made up everything with the posters because it seemed like a good idea to get him back into office."

"He just came out and admitted that?" William asked skeptically.

Gloria shrugged. "I may have pressed him about it."

"Well, I think it's about time someone did," Sakura said supportively from her end of the table.

"I agree—bullies like that need to be confronted to see how ridiculous and hurtful they're being," I said to Gloria with a wink. She nodded back. We both knew I was referring to figures in her past who had once ruled her life.

"Excellent work," Thorn declared. "That leaves the day free

and clear. Did I tell you all that Sloane finally confessed not only to thievery, but to the attack on Miss Krinkle? Said they were worried she might have caught on to something, and wanted to warn her off. Still, it explains the lack of breathing during the attack."

And Luca was right again, I thought, chuckling to myself. *The attacker wasn't a zombie—it was just a ghost who probably smelled bad.*

"I've already sent word to the Council about the arrests," Thorn went on, "and I'd say you can count on the festival happening, just as planned. And we can add my family to the number of attendees!"

"Wait," said Ryuko, speaking up from a shadow beside Saki. "What about the Rangers?"

"Oh, them." Thorn flipped long black locks over her shoulder. "They were watching *us.* They thought *we* had something to do with the attacks—that's why they never showed themselves—to try to see if we'd trip up. They thought maybe I'd got bored around here and created trouble. Blake here had to help me set them straight. Can you believe it?"

"No," Ryuko replied, a rare smile creeping over his face. "I really can't see you as the criminal type. The Witch, on the other hand . . ." He shifted to glare at Trent, who was making obvious lovey eyes at Sakura.

"Hey," Trent said, startled. "I was only helping, this whole time."

"And the attacks were never magic. Just a bunch of show," William said.

I thought of the claws in the lab, and felt sad, especially for Otto, who'd been so moved by Orby's disappearance. *And his family, too.* Across the table, Officer Thorn caught my eye and seemed to know what I was thinking.

"There'll be a remembrance as part of the celebration, of course," she said.

We agreed that this was a good thing, naturally, and before the mood could become too sober, platters of apple pancakes and spiced sausages and a deliciously cheesy-smelling quiche arrived.

Gloria was watching me as we passed the food around. Finally she leaned over and said, "They might as well erect a statue to you while they're at it."

"Gloria, stop," I protested. "It wasn't just me. Not by a long shot."

"Oh, I know. Just checking your ego," she said, leaning back with a twinkle in her dark eyes. "Actually, on second thought, maybe they'd have to make it a double statue. You have the brains and the gumption, but it turns out *Luca* is the one sneaky enough to actually catch a criminal."

36

Halloween

Two days later, the spooks of All Hallows Eve were pure fun. Magical torches had been set up around the Square, and children ran between the trees, scouting for candied apples and caramel pops. Booths lined the street, housing vendors of everything from hand pies to crystal ball readings. Music came from somewhere, most likely the tavern. Since it was a holiday, all of the shops on the Square were closed, but I still set up a basket by my front door with free lightsticks—now that I'd finally been able to catch up with the demand.

"And the wheel turns round again, and all is well," I heard Sir Rowan's voice say as I straightened up. I turned and smiled to see him and Daisy strolling into town. He wore his habitual blue cloak and dark boots, of course, and red-haired Daisy was lovely in a knee-length purple dress. I tugged at my own orange sweater and long red cloak, wondering how she wasn't cold.

But setting small wonders aside, I focused on Sir Rowan's quote. I knew it was from some old epic, or perhaps a poem—

I wasn't sure of the source, but I knew what he meant. "All's well, indeed," I agreed. "I'm glad the both of you could come down. It's nice to see you, Daisy."

"Nice to see you too," she returned, as reserved but kindly as ever. "I'm so glad to hear that everything went well."

I tilted my head. "How did you—"

"Sugar," William explained, coming up beside me. After our experience with Gavin—or rather, Garth—he'd given up his plan of dressing up like zombies, and instead wore wolf ears over his usual floppy ones. "She still reports to the rest of the pixies sometimes. Didn't you know?"

"Oh, I forgot about that," I said. *I forgot all about asking her about Sakura, and then she went and reported on* me *to others. Guess it serves me right!* "Huh. I guess we really are all working together, like Blake said."

"It was the pixies who convinced us to come out," Daisy volunteered shyly. "They want another report on the festivities."

"Let me show you," William said, practically prancing in place. "I already scoped out the best things to do."

I laughed and waved them off—they invited me along, of course, but I didn't feel quite ready to party just yet. Officer Thorn waved as she went by, with a whole party of orcs in costume trailing behind her. As William bounded across the grass with Sir Rowan and Daisy in tow, I couldn't help but think that they looked like dancers headed for a ball.

"Thinking romantic thoughts?" asked a new voice in my ear. Sakura, in costume as an elaborate undead mummy. "After all, darkness and romance go together, I hear."

"You would," I remarked, laughing as I noticed both Ryuko and Trent standing on the street several steps away. "You're feeling better, then?"

"Much. But I've been meaning to apologize to you," she said, stepping closer.

I was confused. "What do you have to apologize for?"

"You brought up a few times that we should go to Gavin for medical advice," Saki reminded me. "Each time, I put you off or disagreed. It wasn't fair of me to do that, especially because I was mostly acting out of my own fear of confronting a scientist directly. I'm sorry I let my personal shadow get in the way of your investigation."

She spoke with clarity and grace—her apology was undoubtedly one of the best I'd ever received. But I still wasn't entirely following her line of thought. "I guess in retrospect I can see how you might've been worried about meeting some random scientist who might look down on your practice," I said, reasoning it out, "but I don't see why you should feel sorry about that. I mean, after all, it turned out that going to Gavin wouldn't have been such a good idea after all."

"But that's just it," she insisted. "If we *had* gone and pressed him for details about the attacks, we might have uncovered everything sooner. At least we would have noticed his magic repelling charm, which was probably helping him try to evade my lures. Maybe we could have put the pieces together before he felt he had to resort to taking hostages."

I shuddered involuntarily at the memory of Luca in that basement. "But still," I said, trying to keep my voice even, "it's not like you could have known that. And everything turned out just fine. Luca—Luca was way more capable than Gavin gave him credit for being."

"Yes, he's good at that, isn't he?" Sakura commented with her unique blitheness. Before I could say anything, she went on, "Anyway, Red, it doesn't matter that it was alright in the end. What matters is that I didn't fully listen to you when I should have. You have very good instincts, you know."

"Well, thanks, that's alright," I murmured, my cheeks aflame. "Is that why you don't mind that *I'm* a scientist, I guess?"

"Oh, I knew from the very beginning that you weren't *just* a scientist," Saki answered, her eyes twinkling in a way that made me vaguely concerned. But at the same time, she made me laugh. "Sometimes, it's just obvious that someone is more than what they appear to be. Or even more than they think they are," she added with a wink.

"I have no idea what you're talking about," I protested, but it came out as more of a mumble than a declaration. I didn't tell her that barely a week ago, William and I had had a similar conversation. "Anyway, you could just as easily say the same thing about yourself."

"I suppose I could. And I'm going to be sticking around a while—so you aren't free of me yet," Saki said, beaming. "I'm going to rent out Gavin's old building."

"Seriously? What are you going to do there?" I asked.

"You'll see," she said, her beam turning mischievous. "But we'll be neighbors!"

"Good." I turned back to look at the Square again, and Sakura turned with me. In fact, I'm pretty sure she noticed Luca moving our way before I did, because she leaned in and said,

"Since it seems like you're going to be sticking around here too, why don't you go ahead and admit it?"

"Admit what?" I asked suspiciously.

"There's no harm in it," she answered vaguely. "Promise. See you later—I'm off to join the pumpkin carving contest!"

I had a feeling that any pumpkin Sakura carved would be

very scary, indeed.

As I was musing on this, Luca made his way up my front steps to join me. I still hadn't made it far from my basket of lightsticks.

"It always comes back to us, doesn't it?" he said cheerfully, watching the others walk off. Fortunately, there was no trace of the mask he'd been wearing days ago. "I never wanted to compete, you know. With the investigation, I mean. Thorn said something just now to me about how it seemed like a competition, and I just wanted to make sure you knew . . . that night when I saw you with Sakura the first time, I wasn't trying to start anything. It's just, I recognized the symbol on that pendant she wears, an old protection charm, and I thought it was odd, that's all. I don't want to compete with you."

"I know," I said, watching the baker's children bob for squashes. Or apples. *Now's the time,* I thought. *Where'd all the air go?* "I didn't—I didn't—

"Luca," I managed finally, turning to him, "what I really didn't want to do was face my fear of losing you. But then I had to. And now . . ."

Luca blinked. Instead of his mask, he'd left his hood off as his Samhain "costume." A dark, twisted horn protruded from his forehead, and mossy green tattoos were visible along the deep brown of his neck. His eyes were incredibly bright, even in the twilight. He was smiling. But hesitant, too. He said, "*Please* don't say 'and now I see it wasn't so bad.'"

The surprise hit me in the stomach and I laughed out loud. "No, I wasn't going to say that. It was horrible, actually. But— we got through it. And I—I should have trusted you. I know that you can handle yourself. I'm so sorry I ever acted like you couldn't. I was just—scared, and not thinking straight. Not *letting* myself think straight."

For a moment we were quiet, him looking at me and me trying to remember what else I had felt I needed to say. *Maybe I should have asked Sakura for more useful advice . . .*

"I like to think I was actually of some use," he observed at last.

"You were." But for some reason this annoyed me, and I scowled at him. "Curse it, Luca, don't you ever want to be anything *more* than useful?"

"You mean like . . . victorious? Safe? Enjoying festive candy?" He grinned, then stepped toward me, so we both huddled on the front stoop of the shop. "Or do you mean like . . . even closer . . . to you?"

His head was right next to mine, our shoulders brushing. He paused. I didn't breathe.

You're going to be sticking around, I heard Saki say. *There's no harm in it.*

It's never about wolves.

It's not about what we fear.

It's about us.

"I want to be your partner, Red," Luca whispered. "Not just in solving crime."

I bit my lip. "Luca . . ."

"Do you . . . do you see me that way? I've always thought you were the one person around here who really does see me, the real me. But if you want to just be friends, that's okay, I understand. It's just that . . . sometimes, I think *I* see something—"

Rather than hear it, or say it, I felt it. In a rush, I flung my arms around his shoulders and kissed him.

At last.

It was a really nice kiss.

That is, until Officer Thorn happened to walk by again. With a broad grin and an absolutely obnoxious wink, she shouted to the two of us, "Happy Samhain!"

Epilogue

A note from Sakura

Red!

I'm sending this over to you so that you can be the first to see the news. I'm hoping you find this note as soon as you open your shop for the day. Don't you just love the design? Isn't it exciting?

Now, because I know you're going to have sooo many questions: 1) yes, I was able to finalize my purchase of the old antiques shop; 2) no, you do not want to know where the money came from; 3) stop worrying, it'll be fine, Ryuko is going to help me renovate the interior; and 4) oh–did I mention that this (enclosed below) will be the new logo?

I'm opening a café –it's official!

Now, I know how you feel about running a business. It's a big commitment, and I know you take your shop very seriously. Actually, that's why I wanted you to be the first to know. From the moment I arrived in town, you've been a sympathetic ear for me. Well, now I want to try things the other way round! I have so much to learn from you.

Yeugh–as I write that, it makes me remember what you said about a certain other newcomer, and how he used that line on you. Well, I am not like him–I think we both can agree on that.

Anyway, obviously I won't be doing this alone. Did I tell you about my friend Glacial? In all the excitement of the holidays and our "wolf"'s trial, I've forgotten. Glacial is used to roaming, a bit like you and William used to, but it's time for a change in business for her. And she happens to be a really good baker. So she's already agreed to move to town and help us out. You'll love her, I'm sure–and even if you don't love her at first, you're sure to love her desserts. They'd make great stakeout food!

Kidding, kidding. :)

I have so many plans for this café –I can hardly wait to talk them all over with you. I wanted to get the details of the name and design just right before I shared anything, but now I'm ready to talk your ear off about it! I don't just want to make tea and coffee; I want to help people, to inspire them, to give them a place to rest and be cozy, even to inspire a little romance in their lives . . .

. . . Not unlike you do, Miss Crime-Solving Alchemist. ;)

In any case, I'm sure I'll talk to you soon. If you can, come over at lunchtime to see the plans Dusty and Ryu are making, and I'll make you our very first cup of tea!

With love,

Sakura

Brand new logo of the Pomegranate Cafe:

Pomegranate Café
TEA, LOVE, & DESTINY

Recipes

The recipes included here have been submitted by the residents of Belville, collected (and at times translated) by the author. Mistakes might have been made at any part of the process, but with any luck, these will bring a bit of fun and inspiration to you, our readers! Always feel free to experiment with the recipes included. And if you do, reach out to info@ellehartford.com to let us know how it went!

That said, without further ado . . .

Red's Taste-of-Home Chai

This recipe leaves lots of room for experimentation. You could use black tea leaves instead of bags, throw in some raw sugar or honey for a sweeter drink, grind up the spices for more flavor . . . this is the one treat Red never makes the same way twice!

Makes two cups

Ingredients:

- 2 ¼ C water
- 1 cinnamon stick

- 3 whole cloves
- 4 green cardamom pods, split open
- 4 black peppercorns
- ½ inch fresh ginger, sliced thin
- ½ tsp fennel seeds (optional)
- 3 bags strong black tea
- 1 C milk

1. Heat water and spices in a medium saucepan over high heat.
2. When the water is boiling, add in the tea bags.
3. Reduce heat to medium-low and simmer for about 7 minutes (longer for a stronger flavor).
4. Stir the milk and any sweetener. Raise the heat so the milk comes to a gentle boil.
5. Reduce the heat to medium again and let the tea simmer for about 5 minutes.
6. Just before serving, raise the heat once more and stir thoroughly. Then pour through a strainer into cups and enjoy!

* * *

Lavender's Hot Apple Cider

As we've seen before, Lavender tends to be less precise with her recipes than Red does. Fortunately, this one is very simple and forgiving—and very warming on a cold, frightening evening!

Serves 8

Ingredients:

- ½ gallon fresh apple juice
- 4 cinnamon sticks
- 1 pinch nutmeg, whole kernels preferred
- 1 pinch cloves, whole kernels preferred
- 1 small sliced apple or orange

1. Add the juice, cinnamon, nutmeg, and cloves to a sturdy pot, and bring to a boil over high heat.
2. Add in sliced fruit.
3. Reduce heat to let the cider simmer.
4. As orders come in, pour cider through a strainer or sieve into mugs.

* * *

Luca's Favorite Toffee White Chocolate Chip Muffins

Luca can't take credit for this recipe himself, of course. In fact, he's rarely been known to give away a bite of one of these sweet treats, so he can't even take credit for sharing . . .

Makes 12 large muffins

Ingredients:

- 2 ½ C flour
- 3 tsp baking powder
- 2 eggs
- 1 ¼ C sugar
- 2 tsp vanilla
- ¼ C butter, melted
- ¼ vegetable oil
- ½ C heavy whipping cream
- ½ C milk
- 2 Tbsp apple cider vinegar
- ½ C toffee chips
- 1 C white chocolate chips

1. Preheat oven to 375 and grease a muffin tin.
2. Sift together the flour and baking powder and set aside.
3. In a large bowl, whisk or blend eggs, vanilla, and sugar until well blended. Mixture should be foamy and slightly stiff.

4. In a separate bowl or measuring cup with a spout, mix the melted butter and oil.
5. Slowly add the butter mix to the eggs, continuing to mix well.
6. Again, in a separate bowl, mix cream, milk, and apple cider vinegar.
7. Add the cream mixture slowly to the egg batter, continuing to stir.
8. Fold the dry ingredients into the wet batter gently, with a spatula. It's okay if there are lumps.
9. Fold in the toffee and chocolate chips. (Those that haven't already been eaten, that is . . .)
10. Spoon batter into the prepared muffin tin. If you like a sweet crispy top, spoon a little extra sugar over the top of each muffin.
11. Bake 20 min, or until a toothpick inserted into the center of a muffin comes out clean.

* * *

William's Recipe for Peace of Mind: The Sea-Monster

You know the drill by now: William is here with another constellation he wants us to brave the cold to look at in the night sky . . .

"The cold is nothing," says William, with a huff. "Today's constellation was way worse back in the day when it was a real live sea monster. You heard me right. After all that talk about monsters and wolves, we're going to find a monster actually worthy of the name.

"This one isn't rare. Maybe that's what makes it scary. You'll be able to find it best in the late fall or winter, but it shows up in both hemispheres. The best time to spot it is probably January, when it's completely above the horizon. Try looking for its brightest stars first; they make two trapezoids, stacked near each other. It's a large constellation, because what kind of monster would it be if it were small?

"Cetus is its name. It was an ancient Greek sea monster–the one that Perseus defeated, if you believe the stories. But then again, Cetus is also referred to as a whale, so maybe it was all a lot of hype. Nothing like what happens nowadays, right?"

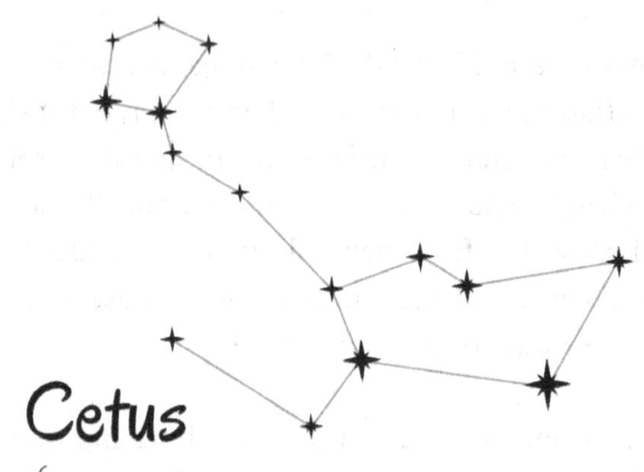
Cetus
the sea monster

Acknowledgments

So, normally I start off this section by mentioning Red and her friends, and how they solve crime by working together. But since Red's a bit preoccupied with newfound romance, instead I'll draw inspiration from Sakura and Ryuko, who rightly remind us that no one is ever alone.

I finished up this book in time for Halloween 2022, and released it as a holiday surprise. Because of my need for speed and secrecy, I did a lot of the polishing on my own—so if you find errors, they are mine! But even so, I am deeply indebted to Richelle of Richelle Braswell Comprehensive Editing, who helped me brainstorm a murderer and his crimes. And I wouldn't have gotten this far without the support of my wonderful friends and family, fellow authors, writing club, cozy mystery community, and amazing ARC reviewers!

And fittingly, like Red, I must acknowledge that my partner is *much* stronger and more helpful than he ever gets credit for being. It's been a hard road editing and releasing the start to this series one after another, and he's been there for me through it all. If I could, I'd give him a Sakura-level apology for each cranky, hangry, stressed-out, worn-out moment. Since I can't (there's been too many of them to count), I'll just say: *you were right.*

Last but never least, thank *you*, reader, for being here. If you have a moment to review this book on your platform of choice, I'll be *extra* grateful, of course—reviews mean even more to authors than cinnamon rolls mean to a certain grumpy familiar. And stay tuned: our adventures in Belville are far from over. You're welcome back at any time!

About the Author

Elle adores cozy mysteries, fairy tales, and above all, learning new things. As a historian and educator, she believes in the value of stories as a mirror for complicated realities. She currently lives in New Jersey with a grumpy tortoise and a three-legged cat.

Find more stories of Red and her friends at ellehartford.com. And while you're there, sign up for Elle's newsletter to get bonus material, behind-the-scenes sneak peeks, and terrible jokes!

And if you're curious about Red's next adventure, just read on for a sample of Chapter One of book five, Cinders to Dust!

Cinders to Dust

Chapter One

Just One Bite

If it hadn't been for Sakura's café , I never would have gotten involved.

Well—to be fair to Sakura—if it wasn't for my love of exotic flavored chai teas, I would never have gotten involved.

Probably.

"I'm so sorry," I said, to the young person I practically bowled over as I went for a personal record in *popping into the pick up counter at the Pomegranate Cafe and dashing back to the potions shop.* Tea splashed everywhere and the scent of cinnamon and vanilla filled the busy café . I kept talking. "Wow, I really didn't see you there, let me help—"

But the person was already on the ground, and not because I had knocked them over. They were on their hands and knees, sopping up the spilled tea with one of the Pomegranate's handy cloth napkins.

Not only did I feel awful, I realized as I stared down at the unfamiliar gray-streaked head that I didn't know this person at all.

"You should also be sorry because you stole his drink," Sakura sang out from behind the counter. "*This* one's yours,

Red. You ought to know by now that yours is always the gold mug!"

I ought to have, and normally I *would* have. But the truth was, I'd been running around like a headless chicken with an overdue to-do list all morning. I was so behind, I might as well have been operating in last week.

Haste is the enemy of speed, I could hear my mother say. *Look, Cinnabar, you were rushing and you made a mess; now you have to take longer to clean it up.*

I took a deep breath. And when that didn't work, I took another, and reminded myself that the best thing I could do was be present.

"I'm so sorry," I repeated, a little less frantically, to the gray-haired stranger. "Please, let me buy you another one. Saki—?"

"Already on it," the café owner chirped back. Her pale face and pink apron bobbed amid gleaming espresso machines and stacks of ceramic cups as she passed another steaming drink over the counter. "One black cherry coffee with cream for Coal!"

"Coal," I repeated, extending my hand down to the stranger to help him up. "Is that you?"

"Y-yeah. I guess," he said, looking down at his hands as he spoke. He accepted my help as if he thought I might have a shocking device or a bit of slime concealed in my palm.

I pursed my lips. Four different custom orders were waiting for me back at the shop, plus I had to run out for more sweet moss later *and* I had a date that night; I didn't have time for "I guess." But as I watched Coal, I reminded myself to be kind. He was barely more than a kid, after all, skinny and a little disheveled, only as tall as my chin. His white collared shirt hung loosely on his shoulders, and his leather boots had been patched and tied with mismatched laces.

"Coal came in with the carnival last night," Sakura informed me. Apparently, she was all caught up on her drink orders, because she found a moment to lean over the counter and speak conspiratorially. "He was asking me about work opportunities here at the Pomegranate, but I have a feeling he'd be more interested in *your* line of work, Red. Why don't you two take a seat over by the window and talk?"

If I didn't have time for guesses, I *really* didn't have time for interviews. But just as I was about to refuse, Coal looked up at me, and I clocked two things: first, his eyes looked much older than I'd expected, and second, he seemed to be biting his cheek to hide a smile.

"Please," he said. "I'm a really good worker, but things just aren't good for me at the carnival any more. I have to get out."

I glanced back at Sakura, but the shadow witch-turned-barista was gone. There was nothing left to do but grab Coal's drink and take it to a table to sit with him . . .

. . . Because by this point, everyone in Belville knows I'm a sucker for a traveler in need. Or a newcomer looking for a change. Or even an outsider who ends up accused of murder . . .

I guess, looking back, I was bound to get involved with the carnival and its silly masked ball—whether tea had been spilled or not.

* * *

A heavy spring rain pounded against the Pomegranate's picture windows as Coal and I took our seats. I did my best to set aside my worries and keep my mind open. An open mind is essential in Beyond—after all, living in a fairy tale world may come with magic and fun things like steam-powered traveling carnivals, but it also comes with hidden dangers. Not every tale ends the way you think it will, and not every hero is, well, a hero. Small-town Belville was a perfect example of this. I'd settled in the alpine town nearly three years ago hoping for a quiet place to practice alchemy—and instead I'd run into murder and mystery at every new turn.

And I myself knew what it was like to be the stranger accused of crime. I'd spent years traveling and studying my craft before I'd scraped together enough money to buy my own shop. Not every encounter in a new town had been pleasant. *How much worse would it have been,* I thought, *if the people giving me grief were actually traveling with me, and I could never leave them behind?*

At least, that was my rudimentary assumption about Coal's problems so far. From the way he watched me across the little wooden table, green eyes wavering with trepidation, I felt fairly confident about my assumptions.

"Hi," I said, since Coal seemed to be waiting for me to start. "Let's start over. You can call me Red. Yes, that's 'Red' like 'Little Red Riding Hood,' and yes, I know my hair is actually black." I smiled at him, trying to use humor to prove I wasn't going to bite. "I run the potions shop right across the corner from here. However, I feel like I should tell you right off the bat that I don't have the budget—or really the need—for extra staff right now. So that's going to be a hard sell. I can give you advice about settling into town, though, if you need it."

"Are you sure?" Coal leaned forward over his coffee. "The carnival itself is twenty-four new people in town. And that isn't counting anyone who comes to see it. We always draw a big crowd. There might be a rush on things like lightsticks or even mending potions."

Well, he sure knows a thing or two about business, I thought, watching him carefully. We had in fact had high demand for *both* those things, on top of the usual spring demand for specialized fertilizers and water-repelling products. That was part of the reason my shoulders were so tense and my feet were already aching at eleven in the morning.

"I could even mop floors and dust, if you'd just let me work for a few days," he pressed.

I shook my head. "I appreciate your willingness to work, Coal, but I already have two assistants." More like one and a half, technically, since the talking canine-shaped magical creature known as William only worked when he felt like it. But that was more detail than Coal needed to know. "And one of them, Sir Rowan, is very particular about his cleaning procedures." That one was true: after just over a year working at the shop, Sir Rowan had pretty much taken over all maintenance. He did have some alchemical knowledge and he could have made potions if he wanted, but he seemed to get more satisfaction from keeping the store in order. *More power to him,* was my thought. "Besides, I have to be pretty careful about the people I hire, even for small things. My workshop is attached to the store, and it's my responsibility to make sure there are no accidents. That makes sense, I hope?"

Coal slumped back into his seat, but he nodded. "Alchemy is the science for people who like adventures and can weather explosions," he said, as if reciting from a textbook. "That's what my dad used to say."

"Well, your dad isn't so wrong about that," I replied, amused. Of course, alchemy was also the science for people who wanted to spend years toiling as an apprentice before they saw so much as a speck of fools' gold, but again, that was a detail Coal didn't need to hear.

"He's gone now, and my mom, too," Coal said. Before I could get out the words *I'm sorry for your loss,* he sat back up and added, "Is it true alchemy is all about transformations? Do you think you could teach me?"

I choked back a sip of my tea, a little exasperated. I'd actually never considered taking on apprentices of my own. And even if I did, Coal was a little older than usual. I would have guessed his age at nineteen—old enough to see independence on the horizon, but young enough to insist on spontaneously-created careers.

All this thinking about apprentices brought to mind my former teacher, Paracelsus. It was like his wizened face was peering over my shoulder, counseling me to *listen* to the results of my experiments. Whatever that meant, I still only had a vague idea. But rather than refuse Coal outright, I asked, "Is it the transformation part that especially appeals to you?"

Coal nodded, and glanced around the café as though he thought someone might be listening in. Then he leaned toward me again, pushing his coffee mug aside. "I'm half naiad," he informed me. "My father's people could transform into full-on lake guardians. Some of my cousins still work with the carnival. That's how it gets around so easy. But I've never been able to," he concluded.

Naiads, I knew, were water spirits—they were to water what elves sometimes were to forests. It took some piecing together, of course, but I could see what he wanted. "Coal, I understand the desire to explore your heritage, especially when you can see others around you who seem more 'in' it than you." Actually, feelings like that reminded me of my own upbringing with mystic Seers in the desert, who had always seemed far more magical and *perceptive* than me. "But that's not really what alchemy is for. Alchemy is about transformation, yes, but not on living bodies, and not into something you're *not*. It's more about making herbs and minerals into the best versions of themselves."

"But I *am* a naiad," Coal insisted. "I'm descended from Melusine. Even if only half."

"Yes, but—"

"And I don't want to be just like *them* any longer!"

I fell silent, watching him again. Something, I thought, was just a little off. The way Coal was nervous around authority and so eager to prove himself reminded me of my friend— well, to be fully honest, my new boyfriend, Luca. Luca was extremely dear and his efforts to overcome a manipulative former boss meant a lot to me. I wanted to be sympathetic to the desperation in Coal's voice, but there was something in his eyes—a hardness—that I wasn't so sure about.

"Just say you'll come to the carnival tonight," he pleaded. "Then you'll see. You'll see how it is for me there. What they're like. You'll see why I have to get away."

Well, we'd already planned to go. "Of course," I said, releasing a breath I hadn't realized I'd been holding. "And if there's anyone else in town you want to talk to, I could suggest Lavender, over at the tavern, or maybe Officer Thorn—"

"No," Coal said emphatically. "Only you can help, Red. Please?"

I hid my frown behind my steaming tea. "I'll do what I can, Coal, but I really think—"

"I have to go," he said abruptly, standing. "Thank you for

saying you'll come. You'll see!"

He left in such a hurry that for a moment I remained sitting, staring out the gray window, wondering if he'd seen something I hadn't.

Also by Elle Hartford

The Alchemical Tales (cozy fantasy meets cozy mystery)
    Beauty and the Alchemist (book 1)
    Cold as Snow (book 2)
    Mermaid for Danger (book 3)
    Cry Big Bad Wolf (book 4)
    Cinders to Dust (book 5)
    Death Pulls the Strings (book 6)
    A Thousand and One Alibis (book 7)
    Tangled Up in Murder (book 8)
    Labyrinth of Crime (book 9)

Pomegranate Cafe Romance (sweet romantasy)
    Worthy in Love (book 1)
    A Tale of Rowan and Daisy (book 1.5)
    Strong in Love (book 2)
    Steady in Love (book 3)
    Sweet in Love (book 4)

Marine Magic (cozy fantasy at the beach)
    How to Care for Cursed Fish (book 1)
    How to Treat Talking Beasts (book 2)

Leonine Investigations (cozy fantasy goes noir)
    The Silver Deck (book 1)